COMPLEMENTARY COLORS

A NOVEL

Kate Evans

Also by Kate Evans

Memoir

Call it Wonder: an odyssey of love, sex, spirit, and travel

Novel

For the May Queen

Poems

Target

Like All We Love

Nonfiction

Negotiating the Self

COMPLEMENTARY COLORS

A NOVEL

KATE EVANS

COYOTE CREEK BOOKS | SAN JOSÉ | CALIFORNIA

ISBN: 978-1-946647-14-6

Cover art by Nancy Larrew

Printed in the United States of America

Published by Coyote Creek Books
www.coyotecreekbooks.com

for the poets

CHAPTER ONE

BEAUTIFUL

I was craving something, but I wasn't exactly sure what. I wanted something new. I wanted something beautiful. My life was at a strange stand-still, stagnant as the smoggy San Jose air. So I'd signed up for a poetry class. I'd been looking forward to it all week, but now as I sat in a university classroom, waiting for class to begin, I thought maybe I'd made a mistake. The students leaned on their desktops, talking to each other in the circle of desks, casual and comfortable in their jeans, while I sat stiffly in my work clothes: black blazer, pink blouse, dark nylons and black heels, my long brown hair pulled back in a clip.

Sitting in the circle with us was Professor Alameida. I knew her name because it was printed on my class schedule. She had long gray hair and a craggy face, and the sleeves of her denim jacket were rolled up to reveal silver and turquoise bracelets. When she opened a folder, silence descended on the group.

Just then, the classroom door creaked open. In walked two

people, two women. They were unlike any two women I'd ever seen. They both had short dark hair, gelled into spikes, and they wore black leather jackets, baggy jeans, and black boots. It's hard to explain now why I didn't think "lesbians" right away. Or "dykes." But I didn't. It was 1992; why would I have known any gay people? Or I should say lesbians. I did have an old college friend, Manny, who was gay, or so I assumed. He now lived in Massachusetts; he'd moved there with a guy I thought was his lover. But my life, not unlike many people's lives, was mostly filled with people like me. In my case that meant straight people, in their twenties and thirties, who were dating, or engaged, or divorced. The lesbian world might as well have been taking place in Massachusetts, while I lived my straight life in California. Until that moment, of course.

I wasn't the only one staring at them. It seemed everyone did. The two women had made a rather dramatic entrance, coming in late on the first day, walking in like they were one person split in two. For women, they took up a lot of space, with their spiky hair and bulky leather jackets and big boots shining with silver buckles. They sat in the two empty seats right next to the professor. The desks seemed too small for their bodies, their energy. They leaned back, knees apart, feet planted like men.

"Sorry," said the taller one, three silver earrings glimmering in one ear, and a smear of a tattoo on the back of her hand.

Professor Alameida looked over at them, half-smiled, and placed her hand on the desk of the woman closest to her. She handed them each a syllabus with a certain ease, a sense of familiarity.

"It's okay, we just started," she said, leaning forward in her desk and crossing her feet at the ankles. "I'm Vanessa Alameida. Please call me Vanessa. Not professor. I don't like that stuff." Her voice was so low and gravelly I had to strain to hear her. "This class is about poetry, poetry, poetry. You will write a poem most weeks, beginning next week, as it says here." She tapped her finger on the syllabus. "You will bring copies for everyone. I don't want you to write a poem at the last minute. You should be writing it and thinking about it all week. A poem is a living thing. If you dash it off and bring it in dead, we'll know." She put her fist over her mouth and coughed a deep cough, her silver bracelets jangling.

Anxiety grew in me. I'd have to write poems and bring them in fresh and vulnerable as kittens with their eyes sealed shut. I looked at the blank piece of paper in my notebook in front of me. If I put my pen to it, thinking "poem," would a bunch of words emerge, words put together in such a way as to create something new, something that at this moment didn't exist? I used to think about that sometimes when I'd begin to write a journal entry—that in a few minutes, I'd be to the bottom of the page even though I didn't know what would propel me, what would get me there, and what it would be like to finish. My living time wouldn't have passed unnoticed. I'd have created something. Could I do this with poetry?

The most I had ever written was when I'd recently lived in Japan for a year. But aside from some journal-writing, most of the writing had been letters. Writing helped alleviate my dizzying culture shock. Could I now write something artful, something that would surprise me and take me to new places? This seemed like a hopeful act. Could I be hopeful like that? The idea of hope seemed to feed something elusive in me that was hungry.

"Now here, let's read this," the professor said, handing the person to her left a stack of papers. The stack continued person to person around the circle. The leather-jacketed woman with the tattoo on her hand leaned over to the other one and whispered something in her ear. They quietly laughed. I found myself curious about what she said, and oddly a little embarrassed, as though maybe they were making fun of me. I knew that was crazy—they hadn't even looked at me. They were probably oblivious of my presence. Yet something about having them in the room, dressed alike and sharing secrets, made me feel a little inept and eager, like I used to around the popular girls in middle school.

When the paper came to me, I saw that on it was a poem by Louise Glück. I'd heard the name before, but I didn't know her work. Maybe I'd read something of hers ten years before when I'd been working on my undergraduate degree in English. That was the thing that always surprised me about having a degree in English: how much literature there was in the world, and how little of it I really knew.

Vanessa read the poem aloud, slowly, as though chewing each word. Its title was "Messengers." Vanessa's voice crackled like electricity through line after line of the long, haunting poem. In the poem, geese and deer waited "as though their bodies do not impede them." Images of animals and nature, imbued with life and death, inhabited the poem's rich language.

When she finished reading, we sat, quiet. A chill snaked through my body. I didn't really understand the poem. But I felt it. I felt it inside me, like it was a fish swimming around in my veins. The poem, it seemed to me, used words to get at something beyond words. The deer, the geese. Beauty. Mortality. I may not have understood the poem, but I thought I knew exactly what the poet felt.

Vanessa uncrossed then re-crossed her legs. A guy with dreadlocks and ripped overalls sniffed. A young woman with short blond hair shifted in her seat. She wore baggy shorts with sandals, and one of those olive green sweaters that looks like the most comfortable sweater in the world, the kind that pretty actresses with tousled hair wear in beach movies. She looked like she'd stepped out of the "casual wear" pages of a high-end catalogue.

The sun was getting low out the window. I could see the dark edges of a tree and the corner of a dirty white concrete building across the way.

"Well," said Vanessa. "What do you think?"

I felt myself flush, as I often did when students don't answer a teacher's question. It seemed to be my fault, that I should have an answer for her. I wanted to say something, but I worried I'd sound like a fool. I wanted to say, "I feel this poem in my veins." But that would sound completely idiotic. As a student with a degree in English, I thought I should instead say something about the images, the metaphor, the use of rhythmic repetition.

Out the window, the tree was completely still. It was a warm, summer–becoming–fall evening. The florescent lights overhead asserted themselves as the light outside dimmed.

"I think it's beautiful," said the tall, leather jacketed woman with the tattoo on her hand. She had dark eyes and thick eyelashes, almost as thick as my boyfriend Daniel's. And a delicate chin that curved up, just slightly, and a small scar on her forehead. She had taken off her leather jacket to reveal a black tee-shirt and a necklace on a long silver chain.

Her words had given me permission to speak. "Me too," I said. "I think it's beautiful, too." I could feel the eyes of the class on me. I swallowed and looked down at the poem, seeing if I could find a line I especially liked, but then a guy who I thought might be Vietnamese was talking, saying, "What does she mean, *wounded and dominant?*"

"What do you think she means?" asked Vanessa.

I lost his answer because as soon as I looked up from the poem, I glanced over at the tattooed woman and saw that she was looking at me. When my eye caught hers, she didn't look away, just smiled. The girlishness of her smile surprised me. She had a mouth full of movie star teeth: large, straight and bright white. I smiled back, trying to say with my smile that I liked her comment on the poem, that I appreciated the way she had spoken up and given me room to do the same.

Then she said something to me, silently exaggerating her mouth movements so that I might be able to read her lips. I couldn't figure out what she was saying. I tilted my head and looked at her quizzically, shrugging my shoulders so she'd try again. She held up the poem and pointed to it.

Then, slowly, she mouthed two words, pausing between. She mouthed the words one more time, very slowly. A surprising tingle scuttled up my spine.

I saw that she was saying, "Yes, beautiful."

On my drive home, I felt hyper-awake as I do sometimes after leaving the movies. The contrast between the dark theater and the bright aliveness of the action on the screen makes me perceive life outside anew. I might newly regard the sound of my shoes on the sidewalk, the exaggerated purple of a blouse in a store window, the blooming white of an airplane trail in the sky. I inhabit a new reality, as though the movie has changed me.

As I drove home that night, the dashboard shone a bright chemical green. The brake lights in front of me vibrated red. The dark asphalt shimmered wet and shiny, although it had been months since we'd had rain. I pushed my foot down on the accelerator and sped up to eighty, eighty-five, ninety, passing five or six cars before I slowed to sixty-five. I imagined if a cop were to pull me over I'd respond in verse, in Walt Whitman exaltations. Maybe the officer would say, "Did you know you were speeding, Miss?" And I'd say, "The night is singing to me! The brake lights and stars are alive!"

When I pulled through the gate of our apartment building and parked, I sat still to the whir of the engine fan. I took out my notebook and, by the overhead light, wrote lines of a poem, a poem about a woman driving down the freeway, exalting in the night. My pen moved quickly over the page, and when I finished I looked at the words. There was that wonder again—the amazement that I had the ability to make something. Those words on the page hadn't been there moments before. I knew the next day they might not be so thrilling, but for now, it was all good.

I ran up the steps to our apartment, hoping that Daniel would be there (often he worked very late) and hoping that if he were, he would let me share my excitement of the night. The excitement had been building all day, in fact. At work it had been hard to focus. I didn't hate my job, but I didn't love it either. Before I'd left for Japan I had been piecing together different jobs: teaching ESL to new immigrants at night at a community college, working in an after-school reading program for kids who hated to read, and babysitting the peevish young daughter of two doctors. I'd felt fragmented driving here and there, not having a single work site, a real career. While I was in Japan, my best friend Lucy got hired as the director of the tutoring center, and when I returned to the Bay Area she immediately offered me a full-time job. I was grateful to her, grateful to have a paycheck. Grateful to have one location to go to work. Although now I could feel the gratitude running thin. I wasn't sure this job was for me. But it was all I had at the moment.

I guess it was the corporate feel of the place. At the learning center, each child had a binder. A hundred fat green binders lined the walls on sturdy shelves. Each binder was embossed with the corporate logo: a blond-haired boy holding a pencil over a piece of paper and smiling broadly. It was my job to write down what each child was to do at the center each day—a script for the tutors. Sometimes I also tutored, sitting at a table in the bend of the U shape, while three children came to me with their binders. I'd open the binders and give each child directions: "Get the yellow reading book and read pages 5 to 10 and answer the questions," or "get the purple math kit so we can do the subtraction blocks."

There were a few kids I looked forward to seeing, the ones who weren't put out by having to do more school after school. The ones who were thrilled to collect fake coins that they could use to "buy" cheap plastic toys and candy in our little awards store. But there was something sterile about the place. The way we had a script we had to follow when a parent called or dropped in to find out about the cost of the program. The way we couldn't wear pants, except on Fridays, and then it was only slacks, not jeans. The corporate logo that was both inane and eerie, clones of that smiling blond kid staring at me from the binders and on the stationary and on every single memo.

It was a small center, just Lucy and me, and a few part-time teachers who taught in the afternoons. During the days, Lucy and I organized binders, tested kids, crunched numbers. Lucy seemed to do it all so easily, as though being part of the business was like cleaning her house or going shopping. She was fast and efficient, and I sensed no resistance in the way she moved cleanly from teaching a kid long division, to filling in a budgeting spreadsheet, to answering the phone with a cheery, "Wellstone Learning, where your child comes first. This is Lucy, how may I help you?" Lucy was freckled, thin and small-boned. As short as she was, she had disproportionately long legs that looked great in suntan nylons.

At lunch time the place was usually quiet—no kids yet, no teachers, no phone calls. Lucy and I sat in the main teaching room at one of the six tutoring tables, eating our sandwiches.

"Quit jiggling your foot against the table, Gwen," Lucy had said. "You seem agitated today."

"Sorry," I said. "I didn't realize."

"What are you thinking about?"

"That poetry class I'm taking. Tonight is the first night."

"Poetry?" She took a sip of her Diet Coke and eyed me over the can. "Are you reading it or writing it?"

"Both, I think."

"Sounds like my worst nightmare." She smiled. I liked the way one of her front teeth overlapped a little with the other one. Combined with her small size, freckles, and frizzy hair, she had the charm of a sprite.

"Really, why a nightmare?" I bit into a carrot and looked longingly at her potato chips.

"*Thou* and *thee* and roses and thorns—it's just, I don't know, weird. All those agonizing moments in high school when the teacher is trying to get us to see the deeper meaning of some obscure poem."

"Have you ever read any contemporary poetry? I mean, some people even use the word *fuck* in their poetry these days."

"Now there's a poem I'd like to read." She put a potato chip in her mouth and held the bag over to me. I took one, just one, and savored the greasy, salty flavor. "Speaking of fucking," she said, "Will is driving me crazy."

"Why?" I asked, taking one more potato chip and relishing the energy in the air, a kind of intimacy that developed whenever we shifted from small talk to a deeper gossip about our lives. I looked forward to hearing what she was going to tell me. There was something about the unhappiness of her marriage that fostered a connection between us.

"Sometimes I feel like he's going to rub my skin off, he touches me so much. He won't leave me alone. We're sitting in bed reading and he absently touches my leg or my arm, up and down, up and down. Driving in the car he has his arm around me and rubs my arm up and down, up and down. It's like a bad habit he needs to break. I wonder if I can get him The Patch or some medication that will dissolve in his coffee."

I'd heard this complaint before, but I never tired of it. Maybe listening to Lucy was my version of watching a soap opera.

"That man," she continued, "would have sex with me twenty-four-seven if I let him. So when he's not on me like a rabbit, he's touching me. It just doesn't seem right that the man I love makes my skin crawl. I wish he was more like Daniel is with you."

"No you don't," I insisted. "I mean, it's like we're with two extremes. You get too much, I don't get enough. We're like Goldilocks searching for the just-right bowl of porridge, the just-right bed."

"Maybe we should swap men," she laughed, stretching out her pretty legs then crossing them again. "Let's just go to each other's houses tonight and see what happens."

"Now there's an idea," I said. "I'm sure Daniel would dig you. Only problem is, I'm too queen-sized for Will."

"You're not queen-sized!"

"Compared to you I am. He likes how little you are. He desires your body. He craves you. He actually has sex with you with the lights on, while you're both fully awake. If I only had your problem."

"Don't say that, Gwen." I could tell by her tone of voice and the lowering of her eyes that she was serious.

"I'm sorry," I said, dusting sandwich crumbs off the table and onto my hand then dropping them into the garbage can under the table. "I didn't mean to make light of it."

"I think I need to face the fact," she said, her eyes still lowered, "that Will and I just aren't compatible. All these months of marriage counseling have not changed a thing."

"What are you saying?" I asked, my heart slightly picking up its pace. Something about the idea of people on the edge of a cliff, ready to make a major change in their lives, gave me a little thrill.

"You know what I'm saying. I'm seriously thinking of divorce."

"Oh, Lucy, I'm sorry."

She finally looked up at me, and I expected her eyes to be shining with tears, but they weren't.

"Yeah, well," she said. "It's not the end of the world. Look at you. You survived a divorce just fine. Divorcing Andy was the best thing you could have done. And now you're with a fascinating man."

"Who drops into silence for days at a time—"

"But at least Daniel's interesting! Maybe it's because you're not married. Maybe living together is better. I mean, all Will wants to do is watch sports on that fucking TV, and he wants me there right next to him so he can pet me like a dog. I want to pull the plug and throw the TV out the damn window. I'm always, *Let's go to the park. Let's go away for the weekend.* Let's—I don't know, let's do *something* that people do." She laughed awkwardly.

"Yes, what *do* people do?" I said in my best upper-class imitation accent.

"I know that—what's that from?" she asked.

"*The Great Gatsby.*"

"Oh, yeah, I kind of liked that book until my senior English teacher went on and on and about the symbolism of eyes on some billboard—"

"The Eyes of Dr. T.J. Eckleberg—"

"Yeah, that—until she went on and on about how they represented some god-like judgment or something like that. Drove me crazy. I just thought it was a good story." She fell silent for a minute. I wished I could say something about how much I loved digging deeply into literature and finding surprises, unearthing hidden meanings. But she was so adamant and practical. I might sound like a flake or a know-it-all.

I drank the rest of my soda and stopped myself from reaching over for another potato chip. I wished I were more like her when it came to food—someone who could forget she had a bunch of chips sitting in front of her.

"Your divorce wasn't that bad, was it?" she asked. "Will and I are like you were. We have no kids, just a house. Not much else of anything, really. Are you glad you got divorced? Are you happier?"

"Yes, I'm definitely happier," I said, not sure that I was. I knew I wasn't sadder. But was I happier? Not quite. I was a little—what? The word *confused* came to mind. *Befuddled.* I had been married to Andy for four short years, having married him when I was only twenty-two. It seemed like a long time ago. I'd heard he was now remarried with a couple of kids. We had been young, hadn't really known what we were doing. At least that's how I felt. I had no idea how he felt. After I'd asked him for a separation, he packed up and went to live with his grandmother. Only his attorney showed up to court. He had friends come get his stuff out of the apartment. He was pissed at me. He left a message on my answering machine calling me a *bitch*, a *whore*. I never saw him again.

Soon after, I met Daniel. I'd thought I'd figured things out after the divorce, but my relationship with Daniel was far from mature, thoughtful, open, and honest—everything it seemed a good relationship should be. Which was why I'd gone to Japan. I thought I could learn independence, could learn to love to be alone, could figure things out (like I had thought after the divorce). If going to another country to live for a year hadn't helped me figure everything out, what would? Even though Daniel and I were living together now, our relationship felt exactly the same as it had before I left:

I was contentious and wanted too much.

He was quiet and withholding.

And my work? I was making okay money, but I had a vague itch of dissatisfaction. There was something I was doing wrong, in both my work life and personal life. I had to remind myself constantly of the little new-age nugget, that life was a journey, not a destination. Sometimes that helped, sometimes it irritated me. I had the sense that something was off-kilter. I was thirty-one years old. When would I figure it out? And, more to the point, what was the "it" to figure out?

Lucy sucked down the rest of her soda, dropped the can to the floor with a clang, and crushed it with her foot. She tossed it to the recycle bin and it plopped in, a direct hit.

"I'm not sure I believe in happiness," she said. I'd heard her say that before. It rankled me, made me want to defend the possibility that happiness exists.

"Of course you do," I said.

"Oh, you're right," she said, pinching me on the arm. "I forgot.

I do. Thanks."

She'd kissed me facetiously and sloppily on the cheek, picked up an armful of binders, and tromped to her office on her tiny high-heeled shoes.

* * *

When I walked in the door that night after the first poetry class, Daniel had on the stereo ear phones (probably listening to Led Zeppelin) and a newspaper in his lap (the sports page of the *New York Times*, the only paper he would subscribe to, even though we lived in California). The TV was on, too, featuring a news story about Ross Perot's fight to be included in the upcoming Bush/Clinton presidential debate. Reading, listening to music and watching TV simultaneously was Daniel's version of a sensory depravation tank—or, sensory overload tank. It was his way to block out everything. He must have had a bad day in the lab. Or maybe he was plunging into one of his dark moods.

Dark moods.

That's what he called the occasional week or two every few months that he lost his sense of humor, his ability to make eye contact, his sense that life was worth living. During dark moods he retreated to his cocoon. There was no touching him there. I had learned over the course of our three years together to leave him alone, to wait for him to emerge. I hated his black moods, hated being left alone in the world to fend for myself while he licked his wounds in his private cave. That's why my stomach tightened when I walked into the apartment. Was a dark mood on the horizon? Or had another one of his papers been rejected? Or had he gotten bad results on a recent experiment? Or had his lab boss screamed at him again, the boss who was an egomaniac and who, I was sure, was threatened by Daniel's brilliance?

I needed to test it out, to see what was going on with him. I pulled the door shut hard so he'd hear it in spite of the headphones (all the neighbors probably heard it too). He looked up. His dark eyes, a little bulging and framed by thick lashes, met mine. I smiled. He smiled back, lifted his hand in a little wave, the hand holding a pen.

So, no dark mood. Just a bad lab day.

I went to him, bent over the couch and kissed his forehead. He put his hand on the back of my head and moved his fingers through my hair. I kissed as close to his ear as I could get, at the edge of the headphone. He pulled my hand to his lips and kissed my palm. I wanted to look into his eyes, but they were closed. He knew that kissing my palm melted me at the center. He knew it had that effect on me, a warm watery feeling that infused my arms and legs. He knew a lot about how he made me feel—good and bad—because I told him.

And Daniel never forgot a thing.

That's why I wanted to see his eyes as he kissed my palm, because I wanted to see him calculating his way into my heart, calculating a way to infuse my veins with desire. I wanted to see that he had planned to make me feel good, even though he apparently felt like shit. I needed to remind myself that he was giving me something at that moment, even though he wasn't in a giving mood.

Because Daniel never forgot a thing, most of what he did seemed a bit calculated—or, rather, planned. Sometimes he seemed like an actor whose off-stage director whispered instructions to him. When he spoke I got the odd feeling that he was reading from a script. Maybe he was an old soul living the exact same life for the second time. Maybe he was so self-conscious that he couldn't act without predigesting the action in his mind. Or maybe he was slow at the regular actions of the world but fast at the extraordinary ones. Whatever he was, one thing people agreed on: he was a genius.

When he let go of my hand, I knew I would be pushing the envelope by standing there much longer. It would be easy to overstay my welcome. It would be easy to ask for more than his palm-kissing generosity in a moment he obviously wanted to be alone. I was like a vampire, he said, always craving more. Perhaps this was something I loved about him: he always left me wanting more. It stoked my desire. What I wanted tonight was to talk, to tell him all about the poetry class. He knew tonight had been the first night. But it was obvious he wasn't going to talk to me.

I turned and left him to his music/TV/newspaper. The apartment was small, only a few steps from the living room to the kitchen. In the refrigerator I found some white wine that didn't smell too bad when I poured it, and didn't taste too bad once I fished out the crumbled cork that floated in the glass. I also found leftover spaghetti, which didn't look too bad after discarding the crunchy pieces that hadn't been protected by loose-fitting saran wrap.

As I walked through the living room with my dinner, Daniel remained engrossed in his music/TV/newspaper. I was sure he was

17

aware of my presence, but it was obvious he didn't want to be. He had let me know with the palm-kiss not to take his need to escape personally. I tried not to, but of course it was impossible.

I sat on the bed to eat. The bed was actually a futon on a low frame, shoved in the corner of the bedroom beneath a window that looked out onto the balconies of other apartments, balconies like ours, cluttered with barbecues and dying plants and plastic lawn chairs and bicycles hanging from hooks. Next to the futon was a large desk with a bulky computer screen on top. On the floor were scattered papers and clothes, all Daniel's. In fact, almost everything in the apartment was Daniel's.

I had moved in just six months before, when I came back from Japan. I'd lived in Tokyo a year, teaching English, and when I came back, I owned not much more than what two suitcases held. Before I had gone to Japan, I had a huge yard sale and sold everything I owned—my furniture, books, heaps of clothes, even my car. I was stripping myself of belongings, trying to make myself clean and free. I even left Daniel behind, a speck on the ground, waving good-bye.

I'd hoped being alone in another country, another culture, would change me. I left as Gwen Sullivan—Californian, teacher, girlfriend to Daniel-the-genius. In Japan, it seemed a little like I was becoming someone else. After a few months, I could sense a new identity building inside, the seeds of something. I could feel myself evolving, as I drank long nights away with Japanese and European friends who said *let's go to Malaysia, let's go to Thailand, let's go to Korea. It's cheap. It'll be fun.* I spent days alone in my tiny studio apartment, reading and writing in my diary, and thinking.

For the first time in my life, I rode subways, willing away my claustrophobia as the train shot through dark tunnels, a stranger's thigh pressed against mine. I wrote long letters to Daniel, telling him the truth about how I was changing. I wrote long letters to my friend Lucy, telling her other truths about how I was changing.

Then one day in Japan, it was as though a light switch flicked in me. Maybe my evolutionary gene was defunct. Or maybe culture shock had rearranged my DNA. I walked down the spiral steps of my apartment, passed my landlord and returned his *konnichi wa* greeting, put my hands over my ears as a screaming motorcycle wove maniacally through cars on the busy street, and then I crossed at the light to the train station, put my phone card into the phone and called Daniel.

I said I wanted to come home.

It felt strange saying that because I didn't really have a home. But he knew what I meant and immediately, silently, he made his home my home. He sent me the money for the ticket, I got on the plane, and he picked me up at the San Francisco airport, drove me to his place, and six months later, there I still was.

Yes, here I was, in the Bay Area, living in a cheap apartment in a sketchy neighborhood in East Palo Alto, bordering elegant Palo Alto, which poured over into Ivy League campus affluence—a constant reminder of Daniel's prestigious yet lowly and low-paid post-doc position that may, or may not, be a stone's throw from an Ivy League professorship. Yes, here I was in Daniel's world, and now those Japan memories were a little like a dream. Coming back to the Bay Area was kind of like that Ray Bradbury story that my seventh grade science teacher read to the class. (Every Friday she read science fiction to us, which fostered in me a brief illusion that I could like science.) In the story, a tour group takes a safari trip into the past. They are told they must stay on the path, but one man deviates from the path and steps on a butterfly. When they return to the future, everything has changed a little: a different person has won the presidential election, the air feels strange, even language is altered just enough so that the usual is recognizably unusual. That's how I felt—that my year in Japan had transported me to another time. And now that I was back, everything was the same but just a little bit changed.

And tonight, the poetry class had heightened that feeling.

I was excited about being a student again. I'd written a little poetry and a few stories, and had kept a diary off and on since I was a kid. There were a few poems I loved, especially Walt Whitman's expansive *Leaves of Grass*. I was looking forward to learning how to write a poem, how to make the magic work officially.

Still in my work clothes, I sat back on the futon and closed my eyes, drifting through thoughts of poetry, of class, and of those two women in leather jackets.

I was only half awake when I felt Daniel unzipping my skirt.

He helped me with my blouse and my nylons. He lay on top of me, kissing my neck, then my breasts, and as he moved inside of me, I felt like I wasn't quite having sex but was dreaming about sex, about tattoos and silver bracelets, and about deer, how they move so gracefully, how *beautiful* they are.

CHAPTER TWO

HOME

When the alarm buzzed the next morning, I quickly shut it off. Daniel groaned and rolled over and pulled a pillow over his head, securing it with his arm. Daniel hated mornings. He didn't want me to say *good morning*. He didn't want to have to say it back. He didn't want to feel obligated to talk before noon. He didn't want to be touched, or for the phone to ring. He'd add another pillow to his head if the neighbors were talking too loudly on the other side of the wall. Usually he worked late in the lab and slept until late morning or early afternoon. I, on the other hand, had to be at work by 8:30.

A slice of morning light slipped through the edges of the curtains. I pushed myself off the futon and quietly stepped over my skirt, blouse and nylons that lay crumpled on the floor. Seeing the heap of clothes brought back the memory of the night before, of Daniel undressing me, of our having sex in the middle of the night. Had he used a condom? I wasn't sure. It had been dark in the room, and I'd been wrapped in the fugue of half-sleep. I reached between my legs and briefly touched myself. I was warm, a little damp.

I hoped he had used a condom. Not because I worried about getting pregnant—I was on the pill. But because I wanted to be fully present during our first condom-free love-making. I wanted to be aware and awake the first time we had sex without even the thinnest layer of latex separating us. For a long time, I had been trying to talk him into it. I wanted him to fully release with me. I wanted to feel him lingering in me even after we pulled apart, to know that part of him swam in me.

When we first began having sex, Daniel's explanation for using condoms was that he wanted us both to get tested for H.I.V. and other communicable diseases. That's how he put it, *communicable diseases*. That's how he put it, *I want us to get tested*. I knew *us* really meant me, not him. I had a much more multi-faceted sexual history than he did. He knew some, not all, of that history. He tried to act like my sex life prior to him didn't matter to him, but I was sure it did.

After our tests came back negative, he said he worried about getting me pregnant. He said if I forgot to take my pill even once, we were at risk. That's how he put it, *at risk*.

We talked about it off and on but mostly left the issue alone. It was always a frustrating thing to talk about, and it usually devolved into a fight.

When I went to Japan, we spent a year apart except for the two weeks he came to visit me. He'd brought condoms in his suitcase, and—immersed in a honeymoon of reconnection after months apart—we didn't talk about the condom issue. Then it became moot because he dropped into a dark mood when we were on the bullet train headed south to Kyushu. His deep funk meant we didn't make love again until the day before he left to return to California. In my tiny studio apartment on the small futon mattress, he held me after sex and told me he loved me, that he would be waiting for me to come home.

When I did come home, I set the pink plastic pill case in the bathroom drawer next to a crumpled toothpaste tube. I never forgot to brush my teeth in the morning. I would never, ever walk out of the house with morning breath. So I would take a pill each time before I brushed my teeth, I told him. A system that could not fail.

Daniel was still assessing the system, it seemed. I picked my wrinkled skirt off the floor and saw that a condom wrapper, torn at the edge, lay beneath it. A surge of prickliness ran through my body, a static charge of frustration. I wanted to go shake him awake, ask him what the hell his problem was. He should know by now I was clean. I was safe. Most men would be thrilled to not have to use a condom. And being on the pill was awful. It made me nauseous in the mornings and my breasts tender, as though I had persistent low-level PMS. And who knew what the chemicals and hormones in the pill were really doing to me, with the way the FDA seemed to be lax about things that might affect women, what with IUD's puncturing uteruses, and diaphragms causing toxic shock syndrome. Who needed it? Who needed to take a pill every day? Who needed this implied judgment that there was something dirty about me, something untrustworthy?

I picked up the rest of my clothes and threw them in the basket in the corner of the room. The zipper of my skirt knocked loudly against the wall before dropping into the basket. Daniel didn't move. I kicked the condom wrapper, and it skipped across the carpet. From the open closet, I grabbed my robe, a cheap nylon kimono I'd bought at a Tokyo department store, a tourist kimono of garish blues and greens. An out-of-focus silk-screened fuchsia dragon spanned the back.

When I opened the bedroom door, the fresh air in the hall brought into relief the bedroom air thick with the smell of bodies. I turned. Daniel's back, clad in a white tee-shirt, moved up and down in the rhythm of sleep. The pillow had slid off his head. Somehow, from this angle, he looked like a little boy. The condom wrapper curled like a leaf on the rug. Why did he always want to keep a sliver of distance between us, even during our most intimate connections?

I remembered last night the way he had undressed me, gently, as though I were a fatigued traveler. He had unhooked my bra, had pulled the straps off my shoulders. He had pushed my hair off my face. In the indigo night, I'd seen the outline of his face as he moved over me. He'd whispered gruffly in my ear, *you're so beautiful.*

When I put my keys in the ignition, I saw my notebook from last night's poetry class on the passenger seat of my car. I opened it. The Louise Glück poem slipped out, onto my lap.

At once I experienced that odd awake feeling of the night before as I'd driven home. It was like the buzz you feel when you've had just the right amount of wine, the exact tipping point that's so fragile, so perfect, that even one more sip might slip you over to the other side of sloppy inebriation. It's the feeling of anticipation. I didn't know what I was anticipating, but my body seemed to be telling me that something awaited me.

I tucked the poem into the back of the notebook then flipped to the page I'd scribbled on the night before: lines of the first poem I'd written in a long time, lines about a heightened awareness, of hearing the click of my heels on the asphalt, about seeing the bright green of the dashboard. In the poem, I rush across the freeway in the night, brake lights pulsing red. A police light throbs in my rearview mirror; I'm pulled over. The police officer is a woman. I tell her *the night is singing to me!* She writes me a ticket—her damp hand sparkling like a mermaid's under the streetlight—and asks me to sign. I do. I smile. We part.

I syllabicate all the way home.

As I read that line, my mouth curled up into a smile. That line of poetry felt like a snug little secret. I imagined my syllabicating as a kind of scatting—me as a mix of poet and jazz singer, riffing in the car, be-bopping, rhyming line after line, moving to the sounds of the night. Driving, free, in my car on the dark freeway of possibility, no idea where I was going but sure that wherever I ended up would be the perfect place.

But of course, that was only in the poem. In reality, I hadn't been pulled over, hadn't interacted with a cop. Hadn't *flirted* with her, is what flitted through my mind, in the vaguest way. I never consciously thought of myself as one who would flirt with a woman. In my mind the woman cop of my poem, of my imagination, sent a prickle through my body. That prickling merged with the half-asleep memory of Daniel making love to me. And before I knew it, as I pulled out of the parking lot and turned toward the freeway, my body was flush with excitement. Sometimes that happened the morning after a night of sex—I'd have a sensory flashback that sexually aroused me. But usually it happened as I lay in bed, quiet, next to Daniel. Not as I drove to work, thinking about a *woman* police officer, or a poem.

On my drive through town toward the learning center, it was a mild Bay Area fall morning, the sky a bluish-gray, the sun thin but gaining in intensity with the promise of a bright, warm day. The car radio played the news, an announcer chattering about the upcoming presidential election. I made a mental note to stop at the Democratic headquarters to pick up fliers. As I sat in my car at a stop light, I saw someone walking along the sidewalk, someone with short dark hair, in jeans, wearing a leather jacket. Could it be one of those women from the class last night? Suddenly I felt dizzy, disoriented, un-integrated, as though I were a partly-finished jigsaw puzzle. Mixed with the odd sexual arousal I'd just been experiencing, the whole thing left me a little breathless.

Sitting at the light, I watched this person. She held a paper coffee cup in her hand and was now leaning against a light pole, waiting for the crossing signal. I sensed that this person—like the two women last night—was completely comfortable in her body. It was as though her body wasn't separate from her mind but was fully integrated into her being. I didn't feel that way about myself. Not that I hated my body (well, sometimes I did)—but it's just that I was always aware of it. Rarely did I forget I had a body. I was like Alice in Wonderland, always shrinking or expanding in relationship to my surroundings. Around a small woman like Lucy, my breasts and thighs overflowed.

Around a person larger than me, I shrank and could feel almost petite. In a dress, I might feel sexy one moment, then awkward and overdressed the next. Wearing black I might believe I was sleek and fashionable, but upon seeing a woman in a yellow blouse, I'd suddenly feel dull. Yes, there was an Alice, a Gulliver, in me.

Then there was this person in the black leather jacket who looked impermeable. It was as though her surroundings were irrelevant, that she was who she was, no matter what. The light changed. I watched the woman begin to cross the street with movements that were so one-to-one with what I perceived to be her solid identity. I stepped on the accelerator, approached her, and then was parallel with her. I saw she wasn't at all who I thought. No earrings, no silver necklace hanging down a white tee shirt between her breasts. As I passed I saw a little goatee, a man's face. An inexplicable disappointment passed through me that the person was a man, not a woman.

That day at work, Lucy was in a mischievous mood. While on the phone, she rolled her eyes in a silly way for my benefit as an upset parent complained on the other end. Lucy kept her voice calm and professional as she said, "I'm sorry, Mr. Vienna, that Evie's grades didn't improve. Often it takes more than two months of working with us. But if you'd like to stop Evie's tutoring and be refunded fifty percent, as per the contract, I'd be happy—" Obviously Mr. Vienna cut her off, so Lucy sat listening, crossing and uncrossing her suntanned-nylon legs. She looked over at me and mimed sticking her finger down her throat, followed by a silent middle finger pointed at the phone in a vigorous flip-off.

When she hung up, she turned on the radio. We weren't supposed to do that, but every so often Lucy would risk it. If the owner, Ed Chambers, walked in the door, he wouldn't be happy. But he rarely walked in the door—maybe once a month, if that. While I worked on student binders, Lucy whirl-winded around the office to loud classic rock, rearranging files, making notes on her notepad, wheeling recklessly in her chair from one big filing cabinet to the other. Every once in a while we'd look at each other and bob our heads in unison to a familiar chorus of a song that had been a hit during our high school days. I smiled at our part-satirical, part-earnest nostalgia. Being in the middle of such energy was great, as though the big stew of feelings I'd experienced that morning had been run through a sieve and only the most playful, least complicated ones remained. I grinned at the subversive way we acted like two teenagers, when in fact we were two grown women in charge of running a business.

At lunch, unwrapping my bologna sandwich, I said, "You're sure in a good mood."

"I was thinking that about you," she said, curling her legs beneath her like a cat as she sat in her chair and popped open a diet soda. "You must have gotten laid last night."

I felt a blush crawl up my neck and light my ears on fire. "God, Lucy, it's uncanny. How'd you know?"

"Something about your disposition this morning is screaming *sex goddess*." She laughed her tight, truncated laugh, her freckled nose wrinkling. Sex goddess? A sex goddess was powerful. Was I powerful?

The phone rang. Lucy turned off the radio, and I reached over to pick up the receiver.

"Wellstone Learning, where your child comes first. This is Gwen, how may I help you?"

"Hi Gwen." It was Daniel. I glanced at Lucy and smiled. She knew exactly what I meant by the smile. She flicked out her tongue at me like a teenage boy crudely feigning oral sex across the classroom when the teacher is writing on the board. I lay my middle finger on my cheek, playfully flipping her off. Satisfied, she turned back to her sandwich.

"Hi honey," I said. His voice sounded a little sleepy. I looked at the clock. 12:30. "Where are you?"

"Just got to the lab and found out that both Ellen and Rich are out for the day. Flu, they say. I say hangovers."

"Really, you think so?"

"Probably," he said. "They found out yesterday their proteins paper got accepted in *Nature*."

Oh. Two of his friends who were also, in essence, his competition, were to have their work published in the most prestigious science journal. No wonder Daniel hadn't wanted to talk last night. He needed to process this reality. In his early twenties, Daniel had been a science prodigy of sorts. With the guidance of his university mentor, he had published and presented a number of prominent papers. But lately, as a post doc, he was struggling. He was hitting one dead-end after another in his work. He researched the brain, with a focus on genetic vision disorders. It was all quite technical. When he'd try to explain his work to me, I'd feel at the edge of understanding. He tried to use layman's terms, but it all seemed so abstract, so elusive. What I did understand was that, as brilliant as he was, he was struggling at work.

"Wow, *Nature*. That's good, right?" I asked, trying to put a positive a spin on it.

"Yes, it's great," he said flatly.

"Maybe you'll be next," I added.

"I know what you're doing, Sullivan. Don't go there." I was surprised he used my last name. He only did that when he was in a good mood. Perhaps his friends' success wasn't bringing him down as much as I'd thought. "Anyway, with Ellen and Rich out, and the shipment of pipettes not here like it was supposed to be, it's going to be a slow day. Want to meet for dinner? At 7:00?"

"The Palazzo?" I said, even though it wasn't really necessary to say the name of our favorite restaurant, the place we always went whenever we had dinner on weeknights. With Daniel struggling at work, those nights had dwindled from once or twice a week to once or twice a month. I loved The Palazzo, and I loved having him to myself in a place outside our apartment. He always seemed different away from home, a little looser, a little happier.

"The Palazzo, but of course," he said, his voice brightening. And then, right before he hung up, he said something he'd never said before. "See you tonight, love of my life."

How could it be, I thought as I hung up, that today the whole world was in a good mood?

On my way to the restaurant, I stopped at the local Democratic headquarters to pick up Clinton fliers. A woman in the office handed me several boxes and a map that showed where, during the two days before the election, I was to distribute them. I felt a surge of optimism in spite of my track record: No president I voted for had ever won. My first chance to vote had come at age 18, when I voted for Jimmy Carter, who was virtually wiped off the map by the hostage crisis and by Ronald Reagan's Hollywood charm. Four years later, I voted for Walter Mondale. I watched the humiliating returns on a big screen television in my college's student union. The memory was stamped in my mind of a beautiful young woman in cowboy boots who shouted out one celebratory laugh after another as it became clearer that Reagan would be re-elected by a landslide. Four years after that, I fruitlessly worked hours and hours as a campaign worker for Michael Dukakis, who was tromped by Reagan's vice president, George H. W. Bush. I had watched the returns numbly, wondering how all my efforts could have been in vain. Deep down an optimist, I believed that if you really, truly wanted something, all you had to do was work hard, which was why I was now working for the Clinton campaign. However, a little bit of my hopefulness had been chopped off, like the tip of a finger: I would no longer be a precinct leader. I'd merely pass out fliers the night before the election. That way, if Clinton didn't win, at least I wouldn't have myself to blame.

When I got to the restaurant, Daniel wasn't there yet. No surprise, since I was twenty minutes early. And he was usually late. Even though it was supposedly a slow day at the lab, I knew it was possible he'd get involved in something and lose track of time.

Natasha, our usual server, brought me a glass of white wine. Natasha was a first-year student at Daniel's university, majoring in biology. She had curly thick black hair that bounced at her shoulders when she walked. I sensed my straight brown hair hanging bored on my head. She placed my glass of wine on the table on top of a little square napkin and said, "It's on them"—indicating with a nod of her head two men sitting at the bar. One large man, one small man. Both were watching us and raised their wine glasses. I nodded my head in a reserved thanks.

"What's up with them?" I said to Natasha.

"They have their eye on every pair of X chromosomes that walks in here," she said. "Daniel will be here in a minute, yes?"

"Yes."

"Okay, then, drink up and enjoy. They'll leave you alone when he shows up." She smiled and tucked behind her ear a thick curly strand of hair that jumped right back out.

"True," I said, a little irritated about getting advice about men from a woman younger than me. But I knew she meant well.

The wine was cool, good. I liked savoring my first glass of wine in the dim restaurant bar, where I sat at my favorite table, facing the door. A candle flickered in a red glass octagon casting shards of pink light on the wall. I tried not to wonder whether or not those men were staring at me. I sipped my wine, flipping through the newspaper, squinting at the words in the low light. Poll results showed Clinton and Bush in a dead heat.

I turned the page and a story caught my eye about a woman who'd had a heart and lung transplant and then became a mountain climber. She climbed some of the most famous mountains, from Kilimanjaro to Mt. Everest to Mt. Rainier. But the story wasn't really about that. It was about how her new heart and lungs had come from a woman who'd died in a car accident. The mountain climber and the dead woman's husband had met. In the press photo, they sat next to each other on a couch, holding hands. How must it have felt for him to know his wife's heart was beating in another woman's chest? I read to the end of the article, but my question wasn't answered. The man just said he was grateful that his wife's tragedy could be another woman's miracle. I wondered if he might fall in love with her, or she with him. Such a connection could not be taken lightly, could it?

I sensed someone standing over me and I looked up, expecting to see Natasha asking me if I might like another glass of wine. But it was the larger man from the bar who had bought me the wine, probably about my age, maybe a little older, standing there smiling at me. At first glance I thought he was fat, but then I realized he just had a round face and a large, bulky body that was probably all muscle. He looked like he might pull a Popeye and burst out of his shirt. He wore wire-rimmed glasses and his hair was prematurely thinning.

"How's the wine?" he asked.

"Fine, thanks," I said.

These kinds of moments were always weird to me, when strange men felt they had the right to approach me. And, of course, they did have the right. If not the obligation. I was a woman alone in a bar. In our society, that meant I was looking for something. Then there were the mixed feelings. I liked attention from men. It was flattering. Kind of. If I ignored what Natasha had said: that they were checking out all women. It meant I wasn't someone special, just that I had two X chromosomes.

"So," he said, "I have a question to ask you." He placed his beefy hand on the table and leaned toward me.

"Shoot," I said, trying to deflect his confidence with my own. Perhaps that was a form of flirting. It kind of felt like it.

"Can I look at the label in your shoe?"

We both looked down at my black pump, dangling at the end of my foot on my right leg, which was crossed over my left. I looked back at him.

"What is this, some kind of fraternity prank or something?"

He laughed. "Ha! No. But that's awfully sweet of you to think I'm young enough to be a frat boy."

"It's dark in here," I deadpanned.

"What's your name?"

"What's yours?" I countered. I was hoping that Daniel would walk in at any moment, although I knew he'd look like Gumby standing next to The Incredible Hulk. It made me wonder if I would look less desirable to this guy if he saw my pale, skinny boyfriend with the big, dark eyes. Although in the world of men, it was likely Daniel would have one-up on this Hulk since Daniel was tall and, more importantly, had a full head of hair. I wasn't sure the Ph.D. would matter.

"Name's J.D.," he said, holding out his hand. I really didn't want to touch him, but I shook it. His hand was warmer and softer than I had expected.

"Nice to meet you, J.D. Now why do you want to look at the label in my shoe?" I asked that only because I wanted to avoid telling him my name. I wasn't good at making up a believable name for myself on the spot.

"I just like to know the brands of women's shoes," he grinned, perhaps a little shyly. Or slyly, it was hard to tell. "It's just a thing."

"A fetish?"

"I guess you could say that." The candlelight threw sparks and shadows onto his thick face. "But not sexual, you understand."

"Of course not," I said. We were in full-flirt mode, which was kind of fun but not completely pleasurable. What I really wanted right now was for him to leave me alone and go back to his friend and fixate on a different XX, perhaps one of the three blondes sitting at the other end of the bar. But of course, they weren't alone and they outnumbered the two guys, so they weren't easy targets like me.

"Well," I said, "thanks for the drink, but the answer is no."

"Oh, come on," he said, an edge of frustration prickling his voice. He smiled broadly as though to compensate, his cheeks puffing out like a chipmunk's. "What would it hurt? Just slip off your shoe. It'll take only a second. I just want to see the label, I swear, then I'll hand it right back. I can even slip it off your foot, if you like, like you're Sleeping Beauty. Or not. I'll do your bidding, Your Highness."

"That's Cinderella," I said. This was getting weird. I glanced around and saw Natasha chatting with the blonde women. The Hulk's small friend was staring at us, an absent-minded grin on his face. A few of the other tables were taken up with chatting couples and small groups.

"No, really, I don't think so," I said, realizing immediately that my refusal contained too many words, too much that could sound like a modification of "no." I needed to speak his language.

"Just a quick peek?" he said. His bulk was so extreme he didn't have much of a neck.

"No."

"No?"

"Absolutely not."

It seemed I was getting through. He took his hand off my table and said, "Hey, I didn't get your name."

"Misty."

The way he frowned a little, I could tell he knew I was lying. He looked deflated. I felt a little bad.

"Well, *Misty*," he said. "I'll have you know you just lost me a fifty dollar bet." He pointed at his little friend. "You're the first woman of four to say no."

Before I could respond, he walked back to the bar and pushed himself, with effort, into the too-small chair.

I was on my third glass of wine when Daniel finally showed. The Hulk and his friend had taken off, but other people had come in, and by now the place was busy. Natasha and the other server were a little harried trying to get to all the customers.

"Sorry," Daniel said, taking the seat across from me.

"It's okay," I said. I was flying high from the wine and no food. Everything really was okay. Besides, he had called me the love of his life.

"I had to kill a mouse today," he said. I knew he hated having to do that. He once described the process to me—the little guillotine, the extraction of the brains and eyes, the careful dissection and freezing of leftover parts to distribute to other scientists. He didn't have to share in this way—many researchers didn't, they just threw away the parts they didn't need. But Daniel didn't feel right about that.

"Bummer," I said, immediately aware of my California slang. Normally I would have been self-conscious about it but warm from the wine, I didn't care much. Daniel was from New York City. Compared to him and his friends who were raised on the Met, lacrosse, prep schools, private liberal arts colleges and the Ivy League, I was a sloppy country bumpkin. I was a product of public schools—and "culture" while I was growing up was a cheap knock-off of a Broadway musical in Sacramento, or a tour of Fisherman's Wharf in San Francisco. I wondered if all native Californians had a bit of an inferiority complex when faced with the cultured, intellectual, international, well-bred East Coast crowd.

"Yes. It. Is. A. Bummer," said Daniel, with a half-grin. He knew it was funny when he awkwardly tried on my Northern California-girl slang, and so did I. I smiled back.

Natasha came by and brought Daniel his favorite micro-brewery beer and took our orders. In spite of the dim environment, I could see Daniel's eyes light up, as they always did around a pretty woman. There was a certain rapport between the two of them that sparked a flash of jealousy in me. At age thirty-one, I was becoming aware that the lure of the young woman was beginning to fall away from me. Natasha was probably ten years younger than I was. I could understand the appeal. There was an openness to her youth, a kind of purity. If Daniel and I ever broke up, I thought he might ask her out. I wondered if she'd go out with him. Was she too beautiful for him?

Perhaps the glamour of his braininess equalized the equation. It was hard for me to judge.

As soon as Natasha left with our orders, I told Daniel about the Hulk and his tiny compadre. It had the desired effect. He reached over and squeezed my hand.

"You saved the crossword for us, didn't you?" he asked.

I unfolded a section of the newspaper, and there it was, clean and undone. He scooted his chair next to mine and pulled a pen from his pocket. It took us a little while but we finished it. I always got the twentieth-century literature and pop culture questions. He got most everything else.

While we ate, I brought up a subject I'd been avoiding but knew we had to face at some point. I figured with good moods and good will in the air, it was possible this conversation might go well.

"My parents invited us for Thanksgiving," I said, scraping a baked potato skin for the last vestiges of buttery potato. "Do you think you might want to come?" Daniel had met my parents when they'd come to San Jose, but he had never been to my parents' house—the house I grew up in—in Suffolk, a small town outside of Sacramento, about three hours from the Bay Area. We'd had only two Thanksgivings to deal with up to this point. One of them was a no-brainer since I was in Japan. During the other, he worked in the lab the whole Thanksgiving weekend while I went to my parents' house alone.

He chewed a bite of spaghetti, slowly. Very slowly, it seemed to me. In general, Daniel was slower than I was—in the way he talked and moved, in the decisions he made. Of course his mind probably worked fifty times faster than mine in most ways, but he generally didn't show that except in the lab. And he got even slower when he was stressed, when there was something he didn't want to deal with.

"Actually, Gwen," he said, "I think I'm going home for Thanksgiving."

There were two triggers in his sentence that made me want to jump up from my seat and run out the door. One was *I'm going*. Absolutely no room for me in that statement. Not even an implied invitation. The other one was *home*. He didn't say "to my parents' house." He didn't say, "to Manhattan" or "to the city," as he often called it. He said *home*. His parents' house, a place I had never been invited, was his home. Home was not the place he lived with me.

And there was more. His home wasn't just East Coast, intellectual, prep school, lacrosse. It was Jewish. Not very religiously Jewish, but according to Daniel, quite culturally so. I regarded my life as having little culture in comparison. Just a basic middle-class white girl who had been raised jack-Catholic. That meant wearing the little bride outfit for communion, and going to midnight mass every Christmas Eve. *Shiksa* was written all over me. Daniel had told me when we were friends, before we'd become lovers, that he didn't know if he could ever marry a non-Jewish woman. I had never again brought up this issue because I wasn't sure I wanted to marry him. Part of me thought I did. But I wasn't sure if my desire was due to his restraint. Did I want him more when I thought he didn't want me enough? Perhaps I was over-thinking things. Perhaps no love is clear. Perhaps all love, all desire, is comparative, qualified, relative.

But there, at that moment, in the restaurant, the candle casting light and dark debris on Daniel's pale complexion, I wanted only one thing. To spend Thanksgiving with him. To have him want to be with me, with my family or his, for the holiday. I had never been to his parents' house. Nor had I met them. I hadn't even spoken to them on the phone or heard their voices except for the occasional message his mother left on the answering machine. The answering machine void of my voice, containing only Daniel's abrupt voice merely intoning after the beep, *Leave a message.* In fact, it wasn't clear to me if he'd ever told his parents the true nature of our relationship. Whether or not there was marriage waiting for us in the future, I wanted to be considered his family right now. I wanted to be his home.

"You're going *home?*" I smeared the word.

"Yes, Gwen, and I really don't feel like talking about this right now." He set down his fork and took his wallet from his pocket, flipping it open to extract a credit card. He set it on the bill in a little black tray on the table, and waved at Natasha who came over and picked it up.

"That's it?" I said. "You're paying the bill and we're leaving? We're not going to talk about this?"

"Gwen, it's been a hard day," he said, a brittle edge to his voice. "Please, please don't ask me to engage with you on this one. It's just asking too much. I need to talk about it later."

"Goddamn it," I said, throwing my napkin on the table and standing up with a jerk. Blood rushed too my head. Too much wine. I blinked, talked myself quickly out of feeling faint. "You've made a decision to go to your parents' house, and you didn't even talk to me about it. Who exactly am I to you?"

"Sit down," he said.

"Fuck you," I whispered, and turned and walked toward the front door. As I squeezed through other customers, I felt queasy. How many glasses of wine had I had? The whole thing seemed surreal. How did we get from doing our crossword puzzle together to this? From "you're the love of my life" to "you're not my home" to "fuck you"?

On the T.V., images of Bill Clinton flashed—his young, hopeful, ruddy face. I pushed open the heavy oak and glass door to a rush of cool evening air. The sidewalk was lit up by streetlights. A car rushed by, its open windows emitting the pumping rhythms of a rap song. The sky was pure black—no moon, no stars. I couldn't remember where I'd parked my car. Was it around back in the lot or on the street?

The intensity of my anger almost felt good. Sometimes lashing out at Daniel felt scarily delicious, as though getting angry was my only way to let him know how deeply I felt. Yet a little something niggled inside me, a little reservation. I wasn't sure my deep feelings were all about him, about us.

But at that moment, I wasn't in a condition to philosophize. The sunburst of my energy had lit my nerve endings on fire. I just had to find my car and drive—where? Back to Daniel's apartment? I was trapped. I had moved back from Japan to California without a plan and without much money. I had sold most of my possessions before I left, so I'd returned virtually empty-handed. I had moved into Daniel's life, and to make room for me he had scooted over, just a little.

I just needed to find my car, I decided. Then I'd figure out what to do. Maybe I'd go to a hotel that night, use my credit card. And the next day, I'd try to find a cheap apartment. Maybe Lucy could help me out.

At my back something moved, a light touch, some breath. I jerked around, ready to strike someone with my purse, my fists. It was Daniel. He took my hand. I tried to pull away, to say something, but he was determined, and I was weak from wine and emotion, so I followed. He led me around the back of the restaurant to the dark parking lot where his little green Volvo station wagon was parked. He opened the passenger door and without thinking I got in. When he got in his side I said, "My car—"

He didn't say anything, just reached across the seat and kissed me hard on the lips, pushing his tongue into my mouth. I opened my eyes. His were closed. He reached under my skirt and pulled at the waistband of my nylons. I helped him peel them off my legs, helped him lean my seat back, helped him maneuver as best he could on top of me. He paused for a moment, pulling a condom from the car door's side pocket and fitting it on quickly, urgently, balancing himself with one arm on my shoulder, pinning me to the seat.

Somewhere down the street, a car door slammed faintly, and a woman's laugh pierced the air.

CHAPTER THREE

PLAYBOY

When I walked in the door for the second poetry class meeting, the two women in leather jackets were already there. So was everyone else, it seemed. I was a few minutes late because one of our tutors at the learning center was sick and I'd had to fill in. But Vanessa hadn't yet commenced class—she was sitting at a desk in the circle, shuffling through papers, while some people talked to each other, and others quietly sat. The room smelled a little dry and dusty, like chalk. I was surprised to realize that there was still an old-fashioned chalkboard on the wall, not a whiteboard. Either way, I doubted it mattered. Vanessa didn't seem like the board-writing type. She looked planted in her seat as though she'd organically grown from it, a magical hoary plant sprouting long white hair and silver jewelry.

I took my seat, the same desk from last week. Funny how that is with classrooms: where people sit the first class session becomes "their" seat and they stake it out through the rest of the semester. So once again I sat between the dread-locked guy (he was wearing those old overalls yet again) and the young woman with short blond hair who last week had been wearing that perfect, slouchy sweater that looked like something out of a beach movie. Tonight she wore faded jeans—a perfect fit—and a pale pink cotton shirt with the sleeves pushed up just right, as though she were ready for a catalogue photo shoot. Even though I was dressed in my usual work attire, I felt like a ragamuffin sitting next to her. My black blazer had seen better days—after traveling with me to Tokyo and back, it was fraying at the cuffs and the buttons were loose. My cream-colored slacks were a little tight at the waist, and they were freckled with stains on the thigh from a blob of coffee that had popped out of my coffee cup that morning. I touched the spots with my thumb. I was running low on decent work clothes, which—I knew—meant doing the dreaded deed soon: clothes shopping. I never liked pushing through all those people and racks of clothes, heaping my arms with possibilities only to find most of those possibilities dashed in the dressing room mirror.

I heard Vanessa clear her throat to begin talking, so I gratefully put surface considerations out of my mind and immersed it with something that filled, rather than chilled, my blood: poetry.

"Welcome back, everyone," said Vanessa in her gravelly voice. I liked the way she greeted us, as though it was a pleasure to have us in her presence. While she reminded us of today's procedure—that we'd read and discuss as many of our poems as we could get through in the given time—she rolled up the sleeves of her denim jacket, revealing an assortment of silver and turquoise bracelets on one wrist. Around her neck hung an impressive turquoise pendant that, from this angle, looked like a distant image of the world, its continents and oceans pieced together.

Vanessa asked us to pass around the copies of our poems. My heart picked up its pace as I pulled my poem from my folder. I had typed up the poem I'd begun in my head on my drive home last week, the one I'd written in an energized splash in my notebook while sitting in my car in the carport, illuminated by the car's overhead light—the poem about driving home after poetry class, filled with joy and energy, and being pulled over by a cop and "singing the night's praises" to the policewoman. And then, as I put it in the poem, "syllabicating all the way home." I'd titled it "After Poetry Class." I hadn't yet shown it to anyone.

It was astonishing to watch stacks of poems pass through my hands. As I took one from each person in the room—twenty-two in all—it seemed we were all connected. Each one of us had gathered in this room last week. Each one of us—no matter what our lives looked like between the bookends of class meetings—had thought about poetry during the week. We had taken time, a few minutes, a few hours, to sit down and write. We had shaped images and lines. We'd painted something of our lives on the page. There on my desk sat a stack of poems, little pieces of strangers' worlds offered up to everyone in the room.

"Okay, let's start with number one and go from there." In the previous class Vanessa had assigned us numbers that we were to type next to our names. Number one said "Sunny King," who turned out to be the dread-locked guy in overalls. Could that really be his name, Sunny King—which shortened to Sun King? Who would name their child that?

"Remember," said Vanessa. "Listen well. He will read it twice. Try to get at what you think the poem is saying and how it's making you feel. Where's the energy? Where's the richness? Where are the gaps? And don't forget, the poet is not to speak until the end. Sunny, take notes on what we discuss. But you are the poet. You get to decide what to do with our feedback."

Sunny's poem looked like it had been typed on an old typewriter. The letters didn't all align. I imagined he lived in a cabin in the Santa Cruz mountains, one without electricity, that smelled like mold and was shadowed by dark, tall redwoods.

He read his poem slowly in a monotone as though he were shy about his writing. The poem was about painting, about applying thick globs of different reds—ruby, burgundy, scarlet—onto canvas. Then blues that dripped down the side. Somehow, in the third stanza, he morphed the idea of painting into writing poetry, where all images and words "gather" and "meld." From his poem I felt there was something elemental, crucial, tangible about the making of a painting or a poem that seemed—what?—sacred? No doubt about it, this was a remarkable poem. I was suddenly self-conscious. My poem was about making a poem too. Could it hold up to his?

After Sunny's second reading of the poem, Vanessa asked us what we thought. The room fell quiet. My face warmed up—both because the teacher's question just hung there, but also because I was a little choked up. Poetry did that to me sometimes, inexplicably. It tightened my throat, sent through me a wave of bittersweet feeling.

"I like it," said the leather-jacketed woman, the one I'd agreed with that the poem we'd read last time was "beautiful." She looked a little different tonight—perhaps her hair was a little shorter? Or was it that it had a little tint to it, a kind of burgundy blending into her dark color? Or had I just not looked closely enough at her last class? Just like before, she and the other spiky-haired woman were wearing jeans and dark boots, sitting back in their chairs, legs apart, relaxed. I uncrossed my legs and planted my feet on the floor.

"Why do you like it, Jamie?" asked Vanessa. *Jamie.*

"I like the bringing together of poetry and art," Jamie answered. Her eyes were big and dark, shining under the florescent light. I was intrigued by the puckered scar on her forehead and wondered how she got it. Most women I knew would hide it with bangs. Instead, because of her short hair, her face was exposed, like a man's, like the moon's. "I like the way the connection is made in the poem. I get it, but maybe just because I do both writing and art."

"So do I," said Vanessa, "but it's not just our experience that makes this work. I think the poem is making it work," said Vanessa. "The way this poem helps us *experience* that connection is really great. There's such energy in the images. The poem feels true."

"I don't get it," said a young woman with curly dark hair pulled back in a clip. She reminded me of Natasha, our server at the Palazzo, with her easy, natural beauty. "What's *impasto* mean? What's *alla prima*? And *sfumato*? I don't like it when you need a dictionary to understand a poem. Why not just use language everyone understands?"

"Those are all art terms," said Jamie, crossing her boots at the ankle and folding her hands on her desk.

"So?" said the curly-haired woman. "What's that prove?"

I squirmed. Curly Hair seemed irritable, even antagonistic.

Something seemed to have gotten under her skin.

"It doesn't prove anything," Jamie steadily persisted. "It's just that those words are integral to the poem since it's about art."

"It bothers me," insisted Curly Hair. "It seems pretentious."

"Are there other opinions about what Jamie and Claire are debating?" asked Vanessa. *Claire*. Perfect. It sounded like a contraction of Curly Hair.

"Doesn't bother me one bit," calmly offered Jamie's leather-jacketed wearing compadre. Her tone suggested an easy dismissal of the argument. Something sparked in me deep down, an intrigue beginning to build. These two women—actually three, including Vanessa—projected a certain forcefulness, a confidence, an assurance that I usually associated with men. There they sat, three in a row, easy in their bodies and solid, yet somehow gentle. Not that I didn't know strong women—I knew a lot of them. I even considered myself one at times. But the strong women I knew seemed so bound, in an intangible way, to certain feminine principles that insisted they qualify their ideas. If they were forceful they could be dismissed as hysterical. Like Claire. She clearly had strong feelings about the poem, but she came across as agitated and cold, not warmly centered in her opinion. She looked about ready to say something else but Vanessa interjected.

"Okay," said Vanessa. "It's time to invite the poet back in. Here's the thing for you to think about Sunny. Do you care if some of your readers won't know all these words upon first read?"

He scooped his dreadlocks up with his hands and then dropped them, letting them fall down the back of his overalls.

"I dunno," he said. We waited for him to continue, but he just sat there, eyes on his poem. I wondered if he was excited that a lot of people, including Vanessa, liked his poem. Or if he was bothered by this particular vein of argument. My heart was racing, bumping in my chest, a mix of anticipation and agitation. I wanted to say something, but I didn't know what. I looked over at Vanessa, but she was still staring at Sunny, waiting out his response.

Finally he said, "I really don't like talking about my work."

I thought Vanessa might push him, as many professors I knew might. But in her deep voice she said, "Fair enough. I would never force you to turn your beautiful poetry into mundane prose."

There was a smattering of laughter. What an astonishing thing she'd just said, that poetry used language to do something regular language didn't do. In all my undergraduate literature courses, we'd analyzed poetry but never quite talked about it like that. It felt like I was walking into a brand new room through a door I hadn't even known existed until now.

Vanessa talked a little more about the strengths of the poem, pointing out the especially effective images and line breaks. I hadn't thought about line breaks before, about how you could carry over the energy of a line with a particular break, or highlight a specific word that way. I shuffled through the stack of poems to glance at my own and immediately saw where I could have created better line breaks or used fresher words. The thought scared me—was my poem good enough to share with this group?

We continued through the stack of poems, reading and talking about them and writing comments to return to the writer. I learned people's names: Jamie's doppelganger was Cat. The Asian man, who tonight wore a black suit with a sharp lavender tie, was David. The blonde woman in perfect clothes was Leanne.

As we moved through the stack, closer and closer to my poem, I got more and more anxious. My palms heated up. Daylight dimmed, casting shadowy darkness outside. We sat warm in the room's fluorescent glow.

Finally we got to my poem. I read it aloud, a little out of breath. But soon I was into the energy of the poem and tried to match the inflection of my voice to the words. Everyone else up to now had read in something close to a monotone. I wanted to bring life into my poem.

When I finished, Vanessa said, "Okay, now read it a second time more calmly, Gwen. We want the poem itself, not your voice, to tell us how to read it."

Feeling chastised, I flushed. It was a familiar critique in my life: that my energy was too much. Daniel said I could be like a tornado when he most needed a calming rain. That analogy depressed me. I liked fierce winds. I took a breath and tried to let Vanessa's truth permeate my resistance. She wanted people to pay attention to the words on the page, not my voice.

I read it again, more calmly. A few people giggled at the part where the cop pulls me over and where I elatedly sign the ticket. How fun, I thought, to be entertaining people through a poem.

"I really like this poem," enthused the catalogue blonde, Leanne. "It's really fun. I like how it's, like, about poetry, like Sunny's poem, but it a different way."

I kept my head down, taking notes on my poem, glowing, as student after student said positive things about the poem. I was a poet. I filled the page with my blue-penned cursive, circling images people noted as especially good.

"Okay," said Vanessa, when the critique had wound down. She had yet to say anything about the poem. I had noticed that was her pattern, that she'd let us talk a lot until she threw in her two cents. "So what I'm hearing is that you all enjoyed this poem, that you were amused and charmed. Is that right?"

I looked up. Several people were nodding, smiling.

"Okay, Gwen," she said, penetrating me with her ice-blue eyes. Her deep voice vibrated in my head. I tingled with the mild electric current of her power. "We now know you can entertain us. And, I'll agree, you do it well. But poetry can do a lot more than that. Let's see if you can go deeper next time."

I flushed. For the second time tonight she had reproved me like a parent scolding a child. Perhaps I was a child in her eyes. How old was she? I would have guessed in her fifties, maybe sixties. But she seemed oddly ageless, as though she'd always been a silvery poet with flowing gray hair. My head was buzzing in embarrassment over her comment. What exactly did she mean? I had loved writing that poem. It had poured out of me with pure exuberance. How would I go deeper?

"Okay," was all I managed to eke out.

She fixed her gaze on me for a moment then cast her eyes around to the other side of the class. We all fell quiet under the sharp wisdom of her look. "Poetry," she said, "is so vast and inexhaustible that you can never be anything but a beginner."

Everyone passed the copies of my poems back to me. As Vanessa directed us to move to the next poem, I glanced through the stack. "I love this poem!" said one comment. "This was really fun, thanks!" said another. Toward the bottom of the stack, I found one with small, tight writing that said, "You intrigue us." It was signed "Cat." *Us*, I thought. I looked up and saw that both she and Jamie were looking at me, almost identical with their dark spiky hair, except that Cat was shorter and Jamie taller with those dark eyes and forehead scar. I half-smiled at them. They smiled back, Jamie with her movie star teeth, Cat with her equally straight and white, but smaller, teeth. A smile is usually a connection, but their smiles made them seem even more enigmatic.

Now Jamie was taking Vanessa's direction and reading her own poem aloud. Her poem was about a grandmother brushing a girl's hair, the grandmother who makes plum preserves and who, when eating fresh plums from the tree, pulls off the skins because her toothless mouth can't handle the skins. The grandmother comes across as a surprising mix of loving and angry. By the last two lines of the poem, the grandmother is braiding the girl's hair,

"hair just like your mother's," she whispers

as if the coincidence should cause me shame.

Those lines almost took away my breath, the way they captured the ambivalence a grandmother might feel toward the granddaughter that reminds her of her own daughter—and the ambivalence the adult narrator of the poem feels toward the memory of her grandmother. An odd bittersweet feeling welled up in me again, similar to how I'd felt with Sunny's art poem. With a tinge of regret I realized Vanessa was right. My poem, "After Poetry Class," did not have the same power. There was something complex and deep happening in Jamie's poem.

I decided to speak up, in part because I wanted to talk about the poem, and in part because I wanted to erase the lingering awkward feelings I had about Vanessa's critique of my poem. I was a beginner when it came to writing poetry—and maybe I'd always be a beginner, as Vanessa had said was true of us all. But with a degree in literature, I knew a thing or two about talking about a poem.

"The images and smells of the house, of the little girl's world, are both tender and fierce," I said. "It doesn't romanticize the grandmother. Her good and bad qualities are both right there, on the page. There's an edge to this poem, a sense of loss or absence. The grandmother mentions the girl's mother, but she's not there. It leaves me wondering where the mother is."

"She's just not part of the poem," said Claire. "It seems weird to talk about what's *not* in the poem. There are many things that are not in the poem. Let's talk about the Empire State Building. It's not in the poem." In just this one class session, Claire had easily established herself as the antagonist.

"Actually," said Vanessa, "Gwen has a good point." I felt a little thrill at the professor's validation. Maybe my poetry wasn't deep enough for her but my critique might be. "We have two females from two different generations. They are connected, but the link in the middle, the mother, is missing. In art, it's called negative space. Meaning the objects that are there create a shape of absence. What is absent is absolutely just as important as what is present."

Claire slouched in her seat. Jamie didn't lift her eyes from her poem. Her tattooed hand was gripping a pen, writing comments on the page. I noticed Cat was staring at me again. I half-smiled at her and flushed, shifting my eyes over to Vanessa who was asking the class if they had more to say about Jamie's poem. Cat had written down that I intrigued her. *I* intrigued *her*? How could that be? I felt so simple, so unintriguing, compared to her and Jamie. Who were they? Where did they live? What were their lives like? It was hard for me to imagine.

On the bottom of Jamie's poem, I wrote, "I like this little girl who makes things with clay and loves dogs. Is this you? This little girl seems like she knows something that most little girls don't. I like her a lot. And the grandmother is such an incredible surprise." My face was burning by this point, my skin alive. For some reason I couldn't quite pinpoint, writing all of this on Jamie's paper made me feel shy, self-conscious, thrilled. I handed the page to the person to my left, and it passed hand to hand around the room over to Jamie, landing in the pile of all the other responses to her poem.

I wanted to see her reaction to my words, but then people stood and were stretching. I lost sight of both Jamie and Cat. Class was over.

As I was driving home, excitement buzzed through me, just like after the last class. But I also carried a stinging echo from Vanessa's critique of my poem. Of me?

I wondered if Daniel was home. He'd been working late nights this past week and sometimes didn't get home until past midnight. I glanced at the green glowing car clock: 10 p.m. For some reason, I didn't want to walk into a dark apartment. I didn't want to be alone.

When I'd been married to Andy, I liked it when he came home late from work or when he'd go fishing for the weekend with his father. When he was in the house, I couldn't relax. When he was away, I could sit on the couch and eat potato chips or ice cream, foods I never ate in front of him. When he was away, I could read or watch T.V. for hours. He didn't like to sit still for long, and when he was at home at any minute he might start cleaning the bathroom or vacuuming the furniture. But not in an easy manner. Aggressively. Grudgingly. The house was never quite clean enough for him. I was an educated working woman at the end of the twentieth century, but still I felt there was something wrong with me if I didn't vacuum every week or iron his work shirts at night or if I didn't make dinner every day. When we first got married, I liked doing those things. It was like playing house. And I could see in his close-set eyes a tenderness toward me when I did domestic tasks. Soon, though, the glow I felt from his loving approval morphed to feeling trapped. This was a *household*. I was the *wife*. The whole history of wife-ness had wrapped around me like ivy strangling tree. I'd had no clue marriage to Andy would be so smothering. We had fallen into an unspoken pattern: I had to ask permission for things I wanted to do. Whenever I wanted to buy something, or make plans, he took offense if I didn't ask him first. But the reverse wasn't so. We were engrained in a crazy double-standard that took me a while to unravel. And unraveling it meant the end of the marriage.

Once I was divorced, I swore I'd never repeat those patterns. I did some things I had never gotten to do since I had married so young, namely going out dancing and partying with single friends. I told myself I would shuck all the "shoulds" of being a woman and eat whatever I wanted and have sex with anyone I wanted (ergo, my complicated past that Daniel wanted to keep at bay with a condom). Fortunately, I didn't get pregnant or any diseases, venereal or otherwise.

By the time I met Daniel I was ready for a change. We met at the swimming pool of our apartment complex—we lived down the hall from one another, this shoddy apartment building in a bad part of town the only place I could afford post-divorce. Sometimes he'd knock on my door and come in and have a cup of tea. Or I'd knock on his and watch T.V. with him. We were friends who became lovers. And he still treated me like a friend in some ways. I could do whatever I wanted. He never demanded an accounting of my time. And now that we were living together, he never expected me to be the one to do the housekeeping. Sometimes, though, his laundry would pile up in the corner of the bedroom and I'd break down and do it because I couldn't stand the smell anymore. Or the grout in the kitchen would be so black I'd bleach it. Every once in a while he'd grab a can of cleanser and scrub the toilet and bathroom sink, but he never did so angrily or aggressively. He did so because for a moment he'd surface from the recesses of his mind and actually see the mundane details of life.

The lab's security guard opened the heavy glass door for me.

I walked down the quiet, empty hallway, the lab's familiar metallic smell infusing my mouth with a chemical tang. I could see through the window of Daniel's lab that he stood at his lab bench, carefully drawing liquid from a test tube with a pipette. His lab coat hung open, revealing a black tee-shirt and jeans, and he wore plastic goggles.

When I walked in, he looked up and smiled.

I smiled back. He was a little hunched, and I saw a flash of him in the future as an old man, thinning hair, bent back. Was that what his father looked like? Would I ever meet his father? We had yet to settle the Thanksgiving question. Our sex in the car had gone uncommented upon, too, like so much in our relationship.

Some punk-like music I didn't recognize played on the boom box.

"What's this music?" I asked him, sitting on a stool at the counter beneath a shelf holding hundreds of glass beakers. Every time I sat there I thought about what might happen in an earthquake, all that falling glass.

"The Ramones," he said. I'd heard of The Ramones in college. A guy down the hall in the dorms was into them. For some reason, it seemed like a guy thing to like The Ramones. It was a guy thing to be a music aficionado, to know obscure details about who fronted which band during what year. Kind of like baseball statistics, all the minutiae that men made important. I wanted to understand the appeal of that, and I'd half-heartedly participated in it at different times of my life, but baseball data and rock-n-roll trivia left me cold.

"You can turn it off," he said, "or change it. I have some Beatles there and some other stuff."

"I'd like to hear The Beatles," said a voice behind me, startling me. I'd thought we were alone. I turned and saw Ellen, short and dark in her bright white lab coat. In my black blazer, I morphed to large and dull.

"Oh, hi Ellen," I said.

"Hi Gwen. How's it going?" She was never anything but nice to me, and I tried to like her, but I was always pierced with a stinging resentment against her. I hated myself for it—it seemed petty. But she seemed to understand things I didn't, things beyond science. She'd been born in New Jersey, and like Daniel was raised in a Jewish household and had attended a private high school and then Brown. Not only was she smart but she was an athlete, a bike rider and mountain climber. She'd spent a number of summers in Europe, and sometimes she'd joke with Daniel in French. She was three years younger than me, but around her I felt like a teenager. Besides, I thought she had a thing for Daniel.

"Things are good," I said. "How about you?"

"I'm good. I can't believe we're here this late," she said, snapping off her rubber gloves and tossing them into a red container labeled *Toxic*. "I'm heading home. Daniel, do you want me to transfer that data over tonight?" she asked.

"No, that's okay," he said.

"Since when are you the boss around here that she has to ask you something like that?" I said, smiling yet unnerved at the edge in my voice. I had meant to make a joke but it came out completely wrong.

"He's the star post-doc around here, not me," Gwen said,

graciously side-stepping the awkwardness of my statement. Was she flirting with him?

"Who's the Walford Fellow?" said Daniel. "Who's getting a paper published in *Nature*? Sure isn't me. You're the one who's the star."

"Gwen," said Ellen, grabbing a paper towel from the dispenser. "Don't ever listen to him when he says crap like that. You're the girlfriend of a future Nobel Laureate. Or who knows, maybe one day the wife?"

"The wife?" I said, laughing, my face flaming in embarrassment.

"Now don't go giving me prizes and marrying me off," Daniel said, grinning. "What, are you moonlighting as a palm reader?"

"God, how can you stand how unromantic he is?" said Ellen, balling up the paper towel and throwing it at Daniel. It bounced off his shoulder and onto the floor.

"What makes you think I'm unromantic?" he said, looking like a bug in his goggles.

She rolled her eyes. "Gwen, am I right, or am I right?"

I felt a ping of resistance at her attempt to align us, while part of me was enjoying ribbing Daniel.

"He has a romantic side," I said, not sure what that even meant. He'd never brought me flowers, but I didn't care about flowers. He did fly twelve hours to see me in Japan. When I was ready to return to the states, he said I could live at his place. Our sex life had its good moments. He said I was beautiful. Was that romance? Did I really want romance, anyway, if it implied the man needed to woo the woman?

"Okay, you two, quit talking about me like I'm not here," he said. "I guess this is what women do when men aren't around, assess men's romantic standing."

"Don't be so egocentric," I said. "Women have much more interesting things to discuss."

"Oh yeah, like what?" He pulled his goggles off and hung them on a hook on the wall. I thought about everything guys talked about, their music facts and sports statistics. Even nerdy scientists spoke that guy talk.

"Like poetry," I said.

"And world affairs," said Ellen.

"And national events," I added.

"And historical injustices," said Ellen.

"Wow, you're busy behind the scenes," joked Daniel. Ellen threw another wadded-up paper towel at him. At that moment, I could imagine Daniel asking her out. And I could see her elated, accepting. Even women who climbed mountains and performed complex scientific research were charmed by a man's teasing them about the inadequacies of women.

I drove home, following Daniel's taillights. When we got in the door, he threw the mail on the table. In the midst of the bills and catalogues, I uncovered a *Playboy* magazine. The shiny cover featured a brunette bursting out of a tight button-down blouse. Her slick lips were pursed at the intended male viewer.

"What the hell is this?" I said, waving the magazine at Daniel who was sitting on the couch untying his shoes.

"What?" He tried to see what I flourished in my hand.

"It's a *Playboy*."

"Oh, yeah. Glen threatened to subscribe me to it for my birthday. I see he's done just that." Glen—whose name, ironically, was nearly a homophone of mine—was Daniel's old college roommate and best friend. He was now a physician living in Maryland. I'd met him once. He'd come to California to stay with Daniel for a week, arriving with a suitcase and a pizza box. On his flight over, he'd deliberately set his layover in Chicago so he could order his favorite deep-dish pepperoni pizza. I imagined being a passenger on the plane with this large, loud, jovial, pizza-bearing doctor, the scent of hot tomato sauce and garlic permeating the cabin. That was Glen. He was a big presence. It was impossible to not notice him. He and I had butted heads a few times in the week he was here with Daniel, but we had also gotten drunk together one night and while Daniel slept (he had a hard time staying awake after drinking too much), we filled the apartment with flirtatious laughter.

"Glen apparently doesn't give a shit that I live with you now," I said.

"What?" said Daniel. The way he paused before saying "what?", and the way he said it with a squint of his eyes, warned me that he felt stressed.

"Why would he think it would be okay for *Playboy* to be floating around *our* house? Did you tell him it was okay?" I had read enough feminist literature and taken enough women's studies classes to understand why this display of women's bodies was an affront to me. I wasn't standing alone here, and I was baffled that Daniel hadn't considered my feelings.

"Gwen, don't you remember that night at Anna and Dave's house?" I could hear him slowing down into a story, a teaching moment. Something hard and strong, like rage, was building in me. I didn't want to slow down. I didn't want him to feel it was time to teach me something. When I sat in the chair across from him, I realized I still held the *Playboy* in my hand. I threw it to the floor. Daniel's eyes followed the trajectory of the magazine as it crashed into the stereo, then he looked back at me.

"What night?" I didn't know how to turn the conversation back to him and Glen and their stupidity.

"We had dinner at their house? And they talked about how they both read *Playboy*? That they liked to read it together sometimes?"

"Oh, yeah, for its brilliant articles," I said. I glanced around the room. Where was my poetry notebook? I realized I'd probably left it in the car. For some reason I thought if I could hold it at that moment, it would anchor me.

"Yes, the articles," he said, ignoring my sarcasm, "and—well. Anyway, we'd all laughed as they told their story of sitting side-by-side in bed, looking together at the pictures."

"Is that what you want?" I said. "For us to wank each other to pictures in *Playboy*?" I suddenly felt very tired. I could hardly keep my eyes open.

"It does have good articles. Look who's been interviewed in it. Jimmy Carter, John Lennon, Gore Vidal."

"And which women?"

"It was just a birthday present," he said. "It's just a magazine."

He crossed his legs beneath him, sitting pretzeled like a teenage girl on the couch.

A horrible thought flashed through my mind, and I hoped I had the sense not to let it come out of my mouth. In a short second, I'd gone from excruciatingly sleepy to petulantly awake. *Just a birthday present. Just. Just. Only. Minutely.* I was a flea. My concerns were those of the teeniest, tiniest nit. He hadn't asked me about my poetry class. Was a poem nothing? He was studying the brain, saving lives. All those scientists raised on the East Coast who went to private schools and Ivy League colleges. Why had I never met his family? His mother a doctor, his father an economist. I was *just* a teacher, *just* a poet, *just* a woman upset at nothing. It was *just* a present. And here came the horrible words, the thought I'd tried to squelch, but I wanted to hurt him, hurt him hard, and I found out I could go far, very far.

"Just a magazine? And is *Mein Kampf* just a book?"

He sat, stunned. A horrible fire burned in my gut. I wanted to jump up, to run out of the room, but I was stuck to the chair.

"What are you saying?" he said. "Don't say that."

I should have shut up, should have said I was sorry, should have done anything but try to justify myself. But I said, "Well that's how this feels. It's oppressive, it's wrong."

"You cannot make that analogy," he said, his voice so soft his words were like wisps of sound.

What I'd said was probably one of the worst, hurtful, outrageous things I could have said. Who was I that I could do that? I hated myself for it, but I hated him too. I jumped up from the chair, my limbs heavy, and limped toward the door, expecting to hear him call out my name. But he didn't. I pulled open the door and ran out of the apartment, slamming the door behind me.

My head was roaring, my ears ringing, as though I'd just spent hours at a loud rock concert. I ran down the dim hallway, along the stained carpet and out the door. I was so disoriented I almost slipped down the stairs.

The swimming pool gleamed darkly in the moonlight. I ran past it and to the gate of the apartment, my breath tight, my head pounding. I didn't have my key or my card to open the gate. I'd have to wait until a car arrived from the other side in order to get out.

Trapped, I dropped to the curb, my knees curling to my chest, and sobbed. What was wrong with me? What was wrong with him? What was wrong with us?

CHAPTER FOUR

TWO GIRLS

All week I struggled to write a "deep poem." I read Walt Whitman over and over, reveled in his exaltations, his celebrations of himself, his connections between him and everyone—and his bizarre images like his body being "stuccoed" with birds. It made sense to me, that everything was connected—all people, all animals, every atom of the universe belonging to everyone and everything. But still I couldn't write anything.

It was Saturday. I woke at nine, and Daniel was still asleep, his pillow over his head. I sat in the living room, trying to write but crossing out every line I put down. I looked out the sliding glass door, at my bike leaning against the railing of the balcony. It would make too much noise to take it out. So I put on the headphones and watched old sitcoms until Daniel got up. He finally emerged from the bedroom wearing wrinkled clothes. Holding his keys in his hand, he walked over and kissed my forehead, then grabbed a soda out of the refrigerator and left the apartment, not saying a word. He didn't talk in the mornings. It was 11:30, early for him to be up and out of the house, especially on a Saturday. He must have been under pressure in the lab to leave this early on a weekend morning.

I shoved open the sliding glass door and pulled my bike into the living room, pushing it across the carpet to the front door. By the time I got to the bottom of the stairs I realized I'd forgotten my helmet. I didn't want to haul the bike back up the stairs. And I couldn't leave it there because I had no lock and it could easily disappear in just a few minutes. So I rode away without my helmet, the cool fall air blowing through my hair.

As I passed through the apartment gate, I remembered the night last week that I'd sat outside for half an hour after Daniel's and my horrible fight about the *Playboy* magazine. It had been cold, and I'd seen two shooting stars in a row through my tear-bleary eyes. I was sure Daniel would never forgive me for my *Mein Kampf* comment. How could I have said that? We'd had discussions in the past—that often degenerated into fights—about feminism and Jewishness. He'd say I'd never understand what it meant to be a Jewish person, to have a background that included family members murdered in concentration camps. I'd respond, *What about the persecution of women over the ages? Witch burning? Foot binding? Female genital mutilation? Domestic violence?* And he'd always say, *Yes, those are horrible things, but it's not the same.* We'd fight round and round in a Sisyphean attempt to get each other to see past their blind spot.

During one of these blow-outs I'd said, "Do you see yourself as a feminist?"

"I'm not even sure what that means," he answered, quietly. I could tell he was about ready to stop talking altogether.

"It means you believe women matter just as much as men."

"That sounds more like the definition of a humanist or humanitarian. I'm definitely one of those."

"But do you or don't you acknowledge that women have been persecuted in our world, in our society?"

"I can't talk about this anymore while you're being this way," he all but whispered.

As though to counter his retreat into silence, I'd stomped into the bedroom and slammed the door so hard his framed Art and Wine Festival poster crashed to the floor, cracking the glass.

That had been bad. But not as bad as the *Mein Kampf* argument. My comment had taken things to a whole new level. Sitting out in the dark that night, all alone and vulnerable, I'd realized I wasn't scared of being attacked and raped as I often was out alone at night, especially in our neighborhood. No, I was scared of myself. This blow-out with Daniel frightened me. I was capable of inflicting much more pain than I'd ever imagined.

I didn't have to dwell on berating myself that much longer, though. Daniel had appeared, sat next to me, put his arm around me. We'd sat together like that in the dark, quiet for a few minutes before he stood, took my hand to pull me up, and led me back to the apartment.

Highway 101 split East and West Palo Alto. While East Palo Alto was filled mostly with black and brown faces—and liquor stores, gas stations, and desolate buildings marred by broken windows—the west part of the town was populated with white faces, upscale cafes and shops, and a high tax base that guaranteed clean streets and state-of-the-art public schools. The university where Daniel worked was sprawled on the westernmost edge of Palo Alto, as far away from the poor side of town as possible. The segregation was clear. Where we lived was the exception, however, a borderland, a transitional space, between the abject poverty of East Palo Alto and the pronounced affluence of West Palo Alto. Our address was East Palo Alto, but our apartment building was part of a mass of apartment complexes on the west side of 101. Only a small creek, not a freeway, marked our separation from the wealthy neighborhood we bordered. The slough of apartment buildings housed a mix of students and low-paid post docs, like Daniel, as well as the workers who kept the downtown humming by teaching in public schools, cutting residents' hair in fashionable salons, and cooking and serving California cuisine.

I rode my bike past our apartment building, shaded by old trees. The sidewalks were cracked and the gutters dotted with litter. Upon crossing the arched cement bridge over the creek, I was surrounded by big, flawlessly renovated houses bordered by impressive green lawns. Huge trees shaded the road, and my tires crunched leaves that had yet to be swept away by gardeners. I wondered who built these houses. Were they initially populated by professors before all the stately professorial homes were built on campus? Were these homes now owned by computer barons?

As I rode toward downtown beneath fat-trunked trees, I felt infused with the childhood freedom of bicycling. I wished writing a poem could feel this effortless. But even though writing poetry was hard, I experienced a rush of pleasure at the thought of poetry, of writing a poem, of poetry class—like an especially delicious secret that you simultaneously want to keep and tell. And blended in with this thought of poetry were Jamie and Cat. They, too, felt like a secret, like something I held inside and was itching to tell. What, exactly, was the secret? That I was in a poetry class with two lesbians? Why should that matter to me or to anyone else? Were they definitely lesbians? I hadn't thought about them that way when I first saw them, but now the word was connected to them in my mind.

No, that wasn't the secret. They were *intrigued* with me. Cat had written that exact word on my poem. She and Jamie were *intrigued*. I suddenly sensed the bicycle seat between my legs, pushing at me. The idea of intrigue rushed through me with a sexual pulse. That was the secret.

I pulled my bike into the park at the edge of town, passed a group of students in university-branded tee-shirts throwing Frisbees, and bumped over the grass to a bench. I leaned my bike against the bench and sat in a patch of sun. It was a warm day, but the air had a cool fall edge to it. A tiny brown bird on a branch above me jumped. A leaf dangled off the tree, just at the edge of falling. It was the edge of fall. I could feel a poem forming in me.

* * *

Fall

A bright blue afternoon, nearly bare
muted branches. That jittery gray bird (there)
hopping foot to foot looks like the bird as a child

I prodded with a stick. A word, I ache
for a word in fall,
splitting a veiny leaf as I pass:
     universe?
     uterus?
     ubiquitous?
     us?
I look up. Fettered brown leaves twitch.
At the bend I switch to another path.
It is like shaking hands with the wind.

Reading my poem aloud in class, I realized how much it owed to Walt Whitman, to his personal narrator connecting with the cycles of life through nature. I looked down to take notes, hearing the students' voices:

"I like the list of words that begin with 'u.' That's surprising and different."

"I don't like 'ubiquitous.' It seems too pretentious. Same with 'fettered.'"

"I don't think so. I like the sound of them. And the poem is about searching for something. So you're going to try different words."

"Yeah, the question marks are really effective."

"Reminds me a little of Robert Frost, with choosing 'another' path, like in 'The Road Not Taken.'"

"There's desire in this poem."

I flushed. When I'd written the poem it had felt like stars were sparking out of my fingertips and through my body, rushing through my blood. For sure, there was desire in the poem. Yes, Walt Whitman. I'd been looking down at my paper, but I knew that Vanessa had made the comment about desire in her rough-hewn voice. I looked up. She was continuing to talk about the poem, tapping her crooked finger on the page as she addressed her ideas.

"The questioning is especially effective." She looked at me with her piercing pale blue eyes, her long gray hair framing her furrowed face. "Gwen, I can see you've gone deeper, tried something new. That's great. I do think, though, that this poem may stop just a little short. There may be more to say about that path."

Again I felt my face heat up and was grateful that my blushing usually didn't show. I wasn't exactly sure why I was blushing, but my body bloomed with energy. I showed I was capable of going deeper, although how I had done it was still a mystery to me. It didn't matter, though. Sitting there in a dusty classroom, in a circle of people who cared about poetry, felt richer than any other part of my life.

Jamie's poem was next, another poem about a grandmother and a little girl:

Grandma's Spoons

Grandma gives me spoons for under the lemon tree
the sacred place, the burial ground
for small plastic animals and green army men
who perish and disappear beneath clay soil tunnels
that collapse under the weight of a child's small fist.
The sacred place where lemon adds cool spice

to the fresh air of pretend,
where small animals in bright blues, yellows and reds
risk their lives rescuing fallen soldiers
whose dirty shelters have swallowed them up. I sit
in the San Joaquin Valley summer heat
under the lemon tree
with Grandma's metal spoons,
digging the dirt,
packing the dirt,
small hands reaching through tunnels
to meet in the cool middle,
a fine place, a safe place for soldiers
to hide from the enemy, a sacred place
to disappear with Grandma's spoons,
under the lemon tree.

As she read her poem the second time, I saw that we both had incorporated into our poems images of a child experiencing mortality: me with the child prodding the dead bird, Jamie with the "burial ground" for soldiers and animals. As the class talked about Jamie's poem, I looked across the room at her. The scar on her forehead shone in the florescent light and her neck curved as her face bent toward the page.

At that moment something came into focus. Complete, clear, unambiguous focus. The word she'd mouthed to me at the first class boomeranged back, as though it had been heading my direction for two weeks in slow motion.

The word was: *beautiful*.

Jamie was beautiful.

Jamie is a beautiful woman. I spoke those words inside in a way I'd never spoken them about a woman before. Of course I'd thought certain friends, or strangers, or actresses were beautiful. But I'd never before allowed the desire in my appraisal of another woman to enter my body.

At that moment, it did.

I simply, easily moved from one position to another. I moved from "I'm attracted only to men" to "I'm attracted to a woman" as simply as you might step over a crack in the sidewalk. As gracefully as you might erase a word from a chalkboard.

After class I sat longer in my chair than usual, slowly gathering my papers and putting my pens in my purse. When I stood, I saw Jamie and Cat walking toward me as though I had willed it to happen.

"Hey," Cat said. She stood about half-a-head shorter than Jamie, who was just about my height. Cat wore what I now thought of as her uniform of leather jacket, white tee shirt and jeans. I tried on the word *beautiful* for her too; it didn't quite fit. But there was definitely something striking about her.

"Hey," I said back, smiling at them both, my heart pounding in my ears.

"We're going to go get something to eat," said Jamie. "Just across the street. Want to come?" Jamie wasn't wearing her leather jacket tonight. Instead she had on a denim jacket, like Vanessa's, and a black tee-shirt with that silver chain glittering on her chest.

"Sure," I said, hardly believing this was happening. I knocked my binder off my desk and my papers went flying. My first impulse was to be mortified, but Cat and Jamie's easy laughter and casual way of helping me gather my things led me to see my blunder as a funny, harmless *faux pas*.

"So who do you live with?" Jamie asked me.

The three of us sat in a booth at Fido's, a dog-themed café near campus. Pictures of pooches lined the walls, and the table cloths were printed with dog paws. Sports banners hung over the tables displaying the university's mascot: not a dog, but a Viking holding a spear and shield. Only one other table in the restaurant had people at it—a group of four guys in the corner speaking in loud voices. We sat in the other corner as far from them as possible. We'd ordered a pitcher of beer and a heaping platter of salty fries. They looked and smelled good but my stomach was too knotted up to eat, an unusual phenomenon for me.

"Well, I live with a—a scientist," I said, jiggling my foot under the table. "Named Daniel."

"Oh, uh huh." Jamie grinned, flashing her movie star teeth. I was sure Cat elbowed her. So they'd been talking about me behind my back. That idea amused and excited me.

"We've been together for almost three years," I continued. "Well kind of. I mean, one of those years I lived in Japan."

"Japan?" Jamie said. I liked when people responded with that kind of surprise. It made me feel like I'd done something unique, something special, with my life.

"Yeah, I was teaching English there."

"And you left your boyfriend for a year?" asked Cat. "How'd that work?" She propped her chin in her hand and looked at me mischievously. Was she flirting? She was playfully teasing me about my boyfriend and probably flirting, I thought. My body was at its apex of tingling.

"It worked alright," I said evasively, in an effort to flirt back, just a little. Something felt precarious about all of this. It was one thing to think of a woman as desirable. It was another to entertain the possibility of following through on that desire. An image flowed through me of two women, kissing, pressing their bodies together … I needed to draw the attention away from me, to turn the interview toward them.

"So who do you two live with?" I asked.

They looked at each other.

"Well," said Jamie, "I live with Rose."

"That's her girlfriend," said Cat, patting Jamie on the arm. "In case anyone here needs any clarification. And not only that, Rose is a minister. A Christian minister. The Most Holy Reverend Rose Altamont of the Holier Than Thou Ministry."

"Fuck you," said Jamie, playfully pushing at Cat with her shoulder and almost knocking her off the booth bench. Cat stuck out her boot and righted herself in an easy way. I couldn't help but think, *in a guy way*. They both had an ease, a comfort, with their bodies that I usually saw only in men—and a guy-like camaraderie fueled by teasing and play. Jamie said to me, "She's a minister in the Disciples of Christ, an open and affirming ministry."

"Which means they're tolerant of queers," Cat said. "Mighty nice of them, don't you think?"

"Yeah, well," Jamie continued, unfazed by Cat's teasing, "it's not my thing, but it means a lot to Rose."

"The minister and the atheist," said Cat.

"Sounds like a sitcom!" said Jamie. We all laughed.

So. Jamie had a live-in love. And they had different religious backgrounds. We had something in common. "Are you really an atheist?" I asked.

"An agnostic."

"What's the difference?" Cat jibed.

"An atheist and a Christian both *believe*," said Jamie with a holy-roller inflection. "A Christian is certain that there's a God and that his son Jesus is Lord and Savior. An atheist is certain that that's all a bunch of B.S. An agnostic says we just can't know. That's me. Not attached to believing or to faith. Life's a big unknown."

"So what does your, your—Rose think of that?" I asked.

Cat interjected. "She hates that she can't convert Jamie! Because," she paused, fixing her gaze on me, "Jamie converted Rose, so Rose wanted to return the favor."

"Oh, give me a break," said Jamie. They were both half-laughing.

"You look confused," said Cat, still staring at me. "Let me explain. Jamie was Rose's first girl. Jamie may be an agnostic but she's evangelical about lesbianism."

"Look who's talking," said Jamie. "The stories I could tell Gwen about you."

"What? What?" said Cat, shrugging her shoulders with feigned innocence.

Jamie turned to me and cupped her hand to the side of her face and said in a stage whisper, "Cat *always* falls for the straight girl. Rose wasn't straight when I met her, just trying to *be* straight."

"And you talked her out of that right quick," said Cat. "And ever since she's been trying to get Jamie to be the perfect Christian wife." They both laughed at that, although Jamie looked a little flushed, maybe annoyed. I picked up the pitcher and poured us each a little more beer to finish it off. The server, a young guy with messy brown hair wearing a sweatshirt with the Viking mascot on it, came over and we ordered another pitcher.

"And you, Cat, who do you live with?" I asked.

"I live alone."

"You do not!" said Jamie.

"Well, I will in about two weeks."

"Yeah," Jamie said, picking up a French fry and putting it on the small plate in front of her. "Emma couldn't take it any more."

"Ha, ha," said Cat blandly.

"Emma?" I asked. I took a drink of my beer.

"Her girlfriend," Jamie said.

"Ex," said Cat. She was looking down at the table so I couldn't tell if she was upset or not. I wanted to know everything about the break-up, about what women do when they fall in love, live together and leave one another. But Cat looked a little hurt, so I moved on.

"How long have you two known each other?" I asked.

"Too long," said Jamie, biting a fry in half.

"Yeah, it's been torturous," said Cat.

"No, really," I said.

"Let's see," said Cat. "It was about, hmm, ten years ago she broke up with me."

"I broke up with *you*?" Jamie said. "See," she said, looking at me, "this is revisionist history if I've ever heard it. Typical Cat."

"Let me refresh your memory," said Cat. "We were eating pancakes."

"Waffles," said Jamie.

"At Howard Johnson's," Cat continued. "And you told me you wanted to break up."

"No, I asked you if *you* wanted to break up."

"Same thing."

"I don't think so," Jamie said. "I had a very specific reason for asking you. A reason equating to our martini-loving, bikini-wearing neighbor, Sherry." Cat was half-grinning at me as Jamie talked, as though I were in on the joke. But I was just on the edges of it. I was still grappling with the idea that Cat and Jamie had been girlfriends. They seemed too much like … well, buddies, to have been lovers. And now was Jamie saying that Cat had cheated on her?

Jamie paused when the group of guys who'd been sitting in the corner noisily made their way past us to the door. Four guys in dark clothes, their energy jostling by like a dust storm. As they passed, one of them grunted out something, a word.

Had he really said the word *dykes*? With disgust?

I wasn't sure I'd heard him right, but Cat and Jamie certainly did. They shot out of their seats and side-by-side confronted the guy, who was taller than them both, lanky and skinny like a spider. A stretched-out black sweater hung on his body.

"What did you say?" Cat said, her voice dropping an octave. He towered over her, but in her black leather jacket and spiky hair she seemed to take up more space than he did.

"What?" he said defensively, taking a step back. His friends stopped and turned. The waiter watched from behind the cash register. This had happened so fast, and Cat and Jamie had responded together so quickly, in synch like the best two players on a basketball team.

"She said *what did you say?*" Jamie said, carefully enunciating each word, her boots planted on the ground. Her face gained a new dimension, one I'd never seen in class nor in our playful banter around the table. As though she'd donned a mask she'd been hiding in her pocket.

I was sure the skinny guy's friends would say or do something, but they just stood there next to the front door. For a disorienting moment, I irrationally imagined him with a knife or gun in his pocket. But, no, he had a backpack slung over his shoulder. He was probably just a student.

"What did you say?" Jamie repeated in the same manner, slowly, decisively.

"What?" said the skinny guy with a bit of a squeak in his voice, sounding suddenly like a little kid getting bullied on the playground. "I didn't say anything."

"You didn't say anything," said Cat, evenly. "Okay. That's what I thought."

She and Jamie stood still as the guy took a few more steps

backward then turned. He followed his friends out of the place. The minute they shut the door, a burst of rowdy laughter filtered through to us. Jamie and Cat slid back into the booth.

"Fucking pricks," said Cat. "Fucking little frat boys." I noticed her hands were quivering as she lifted her beer to her mouth.

"Are you okay?" Jamie asked me. I realized my hands were gripped into tight fists. I relaxed them and took a deep breath.

"I'm fine," I said. "Are you two okay?"

"We're fine," Jamie said.

"All in a day's work," said Cat.

Jamie started to laugh. "Did you see that kid's face?"

"Jesus!" exclaimed Cat, grinning. "My god, can you believe it? The little prick."

"Yeah," laughed Jamie. "Scared of two girls!"

I looked in awe at the two of them—at Cat's aggressive chin and graceful hands, her sleek leather jacket; and at Jamie's long neck, her big striking eyes, the flash of her teeth in her laughing mouth, and the sparkling scar on her forehead.

Cat glanced at her watch. "Oh shit," she said. "I have to go. I told Emma I'd take her to the airport." Something in me drooped. I wasn't ready to call it a night. The idea of driving back home now would be like taking a sleeping pill, when I was wide awake and didn't want to sleep.

"Oh, that's right," said Jamie. "Do you want to stay and finish, or go?" she asked me.

Cat stood and gave Jamie an undecipherable look. "I drove, remember?" said Cat, an edge to her voice that reminded me of my sister and me, the way we easily slid from a playful repartee to an irritated exchange. "I have to take you home."

"My car's in the shop," said Jamie, turning to me.

"Where do you live?" I asked.

"Just a few miles from here, near the Rose Garden."

"Well I can take you home," I offered. "I mean, that is, if you want to stay a while longer." I panicked for a second at the thought of being alone with her, but the panic quickly bloomed into something else, something like the anticipation when the bar locks over your shoulders before the roller coaster jerks forward.

Cat shoved her hands in the pockets of her leather jacket and jingled her keys. Jamie looked up at her and said, "I think we'll stay." She smiled her high-wattage smile. Cat's lips were a flat line across her face. She grabbed her satchel and threw it over her shoulder.

"Well, have fun girls," she said leaning toward me, her lips lifting into a small smile. "Bye Gwen. See you in class next week." I felt a little charge, as though she'd rubbed her boots on the carpet and crackled with static electricity.

"And see you at Judy's tomorrow, eight o'clock. The barbecue," added Jamie.

"Okay, I'll be there. Bye." Cat pulled her keys from her pocket and held them up in mock salute.

"Wait, maybe we should go with you, walk you to your car," said Jamie. "What if those assholes are still out there?"

We all looked out the window. It was dark, and in the streetlights students walked on the sidewalks and crossed the street at the crosswalk.

"I'm okay," she said.

"Really?" Jamie said. "We should walk you to your car."

"Knock it off. I'm late. I'm out of here." She lifted her keys again and turned, exiting the restaurant.

"Do you really think those guys would do something?" I asked Jamie, after the door sprung shut behind Cat.

"Probably not but you never know." She poured the rest of the beer into both our glasses. "Cheers." She clicked her glass against mine.

"Has anything—well, you know, ever happened to you? With aggressive guys like that, I mean. In public."

"Not much more than what you saw here," she said. "What about you?"

"What do you mean?"

"Do men bother you in public? Ha, like I really need to ask."

I flushed. "Just a few weeks ago, something weird happened," I said. I told her about the Hulk in the restaurant who bought me a drink and then wanted to look at the label in my shoe. I left out that I'd been waiting for Daniel.

"Funny, no guy has ever asked me to take off my shoe for him." She laughed, sticking her boot out from under the table and wiggling the thick sole. I glanced down at my sling-back dark blue pumps I'd worn for work. "But," she continued, "plenty of guys have bought me drinks. Mostly gay boys."

I wondered if she meant at gay bars, that she and gay guys hung out together. I wondered if she'd ever had a boyfriend. Or sex with a man. I wondered where she got that scar. I wondered if she was in love with Rose. A million questions crowded my mind, a cloud of gnats. I felt like I could talk to her for days and weeks and still have more to say, to ask. "So you and Cat were, like, really together? Like … girlfriends?"

"Uh huh. For three years. In our early twenties. We lived in an apartment not too far from here, in fact, downtown, over on 4th." I imagined a little apartment with hardwood floors and throw rugs, windows open to traffic sounds, pillows on the floor, bookshelves, an easel. Dust motes dancing in the light.

"And you're such good friends, now," I said. "I don't know many people who are good friends with their ex's. Well, except for my friend, Kaye. She's always on the phone with old boyfriends." It was strange and thrilling to talk causally about two women being ex's in the same breath as talking about a man/woman couple. As though they were basically the same thing. "I—well, my ex-husband would probably turn and walk the other way if he saw me walking toward him down the street."

"You were married?" Jamie asked. I realized my world might be just as extraordinary to her as hers was to me.

"Yeah, for four years. He was an accountant."

"I'm sorry," she teased, smiling.

"About the marriage part or the accountant part?"

"Both! No, some of my best friends are accountants." We laughed.

"Well, he did fit the stereotype. Very detail-oriented. Rigid, even. Kind of old-fashioned, almost like he'd been in the military, which he hadn't. It's hard to explain. I guess at first it wasn't too bad—I mean, I did marry the guy. It wasn't all about him. I changed, I grew. He said I read too much, that it was making me too idealistic." As I spoke, it struck me how Andy was such a serious guy. And so was Daniel. In some ways Daniel was completely the opposite of Andy. But in other ways, they were a lot alike. Or was it not that they were alike, but that I acted in the same way with the two of them? Was I unchangeable in spite of everything I did to try to change— divorce, living in a foreign country, taking a poetry class, working in politics. Was I Sisyphus? Was I repeating patterns, destined to never break out of being the same woman my whole life?

"He said you were too idealistic?" Jamie said. "What was he, a Republican?" She laughed. "Oops, no offense intended. Are you a Republican?"

"Not even close," I said. "I'm not only not a Republican, I'm a fierce Democrat. I was raised that way—it's in my blood. I'm doing some work for the Clinton campaign, and I was a precinct worker for Dukakis. Spent hours working on his campaign, and he was whomped. I was devastated."

"Ah, maybe you are too idealistic," she said. "Just teasing. I admire that, that you do political work."

"Hanging fliers on people's doors doesn't feel like much."

"It's more than most people do. Don't hate me, but I didn't vote for Dukakis."

"What? You voted for Bush?"

"No," she said, "for Willa Kenoyer."

"Who?"

"The Socialist party candidate."

"Okay, how can *idealist* be a dirty word when you're an *atheistic commie?*" I teased.

"Excuse me, that's *agnostic socialist.*" She grinned.

"Are you really a socialist?"

"No, I'm an independent. I do like some things about the Socialist party, though—their focus labor rights and civil rights, especially. And they ran a gay man for president in 1980."

"No, really?"

"David McReynolds," she said. "The Republicans or Democrats probably won't nominate a gay person for, well, a million years."

"The Democrats would do it before the Republicans ever would," I countered. "Look at Clinton compared to Bush. Clinton isn't afraid to talk about AIDS. And he's going to abolish discrimination against gays in the military."

"I have a hard time imagining that really happening," she said. "Maybe he believes in equality, and I do see him as working hard for the gay vote—but I can't imagine that he'll be able to pull it off if he's elected."

"But he's so much better than the alternative. Are you going to vote for the socialist again?"

"I'm not sure."

"Think about it. The polls say the race is very close. I could understand with Dukakis because, bottom line is he really didn't have a shot against Reagan. But Clinton really does have a shot. I mean— it's not just my idealist self speaking, but polls show they are neck and neck."

"I think you're right," she said. "Okay, I'll vote for Clinton."

"Did I just convert you?" I said, flushing the minute I said it, realizing all its implications. I put my hand to my mouth.

She laughed and veered the conversation to a new topic, graciously letting me off the hook. "So let me ask you a question— you seem interested in this agnostic thing. Are you religious?"

"*Leaves of Grass* is my bible. I like Whitman's idea, that everything's connected, that we die and become one with the grass. I guess I do believe in the spirit, that there's something about human beings at our cores that lives on after we die."

"That's a really nice thought," she said. "I hope it's true."

"Me too."

We continued to veer from subject to subject—politics, to religion, to art. Jamie told me she was a painter and sculptor. When I thought of sculpting, I said, I thought of Michelangelo standing before a massive piece of marble.

"No," she said, "I don't do marble. I work with clay and metal."

"I have no idea how you sculpt metal." I imagined trying to bend metal with my hands or taking some kind of hard tool to it to force it into shapes.

"The process I use is lost wax. The easiest way to explain it is this: you mold a figure out of wax and you attach a funnel of wax to it. Then you cast it in plaster so that the funnel part is sticking out. Then when it's hard, you heat it up and melt out the wax, so the empty space is the exact shape of your object. Then you fill it with liquid metal. You see?"

"I'm not sure. Maybe."

"I have a studio on campus, just across the street. I can show you. Do you want to see?"

A giddy, dizzy warmth rushed through my body, not only from the beer but from the awareness of what I was doing. I was alone with this woman who'd been sitting in my poetry class, this woman who I'd had a revelation about, this woman I thought was beautiful. No, not just thought. *Felt.* I could feel her beauty inside me, a jewel of a secret that I had shared with no one—but that, I now predicted, I was on the edge of sharing with her.

CHAPTER FIVE

COMPLEMENTARY COLORS

The night was cool. The air smelled of an oddly comforting mix of car exhaust and the greasy, grilled scents of fast-food. With a group of noisy students, we crossed the street at the light. I wondered what we looked like, Jamie and me walking together, illuminated by streetlights. What did other people see? Two women about the same height, one with long hair, the other with short hair; one wearing slacks and a blazer, the other in denim; one gripping her purse, the other with a leather bag flung across her back, her hands in her pants pockets. Who did they imagine we were?

For as many students as we'd seen on the perimeter of campus, the quad was mostly deserted. In the scarcely-lit night, the vast expanse of grass stretched out like black water. Looming overhead was the red-brick bell tower, the only ivy-covered building on campus, a nod to tradition, to conventions older and more prestigious than this state university. The rest of the campus spoke of outmoded, once modern, mid-twentieth century California, with its flat-roofed, low-slung concrete buildings. The two exceptions were the recent additions to campus, the tall Engineering and Business buildings: elegant, anonymous high rises with opaque glass windows.

As we walked, Jamie told me about her work. She and Cat had a small business they called Home Helper. Most of their clients were elderly people who lived in asphalted mobile home parks that spread across the outskirts of the city. The old people hired them to wash windows, trim hedges and run errands.

Jamie asked me about my work, and I described my job at the tutoring center.

"Do you love it?" she asked.

"Like, not love," I said, distinctly aware of her shoulder moving next to mine. "Well, it's okay." I thought about how excited I'd been when I got the job, when I knew I'd get to work in something related to teaching without having to grade papers, where I'd get a paycheck and get to buy my first car. I'd left Tokyo weary of living in a huge city, in another country. But when I'd first found out about the Japan job, I was so thrilled I spun around in my living room. And when I first got to Tokyo, everything was so wonderfully new, so astonishingly different. And then I hit my limit of novelty and had to leave. Was it inevitable that the excitement of change devolved into discontent?

"Just okay? So it's definitely not your dream job."

"No."

"What is?"

Her question opened up a whirling expanse in me, like the spinnings of Van Gogh's "Starry Night." The night sky tonight looked nothing like the golden swirls of Van Gogh's purple night.

The starless sky was grayish black—and a column of light, probably from a car dealership, slid like a brown illuminated finger above us.

"My dream job's working in a bookstore," I said, surprised that my dream was so available to me. "I love books, the smell of books. Columns of books. Your eyes get to feast on all the possibilities in the titles climbing the spines."

"Have you ever worked in a bookstore?"

"No. I looked into applying to one once, but it was in one of those big chains where everything's clean and smells like glue. And they don't pay anything."

"Well, you should own one then, and run it," she said.

"Now there's a dream."

"And I'll run the café. I'll make lattes with extra foam and ginger cookies and pumpkin muffins."

"You like to cook?" I asked.

"Love it. Especially baking, especially in winter. I love the way the scents fill the house—or in this case, the bookstore-café."

"We can put your art on the walls," I said, the "we" echoing pleasurably, and a little dangerously, in my mind.

"And sell the poetry books of all our friends," she said.

"And what about cats?"

"No, she's not allowed in this dream."

"I said *cats*, not Cat. As in *meow*."

"Oh, yes, we need cats. At least two or three that slink among the stacks."

"What if someone has allergies? Could they sue us?"

"Don't disrupt the dream," she chided me. "Three cats, the fatter the better."

"What would we call it?" I was never very good at naming things. I struggled to title my poems.

"How about Books and Brew?" she said. "And then we could sell beer, too, and there'd be a double-meaning to the 'brew.' Beer brewing, coffee brewing."

"That's good," I said.

"Or Readables and Edibles. Or Books and Bites."

"How about something with cats in the title?" I said.

"Fat Cats and Fatter Books."

We laughed at her riffing like a jazz musician on the title, an expansive act of play. A giddy fullness took over me like I was in sixth grade again, planning a slumber party with my best friend.

We approached the Art Building. I'd never been inside. It looked a lot like the English building, its metal window frames weeping streaks of brown rust down the sallow walls. Concrete stairs led up to a wooden door embedded with small-paned squares of yellowed glass. Above the door, metallic letters spelled out "Art Building" in a lettering style that had once been contemporary but now looked tired.

We walked down the hall. It smelled like old pennies and was lit by overhead florescent lights just like in our poetry classroom. The classroom doors here were all closed. Through the chicken-wire enforced glass square in each door, I could see that some of rooms were dark, while others were lit up but empty.

The men's bathroom door was ajar, and a janitor came out holding a broom and a plastic bag of garbage.

"Hi Jorge, *buenos noches*," said Jamie.

"*Buenos noches*, Jamie," he said, leaning the broom against the wall. "You're here late."

"Yeah, well, just going to go check out the studio. This is Gwen," she said.

"Evening," he said, nodding his head. "Well, you girls have a gorgeous night." He turned with his broom and his bag to walk down the hall.

"Thanks, nice to meet you," I said. I'd seen janitors after-hours in different places but had never had an interaction with one. Maybe I'd said hello. But this man had a name. And he knew Jamie's name. He became a real man, not just a cardboard cut-out of a janitor. Jamie made him visible to me, three-dimensional. Just as she had our dream store. As we'd spoken about it, I could smell the pumpkin muffins and used books. I could feel a cat rub up against my leg as I rang up a sale, as I held the heft of a book in my hand. It felt good to romanticize the vision.

We both needed to use the restroom. It smelled of Lysol and lemons. I thought about the very real person—Jorge—who had cleaned this public restroom, a man in a blue shirt with eyes like my father's, who smelled like cigarette smoke and bleach.

As I washed my hands, Jamie poked her head out of a stall and said, "Do you have a tampon?"

I opened my purse and dug around, extracting one. "Ta dah!" I announced.

"My savior!"

We giggled like girls.

As she washed her hands at the sink, I became very aware of our women-ness. The sloughing off of blood from her womb. The swell of my breasts beneath my bra. The silver necklace between her breasts. The curve of her hips beneath her wide-pocketed jeans.

"Can I see your tattoo?" I asked. I'd caught a glimpse of it as she dried her hands on a rough, institutional paper towel.

She held her hand out to me. Across the room in class, and in the restaurant, I'd seen it on the back of her hand, and now here it was, so close to me: two waves in a yin-yang dance, one orange, one blue.

"What's it mean to you?" I asked.

"It's energy," she said.

"Energy?"

"Artistic energy, life energy, moving together. And in complementary colors."

As we walked toward the studios, I asked her what she meant by complementary colors. She explained the color wheel, that each color on the wheel has its complement, a kind of opposite that intensifies the other color. Each color's complement lies on the other side of the wheel. These ostensible opposites are not merely opposites but together create a kind of gestalt.

"You know," she said, "with two abutting complementary colors, the sum is greater than its individual parts. I can show you. I have a color wheel in the studio."

She pulled open a door at the end of the hall. Through the door an empty foyer was surrounded by thick black curtains like a stage. Jamie pulled the curtain aside. A series of quiet studios lay before us separated by a narrow aisle. We walked down the aisle, each studio its own world of color and jumble. I saw not only canvasses, paints, clay—but also objects, like things you might pull out of the garbage or get at a yard sale. Old broken frames and mirrors, chunks of wood, a bin of old clocks, a table covered in chess pieces and marbles. We paused at a studio filled with women's high-heeled shoes painted an array of crazy colors. There must have been hundreds of shoes—pumps, spike heels, platforms.

"That's Judy's work."

I reached out to touch one. "Oh, it's not a real shoe."

"That one's clay," said Jamie.

"It looks so real."

"Some of them are real shoes that she buys by the truckload at the Goodwill. Others are clay or metal."

We continued down the aisle, and Jamie turned into her studio.

Large empty canning jars lined one shelf. A few canvasses were propped on an easel in the corner, the one on top a half-finished painting of green hills with purple shadows. On a table in the middle of the room were a number of small objects. I got closer and saw they were little sculptures: some of animals, others of boxes. I picked up one animal. It was a black and white dog, sitting cross-legged on a wing-backed chair, reading a book. He looked like a real dog, though, not a cartoon, and so there was something other-worldly about the image.

"Hey, maybe he's our bookstore mascot," I said.

"Sure," she said.

I set down the reading dog and picked up a box. I could feel it was made of clay. It was painted like a fantastical blue sky with puffy white clouds.

"Lift the lid," she said.

I hadn't realized there was a lid. I pulled at the top, and the clouds parted. Inside sat two miniature clay women having a picnic. They were painted blue and white, like the clouds, except they had yellow hair like the sun. I looked closer and realized the women had the faces of pigs.

"It's magical," I said. "And surprising, with those pig faces. Maybe even a little eerie, but I'd still like to be there, in that box, in their world."

She pulled two stools out from under the table and we sat. "That's exactly what I want, to elicit a certain desire like Wayne Theibaud does, only different, my own way."

"Who's Wayne Theibaud?"

"He paints cakes and candies in glass cases. He makes you want to eat his creations. We know they're just paint, but we still want them."

I ran my hands along the surface of some of Jamie's other pieces—boxes, animals, fantastical figures. I wondered what it was like to make something with your hands. Or to want to. I didn't have the impulse to make physical objects. But I liked to see what others did, and to touch them. Whenever I went to museums, it was hard for me to resist the desire to touch. I picked up a box engraved with a crescent and a full moon on it. When I lifted the lid, I saw inside a goddess-like figure with a hole in her belly.

"That's the fertility box," said Jamie. "If you're trying to get pregnant, you put a drop of menstrual blood inside."

I looked up at her. "Is this yours? I mean, for you?"

"Well, I've thought about it."

"You want to have a baby?"

"Sometimes I do. What about you? Do you?"

I had that sense of urgency inside that you get when you're feeling a new connection with someone, someone who is suddenly filling up your life in corners you didn't even know were empty.

"Sometimes," I said. "But other times I think not. Society seems to push the Mom role on me so much that I can't figure out what my real desires are."

"I know what you mean."

So, even as a lesbian she'd felt that pressure to be a mother.

"Are you and Rose—" Saying her name, I felt both the petals and the thorn. "Are you two—?"

"We've talked about it," she said. "But I don't know if I want to have a baby with her."

There it was, what I'd been waiting for without knowing it. Words of dissatisfaction about her relationship with Rose.

"Why not?" I asked.

"We've been struggling for a while, I mean with being unhappy together. I wonder if having a child with her would make it better or worse."

The exact same question about Daniel resided in me. I'd once seen a cartoon man swallow a live frog that bounced inside his body. Every time it jumped, his skin poked out jaggedly in a different spot. That's how the marriage-and-kids-with Daniel question felt in me. Like a crazed frog in my belly.

"I know what you mean," I said. Those words opened up a whole new world to Jamie and me, a place for us to come together through our grievances about our relationships. We sat on the stools in the studio, our arms nearly touching, talking through the richness of what was missing in our lives. It seemed that Rose and Daniel knew exactly who they were. They were invested in their lives as minister and scientist. They *knew* things and imparted them in their worlds, and to us. There was fighting, Jamie said. Lots of bickering, I said. And something, something was missing. We both backtracked a bit, listed Rose's and Daniel's good qualities. They did have good qualities. They were people we'd thought we once loved—and maybe still loved in a way. We weren't sure. We shared our not-knowing, and it wrapped around us like a new coat.

"Oh, I was going to show you the color wheel," she said, reaching over to a shelf. She set on the table a circular piece of cardboard displaying the colors of the rainbow in a variety of shades. A childhood song came back to me: *Red, orange, yellow, green, blue, purple—those are the colors of the rainbow.* That chanting song had been a way for us to memorize the colors, but I'd never before thought of their significance, or of the fact that there was such a thing as "color theory." Jamie explained about primary colors, analogous colors, monochromatic colors, warm versus cool colors.

"And then there are complementary colors," she said, "the colors opposite each other on the wheel—like blue and orange, and red and green." She put her finger on red, then green. They didn't touch on the color wheel, but I thought of them juxtaposed at Christmastime and how put together they jumped out at my eyes. "They're opposites," she said. "When they're placed next to each other, they appear brighter."

I heard something, a metal-on-metal sound, a door opening.

"Jorge?" Jamie said, and stood from her stool.

"Hey, Jamie, no, it's Cat." Her boots marched toward us. Then there was her face, her leather jacket. "Oh, Gwen, hi," she said.

"Hi," I said. And I knew Cat could feel something in the room. She could feel the residue of Jamie's and my connection, as though she'd walked into our bookstore and could smell the pumpkin muffins baking, could see the cats leaning into the sun in the window.

"So you took Emma to the airport?" asked Jamie. Her voice was tight, but she leaned back a bit as though trying to convey a casual air she didn't feel.

"Yeah," Cat said, her eyes scanning Jamie's studio then locking on something on a shelf. "I just came for this." She pulled down a plastic gray box that rattled with what sounded like pencils inside. The rattling was loud, like Cat's boot stomping had been, as though she were deliberately jostling the silent bond between Jamie and me.

"That's mine," said Jamie.

"No, it's not. You borrowed it." Cat's voice dropped low, like when she'd confronted the guy at the restaurant. Her agitation was palpable.

"I gave yours back when I found mine," said Jamie, a sharp edge to her voice. "It'd been at home."

"I don't think so."

"Cat, go look in your studio. Yours is there."

Cat slammed the box down on the table, nearly missing one of Jamie's clay boxes. She disappeared, and next door I could hear her moving things around. "Goddamn it," she muttered. She reappeared, standing at the threshold of Jamie's studio.

"It's not there," Cat said.

"Well, it's okay," Jamie said, not sounding like she meant it. "Just take mine until you find yours. I don't need it right now."

"Fine," she said, grabbing the box. "I'm out of here." She turned.

"Cat," said Jamie, but her boots clomped across the floor and the metal door slammed. Hard. The echo rang in my ears. No wonder the guy in the black sweater at the restaurant had backed down. Cat was powerful.

"Well," said Jamie, seeming embarrassed.

"What was that all about?" I asked, feeling like I might know but then again, maybe not.

"It's something new between us," said Jamie. She sat back on the stool and looked at me. "It's the first time we've both, well, have been attracted to the same person."

The tips of my ears burned, and a warm rush ran down my body.

"Does that freak you out?" Jamie said.

I tried to smile back but my face felt stiff. I forced out a half-smile. "No. No. I'm flattered." The minute those words came out of my mouth I knew they sounded condescending. But Jamie didn't say anything. She just sat there, next to me, letting all these new things churn around us, in us. I picked up the sky box and opened it, peered down into the picnic scene.

"I really need to go," said Jamie. "Rose is probably stressing out."

I imagined Rose with short blonde hair and pink cheeks, kind of petal-ish, Rose-like, sitting on the couch, flipping through the channels, looking angrily at the clock. Or lying in bed, pulling the covers up to her chin then pushing them back down again in frustration.

And what about Daniel? Did he even care that I was gone later than usual? No, he was probably in lab, Ellen at the other bench in her white lab coat. Together they were listening to loud punk rock music. Or he was at home, with a book in his lap, the T.V. on and headphones. Or in bed, sleeping, not wondering about me at all, just hoping, before he drifted off, that I wouldn't wake him when I unlocked the door and crawled in next to him.

CHAPTER SIX

GIANT DIPPER

When I got home it was a little past midnight. Daniel was asleep, a pillow over his head. I quietly took off my clothes and carefully slipped between the covers, not touching him. The bed was small but we seemed detached. I felt that I couldn't get close to him if I tried, as though my body and his were the reverse sides of magnets. My pillow smelled like him, like us. I lay in the gray dark and thought about the shiny scar on Jamie's forehead and realized I hadn't asked her about it. I'd wanted to. I wondered if I'd ever have a chance. We'd been quiet as we walked to my car, silent as I drove her to her house. Our effervescent playfulness had dissipated in the aftermath of Cat's entry into the studio and Jamie's admission that she was attracted to me. And how had I acknowledged that admission? I'd said, "I'm flattered." My memory of those words haunted me. I wished I had said something else, something that more closely expressed what I really felt. But I didn't have the words. Yes, I was flattered. But I was also something else, something much richer, much bigger than that.

Something intangibly edgier. I thought of Vanessa telling me to go deeper in my poetry. "I'm flattered" was like a shallow poem.

As I'd driven Jamie home, it seemed unreal that she sat in the passenger seat in my car, the very same woman who had sat across from me in class, who wrote poetry about lemon trees and a loving, harsh grandmother, poems haunted by loneliness. Jamie, who wore a long, silver chain and paint-splattered boots, and whose face I thought was beautiful. I'd seen that face in my mind several times every day since I met her. And now she was going to get out of the car and go into her house, to lie down next to her girlfriend, the minister. I wasn't ready to let her go.

She'd directed me to drop her off in front of a two-story house on a tree-lined street illuminated by old-fashioned replica gas street lights. She smiled at me, and I thought about how I'd been drawn to that smile in class, that smile that opened up an astonishing sense of womanliness in her face.

"Have a good night, drive safely," she said, opening the door and stepping out.

"Jamie?"

"Yes?" She bent down, peered into the car.

"Have a good night too," I said.

"Thanks."

"Wait a minute." I grabbed my poetry notebook and tore a page out of it, writing my name and phone number on it and handing it to her. She folded it into a small square and put it in her pocket.

And now I lay in bed with a sleeping Daniel. The familiar little rasp in his exhale sent a surprising, sudden pang through my heart.

I'd tried to break up with him once after we'd been together for a year. We were at the park feeding geese the leftovers of our picnic. The picnic had been his idea. He had just emerged from a week-long black mood where he'd worked twelve-hour days in the lab, and when he was at home, he'd write in his journal and not answer the phone. But now life was a champagne picnic on the vast expanse of lawn. He had thanked me for letting him work through his mood, for trusting that he'd be over it. He loved me, he said. And I'd started crying and told him I wanted to break up. I wasn't sure I meant it, but it felt good to say it and good to cry. He held me on the blanket, repeated that he loved me, that I was good for him. I imagined myself the wife of a Nobel Laureate. Daniel, tall, a little balding, at the podium thanking me for sticking with him through everything. For being his rock, his love. I didn't want to be someone else's rock. Was I giving up too soon? Was an amazing life in store for me—a life that might be difficult, sure, but that would be more enriching than one I could ever have with another man?

Those were the thoughts I'd had that day at the park and that continued to plague me while I'd flirted with the idea of cheating on him in Japan with a Japanese man who'd approached me on the train, and with an Australian I met at a bar ... and now I lay in bed after the thrill of connecting with Jamie, a woman unlike any I'd ever known.

In the darkness, I heard a door slam somewhere, perhaps on the floor or two below. A motorcycle thrummed by on the street, for a moment drowning out the familiar whoosh of all the other traffic. I shifted my head slightly on my pillow and wondered what Jamie did with that square of paper I'd handed to her. Did she take off her jacket and throw it over the back of a chair, my phone number falling to the floor? Did she pull it out of her pocket and push it in deep down in her sock drawer? Did she unfold it and set it on her bedside stand, next to the phone? Would she tell Rose she had a new friend, or would she hide me from Rose? I liked to think that she'd keep me a secret from Rose, not attempting to lie and present me as merely a friend.

Or would she not bother one way or the other, forgetting about me until she put her jacket on again and wondered what this piece of paper was doing in her pocket?

Maybe she was in bed right now, too, thinking of me. That idea sent a shiver down my arms, both pleasant and frightening. Compared to a month ago, everything in my external life was exactly the same—and yet internally my whole life was on edge, poised to be completely different. Daniel's innocent breathing whispered next to me while I lay shivering at the thought of Jamie's fingers touching my handwriting on a piece of paper I'd handed to her an hour ago. How could it be that I was lying next to Daniel and thinking of a woman in this way? A month ago I would not have thought it possible. I would have imagined this as a scene from someone else's life. But here I was, right on the edge of something. My inside life and my outside life each had one foot on different continental plates. An earthquake seemed inevitable. Was it? If so, when it happened, what would become of me, of my life?

When I was a little girl, I'd try to stop time by sitting completely still and staring at a spot on the wall, or at the tree outside my bedroom window. I thought that if I paid close enough attention that nothing would change, nothing would slip by. At that moment in the dark, lying next to Daniel, I had that same urge to stop time. Stopping time, I could sustain my desire for Jamie and lie next to Daniel into perpetuity, two lovers in a crypt. My chest moved up and down. There was a marble-sized mattress lump beneath my right heel. I moved my foot. Movement was inevitable. Things were going to change. There was no way to stop time. I turned to my side, facing Daniel's back, not quite touching him but nearly spooning his body like a shadow.

"Will and I got in a huge fight last night," said Lucy, peeling saran wrap off her sandwich. It was two o'clock, and we were finally getting a chance to sit down to eat lunch. It had been a busy morning. We'd had lots of paperwork to take care of, and the phone hadn't stopped ringing.

"What did you guys fight about?" I looked at my Tupperware container of leftover macaroni and cheese. My throat tightened as though to reject swallowing before I even took a bite. Lately I was having a hard time eating. It was very unlike me.

"We were watching *Wheel of Fortune*. I didn't want to be there, on that couch watching T.V., Will's arm around me, his fingers circling round and round on my shoulder. I felt like I was suffocating. During a commercial, I told him I wanted to go back to marriage counseling. He said I refuse to be happy. I told him he refuses to take me seriously. It was the same argument we've had a fucking million times. I saw Vanna smiling, turning a letter, and I lost it. I just thought, *This is not my life*. I did not want it to be my life. So I left."

"You left? What do you mean? Where did you go?"

"I went to a hotel. I spent the night alone in a king-sized hotel bed."

"You should have called me," I said.

"No, it's okay. In fact, it was great. It felt like I was on vacation. I slept naked for the first time in a long time. I don't dare sleep naked next to Will or he'll be on me three times in the night."

"Seriously?"

"The man is a machine. When we first met, I was flattered. I liked it. But now I see that it has nothing to do with me."

"So what are you going to do?" As was often the case, I was experiencing a vicarious thrill about what was happening in Lucy's life. I had a sudden urge to tell her about Jamie, about Jamie and Cat, that two lesbians were hot for me, that I had been in an art studio until midnight. At the same time, telling her that seemed impossible.

"I don't know what I'm going to do," she said. "Maybe this weekend I'll go down to Monterey to my mom's house. She's been married enough times that she might have some good advice for me. Besides, I want someone to cook for me. To make coffee for me." Lucy's eyes were filling. I reached over and squeezed her hand. She linked her fingers through mine. "Fuck this," she said, dropping my hand. "I don't know why I don't just file for divorce."

"Maybe you're not ready," I said. "It's not easy to end a marriage. It feels like something really big. You and Will have been married for almost ten years. The older we get, the longer we're together, the harder it is. I mean, I'm not even married to Daniel and it's so hard to imagine ever disentangling from him."

"What do you mean?" she said, wiping the corners of her eyes with her fingers. "What are you talking about?"

"I don't know," I said, my pulse suddenly racing in my head.

"Are you thinking of leaving Daniel?"

"No, I was just saying—"

"Gwen, what's going on?"

"Nothing. Nothing."

"I don't believe you." She put a potato chip in her mouth, crunching loudly. She held the bag out to me. I took one but my throat tightened, so I set it down on my napkin.

"You know Daniel's hard to live with," I said.

"But at least he's interesting."

"You always say that."

"I do? Well, I mean it. I wish Will were more … unpredictable. I wish he'd surprise me sometimes."

"You mean like Daniel surprises me when he finally talks to me after being silent for days?"

"Yeah, like that," she said, taking a sip of her soda. "Maybe Daniel doesn't talk for days because he has nothing to say."

"Whose side are you on?" I asked, swiftly irritated. The idea of Daniel having nothing to say was absurd. I knew his mind was always churning.

"I'm sorry Gwen." She set down her soda can. "Maybe men and women just aren't meant to live together. Maybe instead of getting a divorce I should rent a house across the street. Or maybe you and I should get a place together."

"Like Laverne and Shirley," I said.

"Or Kate and Allie."

"Or Mary and Rhoda."

"They didn't live together," Lucy said. "Rhoda lived upstairs."

"Yeah, I always thought that was so great, that these women friends lived in the same apartment building. They were always dropping by each other's places. Mary's apartment was so cool."

"I loved her walk-in closet. And her tiny kitchen."

"And her job," I said, "as a news producer. But it always pissed me off how she had to be the one to make the coffee."

"Yeah we always do, don't we? She had boyfriends," said Lucy, "but they didn't hang around. In the next episode, she'd be dating someone else. Or no one. And it didn't seem to matter. Men weren't the center of her life." Lucy took a bite of her sandwich and chewed, her suntanned nylon legs crossed, one of her high-heeled shoes dangling off her toe. She didn't look like a devastated woman who was thinking about divorcing her husband. Had I been devastated when I finally decided to leave Andy? Yes, in a way. What exactly was devastation? Extreme distress. The end of something. I flashed on the bleakness I'd felt, years ago, as I pulled my books off the shelf of Andy's and my living room and placed them tidily in a box. In the midst of that raw blackness of the certain end, of the demolition of a life, I'd felt the sprouting hope of a new beginning, of finding a new way to be me.

Fall was settling in. Most days the sky was bright and clean, the summer smog blown away by the breeze. In the crystalline daytime, everything looked cleaner. Even Daniel's and my run-down little neighborhood looked like it had a face-lift. The three blocks of apartment buildings, inhabited by a combination of students and working-class town residents, seemed like they'd been freshly painted if you didn't look too closely. The spiral of outdoor staircases shone in the bright air, and the swimming pool shimmered as azure as the sky so that your eyes didn't register the cracked tiles and stained pool floor.

It was a nice enough day, this Sunday, for me to take the t-tops off my little red car. That was the best thing about my job at the learning center: I had qualified for a new car loan. I'd never before owned a brand-new car. My first car had been an old family car that my sister and I learned to drive in, a faded yellow four-door Ford LTD pocked with dents. My second car had been given to me by my grandfather when he couldn't drive anymore, a low-mileage, very clean white Toyota Corolla with absolutely no amenities, no power steering, no air conditioning, no power windows.

A month before Andy and I were married, he sold his black Corvette, perhaps out of a notion that married men didn't have such cars, and bought a new Ford Escort because he wanted to support the American car manufacturers. I drove the Escort and he drove his cute classic MG, but when it wasn't running, he'd drive my old Corolla. I told him I'd drive it, but he insisted I drive the Escort, saying, "What if you broke down on the freeway?" After the divorce, I came out from work one day and the Escort was gone, replaced by my grandfather's old Corolla, dented, leaking oil. That was his way to express his anger with me, to get rid of anything connected to me or my family. His gesture said, *fuck you. I don't give a damn anymore if you break down on the freeway. Keep your grandfather's shitty old car.*

And I did. Until a couple of days before I left for Japan when I sold it for $500 to a Mexican guy. I tried out a little of my rusty Spanish, wanted to tell him the car had belonged to my *abuelo*, but I doubted I made much sense to him. As I saw him drive it away, down the hot asphalt street, I felt a clench in my stomach. He was taking my past with him.

My new little red car seemed more imbued with the future than the past. Buying it was an act of independence. Maybe even a bit of rebellion. I hadn't asked my father, or Daniel, or any man in my life to help me buy the car. And in reaction to the memory of Andy's preachy voice insisting we support American car manufacturers, I'd bought a foreign car, a sporty Nissan. I'd gone to the dealer alone, and while I may not have gotten the best deal, I had bought it on my own.

And now, as I tucked one of the glass t-tops into its vinyl casing and placed it in the trunk, I wondered if what I was doing today was an act of independence or rebellion. I was on my way to meet Jamie. We were going to spend the day together.

I drove down the freeway, sipping on a bottled wine cooler. I had never before drunk alcohol while driving, and I never drank in the mornings, but I had seen the wine cooler in the refrigerator before I left and my mouth had watered. The citrus flavor was thirst-quenching. So few food or drink items appealed to me lately that I had to take what I could. I had lost some weight which made me happy, but I was also frustrated at my inability to enjoy the foods I usually did. I was constantly anxious, unable to relax fully, which manifested in my body rebelling against food.

I didn't know if Daniel even noticed. He was one of the rare men who didn't comment on my body or my food intake. When we'd gone out to dinner the previous night, I'd taken just a few bites of my pasta. After we finished doing the crossword puzzle together, he pointed to my uneaten food and said, "Are you going to eat that?" When I said no, he'd pulled the plate over to his side and finished it off. I drank the rest of my wine and took a bite of bread. These days, I could only stomach bland breads, fruits and alcoholic drinks. Seemed biblical somehow.

When we'd returned to the apartment that night after dinner, the phone had been ringing as we walked in. Daniel picked it up then handed it to me. When I'd heard Jamie's voice on the line, I felt a little dizzy. It seemed so strange that she was, in a way, present in Daniel's and my living room. It was like a doubly-exposed photo, my two lives overlapping.

"I was wondering," she said, "if you'd like to go play this weekend. Maybe go to the beach or something?" I'd tingled all over at the thought. We hadn't spoken at the last meeting of poetry class. She'd smiled at me across the room a few times but then left the minute class was over. I'd been wondering if she'd regretted telling me she was attracted to me. She was, after all, as attached to her minister as I was to my scientist. I'd tried to put her out of my mind after that, but that proved to be impossible. I'd been obsessed with thinking about her, hoping she'd talk to me at the next class session. And now, better than that, she was calling me and inviting me out.

When I'd hung up the phone, I sat on the couch and stared at the blank T.V. Clearly I was two people, one who had a "play date" with a lesbian she was attracted to and the other who lived in an apartment with her long-time boyfriend. Daniel was in the apartment somewhere—maybe in the bathroom or bedroom. I stood up and had to grab onto the couch arm to steady myself. My wooziness wasn't entirely unpleasant. Children know the pleasures of dizziness, which is why they like to spin in circles. I walked to the bedroom, gingerly, my feet feeling not completely connected to my ankles.

Daniel sat at his computer, staring at the screen. I came up behind him and ran my fingers through his hair. A flake of dandruff floated down to his shoulder. I brushed it off. He kept his eyes on the computer but reached his hand back and grabbed mine and squeezed. I rested my head on his shoulder. From the front he would have looked like a two-headed, two-gendered being. Usually he was fiercely private; I wondered if he'd turn off the computer to keep me from reading what was on the screen. But he didn't. From that angle, I couldn't focus on the green print anyway. He reached his hands up to the keyboard and began typing. I moved away and undressed, pulling on my kimono, the dragon breathing fire on my back.

In the bathroom, I'd held my toothbrush under the faucet and stared at the water running over the bristles and into the sink, swirling down. And for what felt like a long time, but was probably only a few seconds, I had the odd sensation that I had no idea what I was doing there. Where was I? What was this thing in my hand that I was holding under flowing water? What was I supposed to do with it again? For that moment I was in a foreign place, an alien who'd never heard of tooth brushing. For a moment something I'd done almost every day my whole life was mysterious, unfathomable.

I dropped my toothbrush in the drawer, pulled out my pink plastic disc of birth control pills, and tossed it toward the garbage can. A direct hit.

* * *

Jamie and I sat at a restaurant in the picturesque, affluent downtown of Los Gatos, perched in the foothills of the Santa Cruz mountains. We'd decided to get something to eat before taking the winding hill over to Santa Cruz. After the waitress brought us overpriced cheese omelets and melon, Jamie wanted to know what it was like living in Japan. She had been to another country only once, the previous summer when she'd gone to Mexico to build houses with Rose's church. She hadn't said "Rose's church," but I knew that was what she meant. She'd told me a little about Mexico before turning the conversation around to ask about Japan.

"I loved Japan," I said, "but it was hard at first. I didn't understand culture shock until I lived there. It's a real, visceral thing."

"What do you mean?"

"Well, I'd been there only a few days when I took a subway to one area of downtown Tokyo. When I exited onto a street that was unbelievably crowded and chaotic, I felt exhilarated at the people walking around, at the massively tall skyscrapers, at the huge video billboards booming Japanese words and American music. And as quickly as I'd felt that excitement, I felt crushed under it all like I was the size of an ant. My limbs got really heavy and I had to sit down. I found a bench and sat and cried and cried. I felt like I could die right there and no one would even know."

"That was culture shock?"

"Yeah, these crazy mood swings like I'd never had before. I mean, I'm very emotional anyway," I said, feeling a hint of apology in my admission, "so maybe I was just more susceptible. But, yeah, it's this overwhelming feeling, like you don't know who you are when you're surrounded by so much foreignness."

"I think that's something I've felt all my life, being immersed in straight people." She laughed in a way that suggested she was only half kidding.

"When ... when did you first know?"

Jamie sipped her coffee. "That I'm a lesbian?"

"Yes."

"Second grade, when I wanted to marry my teacher, Mrs. Freemont. I was devastated when I learned that 'Mrs.' means married."

I laughed. "Really? You were that young?"

"Actually, maybe it was even before that. I had fantasies about my Mary Poppins doll. Maybe it was more of a crush on Julie Andrews. Didn't you ever have crushes on any of your dolls or actresses or teachers?"

I flashed on examining Barbie's curves as I pulled off her pink, spangled dress. Had I felt a little flame of something inside? "I sure loved Barbie," I said.

"Her feet always freaked me out," said Jamie. She took another sip of coffee. "Those unnaturally high arches and teeny tiny toes all smashed together."

"Yeah, they are bizarre, now that I think about it," I said. "As a kid, I thought of them as dainty, though. But I guess they are kind of like foot-binding, if you really think about it. Have you ever been to the Barbie Museum?"

"Is there really such a place?"

"Yeah, in Palo Alto, just about a mile from my house, but I've never been. I read about it in the paper."

"We should go sometime," she said. I loved the "we" in her statement. And the "sometime," which intimated a future.

"Did you play with Barbie?" I asked.

"My mom always wanted me to. She was a Barbie-pusher, buying me Barbie clothes, Barbie cars, Barbie houses. But I liked Mary Poppins. And G.I. Joe. I always stole my brother's and played with it when my mom wasn't looking. That was another great thing about Mrs. Freemont. Not only was she pretty but she didn't give a shit if I played with G.I. Joes."

"What about plastic soldiers?" I was obliquely referring to the poem she'd read in class about a girl under her grandmother's lemon tree. "Did you really bury them in your grandmother's backyard?"

"Yep. That whole scene of me in the backyard, all those details are true, from my life."

As Jamie took another drink of her coffee, I cut into the middle of my untouched omelet with my fork and watched the cheese run out. Normally that would have appealed to me but my throat rebelled. I pierced a piece of melon and held it up to my mouth, taking a small bite, trying to swallow past my tricky throat. I noticed Jamie had hardly touched her food either.

"Are you close to your mom now?" I asked.

"My mother's not alive. She died when I was eight." She said this matter-of-factly as though it was someone else's life she was telling me about. I swallowed, almost unable to speak.

"I'm sorry. What happened?"

"A car wreck. My brother and I had been at our grandparents' house in Ceres for the whole week waiting for her to come home. She was working in San Jose—a waitress job, and a job at a storage facility—while we lived during the week with my grandparents. You have no idea how right you were that day in class when you asked about the absence of the mother in the poem. Even before my mom died, my brother and I were mostly living with my grandmother. My mother—well, she was very young when she had us, and my dad wasn't in the picture. He left her for another woman when I was still a baby."

"Do you ever see him?"

"No. He has a family up in Oregon, a wife and an adult son, a half-brother I've never met."

"What about your grandparents?"

"My grandfather died ten years ago, suddenly, from a heart attack. And my grandmother, two years ago from cancer. If it's possible for an adult woman to be an orphan, that's what I am."

"Where's your brother?" I wanted family for her. My questions were seeking it for her.

"He lives in Florida with his wife and two kids. I haven't seen them in years, but I'm going there this Thanksgiving." She sipped her coffee. "You have a look on your face. I didn't tell you all of this so you'd feel sorry for me."

"I don't. I mean—well, you did say *orphan*."

"Touché," she said. "You're right, that's a pity word. I do miss my grandmother horribly. But I have Cat. She's like a sister. And her parents live in San Jose—they're like an aunt and uncle to me."

"Speaking of Cat—is she okay?"

"Not really, but she'll get over it. She's pissed because she's not getting her way. When she found out I had your phone number she asked me for it, but I wouldn't give it to her. I told her she'd have to ask you. So that's just a head's up."

"It's hard for me to imagine you two together."

"It was a long time ago," she said. "We've been through a lot together. That's part of the problem. She's helped me a lot in my life, so sometimes she has a hard time thinking of me as a separate person who can make her own decisions and make her own way."

"Helped you how?"

Jamie paused while the server poured us more coffee. "She helped pull me up out of the depths. I had a pretty bad drug problem for a while."

I was a little taken aback. "What kind of drugs?"

"Cocaine. I was working as a waitress. A whole group of us at the restaurant were into it. When I met Cat, she wouldn't have anything to do with it. She whupped my ass about it, truth be told. And to this day I'm grateful. Who knows what would have happened to me if I hadn't met her."

"You might have quit anyway."

"Maybe. Or I might have burned a hole through my septum like someone I know did. Or lost all my money. Or died of sudden heart failure like someone else I knew."

"Did you do rehab?"

"No. Fortunately I wasn't quite that far gone. I just needed to change my friends, my lifestyle. Cat's actually pretty straight-laced. She's very moderate in all things. I'd been so lost in the party scene that I'd forgotten that people do things like drink just one beer before dinner. And that they even have dinner—I mean, set the table, make a meal. So when I began living with her, I began living like her. We started our business, worked regular hours, did regular things like bike riding and going to the movies. Leaving that job at the restaurant helped a lot. Every Sunday Cat and I went to her parents' house for dinner. We were like a nice little nuclear family." She laughed. "So what about your family?"

"My family's an anomaly," I said, almost apologetically. "My parents are still married, have been for thirty five years. When I got divorced from Andy, my cousin Thomas called me and thanked me for taking the heat off him because he was the first person in my extended family to get a divorce and he'd felt like a freak. Well, now I could join him in freakdom."

I told Jamie about Andy, that I still wasn't sure why I'd married so young, at age twenty-two, even younger than my mom when she'd married my dad.

"It was like I was trying to grow up fast," I said.

"Or maybe you were born old and are getting younger as you go."

For some odd reason, tears sprang to my eyes. I looked down so she wouldn't see. Why did that idea touch me, the idea of getting younger? If I'd been going in one direction my whole life, was it possible to just turn around and go the other?

"Are you okay?" she asked.

"I, I'm fine. I don't know what happened. The idea of getting younger … it just touched something in me. God, I feel stupid."

"Don't feel stupid. That'd be stupid." She smiled. It was as though the space between us had filled up. Sitting across the table too far from each other to touch, it was as though we were nevertheless touching.

The winding drive to Santa Cruz was a little on the chilly side with the tops off the car, but I didn't care and Jamie didn't seem to either. My ponytail blew all around, and Jamie took advantage of the topless car by lifting her arms up over her head on the hard turns, like on a roller coaster. As the car climbed the wooded mountain highway, we were stippled in sun and shadow. Every so often I'd inhale a surge of eucalyptus smell, then redwood. A pure kind of happiness swelled in me, the kind of summer joy I felt on the swings in the park when I was a little girl. Maybe Jamie was right. Maybe I was magically getting younger.

It was a typical dazzling late-fall day in Santa Cruz with the summer fog vanished and replaced by eggshell blue sky. Jamie and I found an isolated spot on the beach down from the Boardwalk, with its carnival rides and games entertaining a sparse post-summer crowd. In the distance, faint screams of delight emerged from roller coaster riders and brave wave jumpers. The water was cold. A few surfers in wetsuits bobbed on their boards, gleaming like sea lions. Without a blanket, we sat under the mild sun, the sand warming our legs through our jeans.

"I used to hitchhike here sometimes," said Jamie, dropping sand through her hand, a makeshift hourglass. "My friends and I would spend the night on the beach."

"I've never done anything like that in my life," I said, quickly, happily settling into the comforting texture of our conversation. "I mean, hitchhike or sleep on a beach. It seems, I don't know, brave."

"It wasn't brave. It was stupid. But a good kind of stupid. The kind where you feel free. Bravery is selling everything you own and moving to Japan, living in another country without knowing the language, having an experience like that."

"That's what people always say to me. But it didn't feel brave. It felt desperate."

"What do you mean?"

"I needed to go. I had to go. Somewhere."

"Why?"

I wasn't sure how to answer her question. The way I best understood my answer was with one word, *Daniel*. But did I want to conjure him up here and now?

"Daniel. I had to go because of Daniel."

We sat quietly for a few seconds. A gull, wings outspread, landed at the edge of the water and pecked at a bulbous piece of seaweed. A wave lifted in slow motion, its gelatinous arc gleaming then falling in a rush of green and gray.

"Daniel lived in Europe his junior year of high school. He spent many summers in France, Italy, England. He thought I needed … something." *Experience.* But, no, I was more "experienced" in many ways than he was. *Sophistication.*

"So it was his idea that you move to Japan?"

"Not really. It was just always something between us. He thought I could benefit from, grow from, travel. All his friends, his co-workers at the lab, they've all been everywhere. They all speak French or Italian. Some speak Latin, even."

"They sound privileged." She said this in a matter-of-fact way. Her simple statement was like opening a window to let in fresh air. Yes, that's what they were. Privileged. And funny thing, I'd always thought I was the privileged one. And sure, I was in a way. Compared to many of my friends, my family had a bigger house, more money, more experiences like going to see plays in San Francisco or taking summer camping trips. But Daniel's world—private schools, parents with Ph.D.s, European vacations—it was a world I'd never known existed, really, until I met him. I tried to explain this to Jamie. She listened intently, I noticed, as though she were involved with me in making something, like a quilt or a meal. I told her about the differences between Daniel and me. It struck me that emphasizing Daniel's and my differences made me feel closer to Jamie.

As though to highlight his absence and her presence, she asked, "Where is he today?"

"In the lab."

"On the weekend?"

"Yeah. It happens that way sometimes. Where's Rose?"

"Church. It's Sunday."

"Oh yeah," I said, laughing a little. "I guess it makes sense that *she* works on Sundays. Do you ever go and hear her preach?"

"I have a few times. But it's been a while. Although on Fridays

I usually read her sermons and make a few suggestions."

"Funny, I never really thought about that, about preachers writing sermons. I guess I always thought of them as standing up there and talking extemporaneously. Or reading at random from the Bible and making a few comments about it because they know it so well. Do they take classes in Sermon Writing 101?"

"More or less. Rose went to Princeton Theological Seminary."

"Impressive," I said, trying not to sound derisive, because truly I was a little intimidated. "But not as impressive as hitchhiking to Santa Cruz. I want to hear about that."

Jamie grinned, perhaps acknowledging my desire to steer the conversation away from Rose and Daniel, the two people whose ghosts I suddenly wanted to exorcise from our day together.

"I had long hair then," Jamie said, pointing to her waist. "I was such the hippie chick. Wore sailor pants and played the guitar." I tried to picture her that way but drew a blank. "Well, sort of played the guitar. Did my best. I carried it on our little trips. My friend Nancy and I would stand at the entrance to Highway 17 and stick out our thumbs."

"Were you scared?"

"I only remember one time being disturbed by a guy who wanted us to sit in the front seat with him. We almost turned down the ride, but he relented and let us sit in the back. He kept looking at us in the rearview mirror. He was really stoned and he kept handing back his joints for us to share with him. Which we did, of course. But nothing happened. He just dropped us off downtown and that was that."

"My parents drilled in me that people who pick up hitchhikers are rapists and murderers."

"I was lucky, for sure." Jamie reached her hand into the sand and began digging. I joined her, digging a hole next to hers. "My grandfather would have killed me if he knew."

"Your grandfather." The idea of a grandparent disciplining a grandchild was foreign to me. My grandparents had been on the edge of my life. "The grandfather in your poems, the one who plays solitaire?"

"Yes, the only grandfather I had—my mother's father, the one who raised me along with my grandmother. My other grandparents—my father's parents—I never knew them."

"Did you like living with your grandparents? I mean, before your mother's accident?" We were side by side, our hands moved steadily in the sand, digging and digging. Beneath the warm, dry surface, the sand was chilly and damp.

"I loved them. But I missed my mom. When she was in the hospital, after her accident—she'd broken her pelvis—my grandmother would take me to the hospital parking lot. My mom would look out her window from up above and wave. Kids weren't allowed in. Then, when she got out, she'd visit us. And every time she had to leave, I'd beg her to take me with her. She'd always hug me, tell me she loved me. She'd say *soon*, that Bobby and I could come home soon."

"But I thought she died in the accident."

"Not that one. She had another one, a year later."

"God, that's terrible luck."

"It's really unbelievable, if you think about it. Neither one was her fault, either. After the first accident, after she recovered, she married a guy, Johnny Wagonner, who—well, I don't think he wanted us around. He disappeared after she died."

"How well do you remember your mom?"

"I remember she'd come to Grandma and Grandpa's wearing a uniform that looked like a candy striper's and smelled like French fries. That was when she worked at Foster's Freeze." I pictured a 1950's-looking woman with permed hair and plushly lipsticked lips. Pretty. And younger than I was now but looking older like they did back then. Sometimes I thought people of my generation were perpetual teenagers. Jamie and I seemed like teenagers right now, talking and digging in the sand—me with my hair in a ponytail, Jamie with her paint-splattered boots. I had a hard time imagining my mother doing this at my age; at my age she had been married eight years and had two children.

"It's really sad that you lost your mother so young." I was amazed Jamie was sharing all of this with me. I knew next to nothing about Daniel's family after three years. I liked the way Jamie talked, like there were no taboos, nothing to shy away from. Life was to be talked about, to be sculpted and painted, to be written about.

"Yes, it's awful but it could have been much worse. We could have been placed in foster care. My grandparents were really good to us. Still, I yearned for not only my mom but for what I thought was a normal life. Like yours. Yours was one I would have watched on T.V."

"And yours," I said, "is one I would have read about in a book. It would have, I hate to admit it, sounded like an adventure to me. In all the best books, the parents were gone a lot or absent. Like *Harriet the Spy* or *Pippi Longstocking.*"

"Oh god, I loved those. I also loved *Treasure Island* and *Hardy Boys* and, in a pinch, *Nancy Drew.*"

"What about *The Happy Hollisters*?"

"They were great!"

"I can't believe you read *The Happy Hollisters*! No one has read *The Happy Hollisters.*"

"Family of five freckled kids, two parents, dog, cat, travels the U.S., solves mysteries."

"Well, damn," I said, laughing. "I can't believe this."

"Talk about normal," she said. "The Happy Hollisters were Über-normal."

"But they solved mysteries," I said. "Ergo, the appealing adventure. And did you notice how the kids had free rein? They could go anywhere they wanted, it seemed, at any time. Parents in the background. My parents were so ... so in the foreground."

"Are they still?"

"In a way," I said. "Well, yes. Okay truth is, as a 31-year-old woman, I sometimes feel like I'm twelve around them. I want their approval. I mean, I don't want to want it. But I do."

"Your parents are *supposed* to be your superego," she said. "Wasn't that Freud's definition of superego? Parental?"

"Right. I think people become parents," I said, "because they want to fix the past. They want to perfect their childhoods."

"Is that what you want?" she asked.

"Sometimes," I said. "Sometimes I want a daughter so I can

teach her to be freer, to be less concerned with worrying about how she looks to men, how she acts in relationship to men."

Jamie was building a kind of a mound inside the hole she dug, the tattoo on her arm obscured by sticky sand. Like her I began to build a mound in the hole I was making.

"Hannah," Jamie said. "Her name should be Hannah. I love names that are palindromes. Can't you see Hannah at our bookstore?"

"Her job is to feed the cats," I said.

"And to help me bake muffins."

I couldn't add to the perfection of that statement. I let it float in the salt air, while we silently dug and built to the buzz of the waves. The bookstore played around in my mind, the smell of books and baking. Jamie's shirt was pulled up a bit in the back as she leaned forward, revealing a line of pink skin. I wondered what it would be like to touch her there, to run my fingers across her lower back.

I wondered why she didn't talk to me last time in poetry class. But I didn't want to ask her. We were here now, together.

She pulled her hands away from the sand and sat back on her heels. I did the same. We had created two mounds surrounded by moats. Jamie stood and picked up a stick of driftwood. In the sand she outlined our creations, connecting them with a figure-eight. The form we'd built together now looked like the sign for infinity.

Later, we walked along the Boardwalk, chewing on pieces of saltwater taffy, looking at the carnival games but passing up every barker who tried to get us to waste a few dollars. We talked and talked as though we'd never run out of words, as though our lives and our thoughts were as abundant and continuous as ocean waves. When we got to the Giant Dipper, the old wooden roller coaster, we decided to ride. There were only a few passengers. We lucked out and got the very front seats.

The car lurched forward then thrust us into darkness. When it jolted up and climbed into the daylight, I saw our hands gripping the bar, her colorful tattoo next to my gold and ruby ring. Her thigh pressed warm against mine igniting all the cells in my body. We were pulled up, and up, and up, chains chattering beneath us. At the very top came that moment when you feel suspended.

For an instant, a millisecond, time stopped.

A dot of a white gull hung in the aquatic sky. The air was so neutral that I couldn't feel my skin. The vast expanse of ocean held its breath.

And then, we plunged.

Chapter Seven

"Divinest Sense"

When I walked in the door, Daniel looked up from the couch where he was watching T.V. and listening to music with headphones on, a book on his lap. He took off the headphones, hit the mute button on the T.V. and said, "Hi."

"Hi," I said.

He stood up and came over to me, put his arms around me and kissed the top of my head. A bone in his chest pressed against me.

"Did you have a good day?" he asked into my hair. He rarely asked me that question. Funny that he would ask this today of all days, the day that I spent ten hours with Jamie. It had been an incredible day. I'd been hoping Daniel wouldn't be home, that I'd have time to be alone in the apartment with a glass of wine to think through everything that had happened. But his hug soothed me, as though he sensed the jagged turmoil running through my veins and was comforting me.

"Yeah, I had a good day. Did you?" I asked, my voice muffled by his shirt. I was immersed in his familiar vinegary smell. Suddenly I felt very, very sleepy.

"It was horrible," he said.

I made a move for the couch and he followed. There, I lay back and he sat, lifting my feet onto his lap.

"Why was it horrible?" I leaned back my head and closed my eyes.

"Bad results again," he said. "This post-doc is such a horrible disaster. I feel like I've wasted two years, with no end in sight." He said all this in such a low-key way that a stranger might think he was kidding or being sarcastic. But I knew he spoke in an even-keeled manner, no matter what he was talking about. His tone of voice seemed to imply that happiness and despair held equal weight. Still, his continual talk of disasters in the lab was a little confusing to me in light of how everyone proclaimed his brilliance.

"I'm sorry," I said, foregoing my usual pep talk, my usual suggestions that he try another lab, apply for another post doc— suggestions he would sometimes expand upon and imagine with me, but that more often he'd reject outright. I couldn't give anything to him right now as immersed as I was in the surreal juxtaposition of my day with Jamie set against being here with him, now.

"It's okay. Well, it's not okay, but there's nothing to do about it tonight." He picked up the remote and un-muted the T.V.: the frantic sounds of a commercial melted into the familiar whistling music of the old *Star Trek* theme.

He untied my shoes and pulled off my socks. He took my right foot into his hands and ran his thumbs up the sole. I remembered the first time he'd rubbed my feet, when we were still friends, neighbors. I'd been watching a movie on his TV, this same TV, and he'd reached over and touched my feet. We were friends, just friends, so it had been surprising that he'd done such an intimate thing. Surprising, sweet and sexy. A few weeks later, we'd begun kissing on this very couch. I'd said to him, *What are we doing?* And he'd replied, *Do we really need to talk right now?*

Behind my closed eyelids, my eyes began to burn. I'd been drawn to Daniel, I'd loved him, I'd entertained ideas of marrying him, of being with him forever, and now … what was I doing? Tears threatened to escape my eyes. I rolled over to my side, pushing my face into the sagging couch cushion. I thought about how Jamie and I rode the roller coaster three times. There were so few people there that the attendants let us stay two more rounds, free. When we finally disembarked, we saw that a secret camera somewhere on the ride had taken pictures of us. At the exit, on a screen, was a photo of us, my hair obscuring my face, Jamie laughing so hard she appeared to be stiffly grimacing. *Cousin It and Frankenstein*, she'd joked. We'd laughed so hard we had to run to the bathroom to pee. Soon after, she'd said she'd better get back home. Rose was sure to be angry, suspicious.

"Maybe it'd be better if I met her," I'd said, not sure what I was saying.

"No," said Jamie. "I don't think so. I think it would make it worse. Rose is the jealous type. She'd take one look at you, and well…"

Something in me had surged. I wanted to touch her. But the idea panicked me. I felt like I couldn't quite catch my breath. We had made our way to the car. I opened my door quickly and sat, deeply breathing.

"Are you okay?" she asked.

"I don't know. Yes. No. I feel kind of crazed."

"Me too," she said, looking over at me. I realized how self-centered I was being. I wasn't the only one grappling with what was going on between us, whatever that might be.

"Do you love Rose?" I asked recklessly, as though I had nothing to lose—or everything.

Jamie took a deep breath, like the one I'd just taken. "Yes. Well, I don't know," she said. "That's a complicated question, with an extremely complicated answer. I care about her. I would hate to hurt her."

What about hurting me? I thought, knowing the thought was childish, selfish, out of line. Dusk was settling in. The sky had turned dark gray, the sun a purple glow on the watery horizon. A hooded guy on a skateboard rushed by, wheels scrambling against the asphalt.

Jamie and I hadn't touched at all except thigh-to-thigh on the roller coaster. My thigh still felt the ghost of hers. I wanted to reach over and hold her hand, to feel her fingers slip through mine. The thought sent a prickly charge through my body. But it was as though my brain signals weren't reaching my limbs, as though I couldn't physically follow through on my mind's desires.

I thought she'd ask me if I loved Daniel. But she didn't. Instead, she said, "I'm not exactly sure what's going on here." It seemed a version of my question to Daniel when we'd first kissed, *what are we doing?*

"I'm pulled to you," I said. Saying that out loud made it real, injecting me with a peculiar combination of composure and nervousness. "I don't know. It's the first time in my life I've felt this way about another woman." My statement felt utterly inadequate, like the words of a teenager with a crush. I hoped Jamie would be able to find the poetry, the depth, in my words.

"Are you okay?" she asked.

"I … yes, I'm okay," I said. Deep down that felt true.

"I'm glad," she said. "I'm glad I'm not alone in this." I saw for the first time that she was nervous, excited, bowled over, like me. This was new to me, to be falling for someone else and to believe that person felt exactly the same. Usually there was some kind of imbalance—the guy wanted me more than I wanted him or vice-versa. Did I now feel this sense of balance because Jamie was a woman? Did I not have to second-guess how she felt because I was a woman, too? Was it like our double-X chromosomes could dance together equally, no one-legged Y creating disequilibrium?

"What are you thinking?" said Jamie.

I told her about my image of the double X's dancing together.

"I can see them," she said. "Our X's bow to one another, and then hold hands, little X hands. And they dance." The image was fanciful, silly and serious all at once. I smiled.

"God," I said. "What are we going to do?" A huge, huge question. I knew we both felt its weight.

"I don't know," she said. "I think we need to think, to sit with this, to look at our lives. As much as that's the opposite of what I really want to do."

A charge ran through me at what she was intimating—that she wanted to act, not think. That she wanted me. It was as though the car had suddenly dropped off the road into the ocean and was submerged in the salt water of our desire. I could feel it. I knew she could feel it too. It was compounded by the extra thrilling pleasure of withholding, of not touching, of being engulfed in electric longing.

As I had driven back over the hill in the falling darkness, we didn't talk anymore about this thing between us, but it hung there like a richly-textured quilt drying on the line. I asked Jamie about her art. She told me about her master's degree show she was preparing, a combination of art and poetry centered on memories of her grandparents' house. She was collecting childhood objects and also making small paintings and sculptures that would probably figure into the project. She was haunted by her grandparents' love, she said, and the loneliness she'd felt, waiting for her mother—and the sense of anger and abandonment when she realized her mother would never come back. Somehow she wanted to explore those feelings in her art.

Too soon, we were in front of her house, the car illuminated by the old-fashioned faux gas streetlight. She was just about to open her door, when I said,

"Can I ask you something, Jamie? That scar on your forehead—"

She reached up and touched it, a talisman. "When I was four, I fell out of a tree in my grandparents' backyard. They'd been sitting there drinking lemonade, so the story went, and watching me be my tomboy self. And then, I just dropped."

"Did you hurt yourself badly?"

"I had some blood, a few stitches. I think I did it on purpose.

I think I was trying to fly. I remembered feeling like I was flying, for just a second. When I hit, I was stunned. Then I wanted to do it again even though I was hurt. I think my grandmother thought I was crazy."

"I can imagine," I said. "You were so little, and fell out of a tree, and wanted to go up again."

"I liked to climb. And falling didn't stop me. You'd think it would have but it didn't."

A porch light went on in the house next to Jamie's.

"I need to go," she said.

"I feel like dropping out of a tree, right now," I said. My heart throbbed in my chest. "And then climbing back up to do it again. I feel crazy, too."

"I'm glad," she said. "I'm glad to not be crazy alone. I'll see you in class." She opened her door. Cold air rushed in.

"Will you talk to me this time after class? Don't just take off, okay?" I knew I might be asking too much.

""I promise. I'm sorry that last week—" It seemed she was going to say something but stopped herself. Her hand still on the car door she said, "Good night, Gwen."

"Good night." Then I couldn't help myself; I had to add: "XX and XX."

She smiled. "XX and XX, dancing," she said. She got out and quietly shut the door. I watched her walk down the walkway, moved by the quiet vulnerability of her exposed neck, her rounded, womanly hips. She reached the porch, mounted the stairs, then turned and gave a small wave before opening the door. A light flicked on in an upstairs room. I wondered if that was where she was headed, if that was the bedroom. If she'd climb the indoor stairs slowly, or take them by two's. If she'd feel the gravity of going up and up and up as the opposite of falling out of a tree, of trying to fly.

I felt Daniel kissing me before I registered what was happening. As he'd rubbed my feet and watched T.V., I'd fallen asleep on the couch. And now he was lying next to me, kissing me awake. I could feel him pressing into me, his body taut. He was running his hands up the back of my shirt. I closed my eyes, imagined Jamie was the one kissing me, her tattooed hand slipping beneath my bra. My body ignited. I pressed my body into her then eyes still closed, pushed my body over and slid on top of her.

My eyes opened as though of their own volition. I looked down and saw Daniel beneath me, his dark eyebrows pressed together in the dim room, his face mottled by the movement of the blue TV screen. As if for the first time, I really saw him—his oval face, his thick eyelashes, his fleshy earlobes, the man beneath my body. I felt myself, my full essence, behind my eyes, looking out. I didn't think about how I was being seen. My body was not receiving; it was acting. At that moment, I thought only about my gaze, both outward and inward. I closed my eyes and didn't think about what he saw or what he wanted. Instead I saw what I wanted to see, and took what I wanted.

I woke the next morning, feeling hung over even though I'd had nothing to drink. My limbs were heavy, my head throbbing. It took me a moment to realize I was on the couch, naked and covered with a blanket. The clock on the VCR blinked 12:00. I got up, pulling the blanket with me, and walked into the bedroom. Daniel was asleep on the futon, a pillow over his head. The clock radio said 9:30. I was supposed to be at work at 8:30 a.m. How could it be? Hadn't the alarm sounded?

In the kitchen, I called the learning center.

"Good morning, Wellstone—"

"Lucy," I said, interrupting her phone-answering-mantra, "I'm so sorry. I don't know what happened. I just woke up."

"Are you feeling okay?"

Yes, no, yes, no, yes no. "I'm … well, I think I need to stay home today." I realized I was speaking quietly, out of habit, so as to not disturb Daniel. I raised my voice to its normal pitch. "Would that put you into too much of a bind?"

"I think it's okay, Gwen. I'll call Evelyn to see if she can come in before the kids to help me with a few things."

"Thanks, really," I said, flushing with gratitude for this friend.

"Are you sick?"

"Maybe I'm coming down with something. I think resting at home today would be good."

"Okay, because you better not have a job interview or something like that. I'd kill you if you abandoned me. Sorry, I sound like Will."

"Will says he'd kill you if you abandoned him?"

"Yeah, well, let's just hope it's a figure of speech."

I couldn't believe she was making light of this. I flashed on Will's large, handsome face, his massive, rugby-playing arms. "Did he actually say 'kill'?"

"Gwen, don't worry about it. Really, he didn't mean it that way."

"So you're back with him? You're not in the hotel?"

"I was at my mom's this weekend and he came down. We walked on the beach, talked. He agreed to go back to marriage counseling if I came back home."

It was odd to think of her walking on a Monterey beach with Will, just across the bay from where Jamie and I had been. I imagined an aerial shot, two specks of couples dwarfed by the white and blue vastness. From so far away, you wouldn't be able to tell that one couple was a woman and a man, and the other two women.

"That's great," I said, lilting the tone of my voice to try to belie the flatness of my sentiment. Whenever Lucy talked about leaving Will she emanated a feisty vitality. Whenever she talked about trying to work things out, she sounded like a bored eighth-grader giving an oral book report.

"Yeah, and he better fucking mean it this time. I swear to god I'm leaving if he doesn't try." That was more like it. I had a sudden urge to tell her about what was going on with me, with Jamie.

"Lucy," I said. "I … well, can we talk?"

"Sure, go for it."

"No, I mean … maybe after work, we could go out for a drink or something?"

"Great. How about tomorrow?"

"No, can't. Wednesday?"

"We have marriage counseling. Can't miss that. Ha! Um, Friday?"

"I think it will have to be next week." I was both anxious and relieved at the possibility of a reprieve.

"Give me a hint. What do you want to talk about? It's going to drive me crazy."

"Well … hm. I can't give you a hint. There's no hinting."

"Damn, girl, you've got a cruel streak!" I knew she was joking, but her comment felt like a hard pinch. Was I cruel? I thought about last night, innocent Daniel beneath me on the couch. Or this morning, Daniel in bed, my voice drifting through the wall, grating at him, waking him up.

"I don't mean it," I said lamely. "I wish I could tell you now, but we need to be alone somewhere with lots of time to talk, away from the phones at work, away from the possibility of anyone walking in on us."

"It's okay, don't go explaining things away. It won't kill me to wait. Maybe I'll get *something* out of you at lunch tomorrow. You are coming in tomorrow, aren't you?"

"Yes. I'll be there. I just need some extra rest today."

"Gwen, is everything really okay?" The tenderness in her voice made my throat catch.

"I'm not sure." My admission was like a leak in a dam. In the midst of heavy pressure came a tinge of relief. I needed to talk to someone to see if I was crazy.

I was sitting on the couch, reading through a poetry anthology for inspiration to write my own poem. I was still naked and wrapped in the blanket because I worried about waking up Daniel if I were to go get some clothes out of the bedroom. No work today. I had the whole day ahead of me to write my poem, to do whatever I wanted to do. It made me feel like I was in a free-falling elevator. I took a deep breath to ward off a shard of panic.

Daniel was up. I could hear him in the bedroom, opening a dresser drawer, mumbling something to himself. It sounded like *forty-two, forty-two*. He did that sometimes, mumbled numbers under his breath. I'd once asked him why and he looked at me like a blind mole. *I didn't know I was saying it out loud,* he'd said. When I assured him he was saying it out loud, he said it didn't mean anything.

He emerged from the bedroom rumpled like a little boy, his striped shirt untucked, his hair fittingly Einstein-esque. Something in me—the something that had spoken loudly while on the phone—felt an urge to break his rules of no speaking in the morning. I said, "Good morning."

He looked up at me, clearly startled.

"You're not at work?"

I was amazed—it was only 10:30 and he was speaking to me. His voice was thick, like he needed to clear his throat.

"I'm staying home sick today," I said.

He grunted out something that sounded like "uh huh" and then walked to the refrigerator and opened it. He pulled out the orange juice. I resisted reminding him to shake it. He never shook it. He put the carton to his mouth and took a few heavy gulps.

He went into the bathroom. I heard water running in the sink, his toothbrush scraping against his teeth. His electric shaver purred. When he came back into the living room, his shirt was tucked in but his hair was still wild. He walked toward me and grabbed his keys off the top of the T.V. The freefall feeling hit me again, a surge of dread at the thought of being alone in this apartment, surrounded by the things of his life, our life.

"I'm not feeling too bad," I said. "I just needed to stay home today." I was unnerved at the sound of my voice in the house this early as he stood there still pulling himself out of sleep. He'd asked me a long time ago not to talk in the mornings, and it had been a long time since I had. "Thanks for covering me with a blanket last night. I must have really been out of it, that you couldn't even get me up to go to bed."

He opened his mouth then closed it. He put his keys in his pocket. "I'll call you later," he said. A manic surge ran up my spine.

"I couldn't believe it, when I woke up and it was 9:30. I called Lucy. She was very cool about the whole thing."

He stood looking at me like he didn't recognize me. Like I was an alien who materialized on his couch, robotically speaking an awkward version of translated English. I felt a little sorry for him, but I couldn't help myself.

"She told me to go ahead and take the day off. She's going to see if Evelyn can come in to do some things." He didn't know Evelyn. I'd never mentioned her. She was one of our tutors who worked in the afternoons. "And I'm sure I'll go back tomorrow. I'm just going to stay here today, working on my poem. Do you want to read one of my poems? You know, I've written several now for the class. It's a really great class. Let me tell you about it, Daniel. You've never once asked me about the class."

"I need to go," he croaked. He had a sour look on his face, like the one I'd seen just two or three times before when he was close to tears. He turned to go.

"Okay," I said to his back, "let's talk later. I'll tell you all about my class." My voice by now was brittle, like stepped-on ice, cracking. "I'll read you some of my poems." He had disappeared behind the wall. I heard the front door open. He was going to leave without saying anything. He always did. Why would that surprise me? Why would I care so much now?

To the sound of the door closing, I yelled out something I'd never said to him, something I knew he would hate: "Have a nice day!"

I sat in the silent apartment on the sagging couch, where we'd had sex last night. Then it struck me. I scanned the floor. My shoes lay on their sides, next to a wrinkled magazine. I reached my foot out and kicked my shoes aside, then the magazine. Nothing. I lifted the blanket, lifted my body, looked all over the couch. Nothing. I reached between my legs, touched myself, brought my fingers to my nose. My fingers smelled of Daniel. What I had wanted for so long had actually happened. We'd had sex without a condom. And I'd missed it.

I spent that whole day on the couch, getting up only to put on sweats and a tee-shirt, and to get a glass of diet soda and a cheese sandwich from the kitchen. I worked out lines of a poem, then when I'd get stuck, I'd go back to reading the anthology. It felt like my limbs were unfixing, and the poems in the book and the lines I eked out were connective tissue, keeping me in one piece. I thought about

Jamie and me, telling each other we felt crazy. Crazy, crazed, cracked like the crazing on a piece of pottery that Jamie had showed me in her studio. Was that just a few weeks ago? It felt like a memory I'd always had, one that was gently embedded in a fold in my brain.

I ate the last of my cheese sandwich and turned the page in the anthology. And what jumped off the page at me was the perfect poem about craziness. The perfect antidote by Emily Dickinson:

Much Madness is divinest Sense—

To a discerning Eye—

Much Sense— the starkest Madness—

'Tis the Majority

In this, as All, prevail—

Assent— and you are sane—

demure— you're straightway dangerous—

And handled with a Chain—

I copied the poem in swirling cursive onto a piece of lined paper. Beneath it I wrote, "Jamie: Emily knew what craziness really is: divine sense." My pen paused, hovering over the page.

Then I signed it, "Love, Gwen."

A sign-off, an invitation, a command.

CHAPTER EIGHT

FLIES ON THE WALL

As I drove to work, I saw groups of kids in costumes clustered around the front of an elementary school. It was Halloween, my least favorite holiday. I was never entertained by unsettling stories and costumed portrayals of ghosts, ghouls, witches. As a girl, I dressed as a gypsy or a princess, but I never experienced the thrill that other kids did by wearing a costume or a mask. I loved the candy, though. Finally out of our costumes and secure in our pajamas, my sister and I would take our brown paper grocery bags—now soft at the edges from where our damp hands held them all night—and dump the thick-smelling booty on our beds. We'd sort by color, kind, size.

My sister, Barbara, now lived in La Jolla, near San Diego. No doubt she would be out trick-or-treating tonight in her exclusive neighborhood with her oldest boy, while her husband stayed home with the baby, handing out candy and watching movies. Thinking of Barbara, I felt a twinge of loneliness. That life, of us in our shared room, sorting out our candy, bartering caramel for chocolate, teasing each other, laughing, fighting—it had disappeared when I wasn't looking.

I wondered what Barbara would think if I told her about Jamie. I couldn't imagine. It had been years since we shared our secrets. When she moved away, she took her secrets with her, leaving mine behind.

Because it was Halloween, we were especially busy at work, setting out pumpkins, taping cardboard black cats to the windows, preparing candy treats for the kids. Lucy didn't press me about what I wanted to talk to her about. We'd had to wait longer than just a few days to talk; things kept coming up, and now a couple of weeks had passed. We finally had our plan secured to meet in three days. I was grateful for the ongoing delays because I was wavering about whether or not I could really go through with telling her that … what? That I had a thing for another woman? That I was falling in love with another woman? That I was coming out as a lesbian? None of those seemed quite right. None of those statements captured the intangible nature of what was happening to me.

Besides, maybe nothing would come of it. Jamie stayed obsessively on my mind—and I couldn't wait to see her in class each week—but we had spent no more time together since the beach. The past few weeks after class we'd talked for a few minutes, each one of us clearly meaning more than we could say. I was dying to be near her, but I understood her need to stand apart a little and think. Just standing next to her made my breath tight and shallow. I wanted to give her the Emily Dickinson poem, but I felt shy about it. And guilty. What was I doing to Daniel and me?

Finally, three weeks after our day at the beach, Jamie wrote me a note on one of my poems. "Let's go out for a drink after class next week, okay?" I'd looked at her across the room and smiled, wondering if anyone else noticed. I knew she knew I meant yes. Our desire to be alone together again was clearly trumping any guilt crawling around in my heart.

I kept thinking about being alone with Jamie as I taught a boy subtraction with red plastic blocks, and then as I corrected a girl's reading comprehension questions. Every so often Jamie's face flashed through my mind, a visceral memory, a sensual shiver of adrenaline. I wondered how she'd react in class tonight to my poem that I'd be turning in, with its image of two women on a roller coaster, plunging into the dark and pulling up and out, into the light.

When I walked into poetry class I saw that the Vietnamese guy, David, was dressed as Dracula, with a black cape and pointy teeth. Claire, the crabby one, had on a tattered prom dress, fake blood streaking down her neck. I wondered what their lives were like that they'd be dressed in costumes. Were they going to parties right after class and wouldn't have the time to change? Or had they been in their costumes all day? Their poems, up to now, hadn't revealed much about their lives. David wrote enigmatic poems with complicated patterns and surprising rhymes that Vanessa called, with a mix of admiration and irritation, "intellectual puzzles." Claire's poems were mostly about nature. Vanessa pointed out the beauty in her poems but pushed her to more deeply mine the metaphor: "Poems," Vanessa said, "are not merely descriptions of things." I'd written that down in my notebook along with other Vanessa gems, such as "Don't turn good poetry into bad prose" and one that she attributed to Plato: "Poetry is nearer to the vital truth than history."

I'd avoided seeking out Jamie when I first walked into the room, prolonging the moment so I could relish the instance I was finally seated and could look up and see her looking at me, our gazes locking in acknowledgement of what we shared—and that tonight would finally be our chance to be alone together in weeks. I took my seat and looked up. Cat sat next to Vanessa, their heads leaning toward each other as they talked amidst the chatter of other students entering the classroom. Usually Jamie sat between Cat and Vanessa. I scanned the room but didn't see Jamie, and with a sinking feeling I wondered if she wasn't going to show up tonight.

Throughout the whole class session, with every turning of the door knob, with every creak in the hallway, I looked up optimistically, hoping Jamie would come. She didn't. The usual richness I felt in the room as we discussed poetry fell flat. When it came time to discuss my poem, my stomach sank in disappointment at Jamie's absence. The class and Vanessa thought the poem was strong, that the images and line structures captured a sense of risk and hope. While normally I would have been thrilled with that critique, it felt lackluster in Jamie's absence. I realized that for weeks now, I'd been writing my poems for Jamie.

When class was over and I was putting my notebook and papers into my backpack, I felt a presence near my desk. I looked up and there stood Cat in her glossy leather jacket. I hadn't talked to her since she'd barged out of the studio, slamming the door.

"Hey," she said.

"Hi. Where's Jamie tonight?"

"I don't know," she said, a flatness to her voice that made me think there was still a rift between them.

"Would you tell her I said hi, when you see her?" I asked.

"Sure. So I was wondering, do you think you might want to go have a beer?"

A spider of prickliness scooted up my spine. Go have a beer, with Cat? Alone? The woman Jamie had told me also had a thing for me? I saw she had a new nose piercing, a little silver hoop. Or had I just not noticed it before?

"Is this new?" I asked, pointing to my own nose. She reached up and touched the hoop.

"Yeah. Not sure about it though. What do you think?"

"It fits you. It looks good." Giving her a compliment, I suddenly felt a little shy.

"Thanks. So, what about a beer?"

Walking into Fido's provided warm relief from the cold night. I scanned the room for the belligerent guys who had called Cat and Jamie "dykes" the last time we were here. The place was more crowded than last time. I didn't recognize anyone, but a few people wore Halloween masks so it was possible one of the guys was hiding behind a rubber face of Freddy Krueger or Ronald Reagan. At one table sat a group of young women wearing black satin leotards, fishnet stockings, heels and bunny ears. Playboy bunnies. As we walked past some tables toward an empty booth in the corner, I noticed that some of the people we passed looked at Cat. I couldn't read their faces, whether their stares were hostile or admiring. Or maybe they were just curious. I understood. Cat was someone you noticed. I wondered who people thought I was, with her.

"Are you hungry?" Cat asked, scanning the menu.

I was but I wasn't. That feeling of both wanting and not wanting food had been with me for weeks now. I said I might be able to eat something. When the messy-haired waiter came by, we ordered beers and onion rings. I added a side salad with blue cheese and Cat said, "I'll have one of those, too."

I was a little nervous, sitting with her. I wondered what she thought we were doing, exactly. This felt different from having a drink with a friend, and different from a date. Not too long ago, such complications weren't part of my life. A drink with a woman meant an outing with a friend. A drink with a man meant a date.

I wished Jamie were here, that she and Cat were bantering across the table, nudging each other about the past and about me, like last time.

"How did you and Jamie meet?" I asked.

"At a bar," she said. Again, a flatness to her voice. She wasn't offering much more information. I got the feeling she didn't want to talk about Jamie.

"And how old were you two when you met?"

"We were about nineteen, twenty. Fake I.D.'s, you know. What were you doing when you were twenty?"

"I was in college, and engaged," I said.

She looked at me, as though expecting me to go on. Her eyes were intense, like she was trying to pull something out of me. It startled me, made me feel like I'd opened a door to leave the house and unexpectedly was face-to-face with someone who stood on the stoop, about to knock. I lost my words, as though I had nothing to say about the ocean of feelings and experiences that accompanied my memories about being in college, and engaged.

Cat unlocked her eyes from me to look up at the server, who handed us our beer mugs. Cat held hers up and said, "*kampai*," the Japanese version of "cheers."

"*Kampai*," I said, relieved to have another thread of conversation to follow. "Have you been to Japan?"

"No, never have. But I'd like to go sometime."

"So how do you know *kampai*?"

"I have a friend, Reiko, whose family is from somewhere there. Okinawa, I think."

"I never went to Okinawa. All I know about it came from a history class, that in World War II there was one of the most devastating battles there. Thousands of American soldiers killed. More Japanese soldiers. And even more Japanese civilians."

"That kind of talk makes me realize I'm glad I never joined the military."

I looked at her, surprised. "You'd thought about joining the military?"

"Yeah, at one point, in high school, I thought of enlisting in the Air Force. I liked their uniforms." She smiled a small, careful smile. The way she lifted her beer to her lips looked like a practiced ballet, smooth and controlled. I could see her in the military. She continued, "I had a high school friend, Georgia, who was going to enlist with me. When I backed out, she didn't. But after about six months, she was dishonorably discharged, for being a dyke."

I hated all things military. I was a pacifist to the core. But the complete injustice of what Cat had just told me made the red heat of outrage sweep through me.

"What? You mean she was kicked out for being a lesbian?"

"Yep." She sipped her beer in a way I might have described as daintily, but that word didn't quite fit Cat.

"Wasn't there anything she could do about that? Did she fight it?"

"Fight it? It's the government's policy. What could she do?"

I knew that, but it still shocked me that people were actually kicked out. I thought about Bill Clinton's campaign promise: that there would be no more discrimination against lesbians and gays in the military. I'd always known that gays and lesbians weren't allowed in the military, but I'd never given it much thought until it came up in this Presidential campaign. I'd never given many things related to lesbians and gays much thought, I realized. A meek bafflement overtook my indignation.

"Well, how did they find out?" I asked.

"Her lover, another enlisted woman, told their superior. I'm not exactly sure why, but she told, they believed her, and they were both kicked out. It's random, really. I mean, the military is crawling with dykes. Only a few get kicked out now and then, I guess, to remind us of our place."

It seemed to me she relayed these unjust events without bitterness, as though they were benign pieces of information. She was used to such inequities.

"So what's she do now?"

"She's an electrician. Has her own business. Makes so much money, you wouldn't believe."

"Revenge as the best medicine, or whatever they say."

"Exactly."

The server appeared and placed a plate of hot onion rings between us, followed by our salads.

"I'd like to use a woman electrician," I said. "I've never known of one before."

"If you give me your number," said Cat, picking up her fork, "I can call you with her info." She took a careful bite of salad.

"Okay," I said, not sure how to say no, my landlord takes care of electrical problems in our apartment. I flushed. Jamie had warned me that Cat wanted my number.

"Yeah, it's funny," Cat said, "that Jamie met Rose through Georgia. Georgia had invited Rose to a party. Jamie and I were at that party, and that's where she and Rose hooked up. I really don't get what she sees in Rose, with all that religious bullshit. They even had that commitment ceremony and everything, like a church wedding. Creeped me out but, hey, whatever."

Jamie was married to Rose? When I'd told her I'd been married to Andy, why hadn't she said anything then? A white heat raced before my eyes, a chasm of loneliness opening up in me. Where was Jamie? Was she so sick that she couldn't come to class? Why hadn't she called me to let me know what was going on? We had spent all that time together at the beach, and all that time in her studio, and she had never mentioned that she and Rose were married—or whatever the equivalent was for two women. I thought about her in that two-story house on that quiet street, with perfect lawns and shade trees.

"Excuse me, I need to use the bathroom," I said. I found my way to the restroom, a one-person bathroom with a cracked mirror and walls plastered with yellowing dog posters. My heart was racing. I tried to take a deep breath, but the smell of cleaning chemicals repelled me. I turned on the water and splashed some on my face, avoiding my eyes so my mascara wouldn't run. Then I looked at myself in the cracked mirror, half of my face lifted higher than the other half. One reddish eye out of synch with the other. A Picasso—jagged, animated, serrated. I wanted to be in bed, my mother's cool hand on my forehead, a bowl of chicken noodle soup steaming on the bed stand. *As soon as she takes the thermometer out of my mouth, I'll eat the soup, extra pillows at my back, the oak trees out the window gleaming from rain.* It was pitiful, a thirty-one year old woman thinking *I want my mommy.*

In the dark kitchen, I saw the message machine light blinking red. I hit play.

"Hi Gwen." It was Jamie. "Give me a call when you get in. Doesn't matter what time." Casual, but with a hint of urgency.

I picked up the phone and dialed.

"Hello?" A thin, low voice. Not Jamie's.

"Hi. Is Jamie there?"

"Yes. May I tell her who's calling?"

"Um, yeah, Gwen, her friend from poetry class." Too much information. I sounded guilty of something. But I wasn't, really, was I? Of course I was, kind of. Rose wasn't only Jamie's girlfriend, she was her *wife*. Did they really use that word?

"Hi Gwen, this is Rose," she said. "I'll get Jamie." In just those few words, I could feel Rose pressing herself into my life. She wanted to make sure I knew who she was. Jamie's minister wife. I felt a little sorry for all three of us.

"Hey Gwen," said Jamie.

"Hi Jamie. Are you feeling okay?"

"Oh, yeah, I'm fine. Something just came up tonight, so I couldn't be in class. But thanks for calling. Nice of you. Sorry, but I really need to go."

How strange. Maybe she couldn't talk because Rose was right there? But why had she told me to call her, no matter the time, if she was just hanging up without saying anything?

"Oh, okay," I said, swallowing my impulse to blurt out something, but I wasn't sure what. "I'm glad you're okay."

"Thanks. See you next week."

I stood there with the phone to my ear after she'd hung up. Would it really be another week until I saw her again? Something was off. Something wasn't right. I put down the phone, suppressing the urge to call her back. It was late, 10:30, and Rose had picked up the phone like it was the middle of the afternoon. Well, it was Halloween, and they lived in the kind of neighborhood where kids still actually trick-or-treated. Or maybe they went to a Halloween party? What would a minister dress like for Halloween? A demon? A nun? My stomach was knotted. I hadn't been able to eat the salad I'd ordered with Cat. After my moment of panic in the restroom, I had rejoined her at the table and tried to eat, tried to continue the conversation. But it was no use. I'd felt jumpy. I couldn't sit there anymore. Cat hadn't seemed too happy about my wanting to leave the restaurant so soon. But she tried to hide her funk and said that she needed to get up early, anyway. She'd reminded me about her friend, the electrician, and that she could get me her number. So I wrote down my number and gave it to Cat, a little tremor of something running through me as our fingers touched when I handed her the paper. It was like she was electrical, sparking anyone who touched her or looked at her. Cat's magnetism was palpable, and a little scary.

I went into the bedroom. As usual, the bed wasn't made. I used to always make my bed, but Daniel never did so I'd fallen out of the habit. The comforter looked abandoned. I took off my clothes and put on my kimono. My stomach growled. Back in the kitchen, I opened the refrigerator, scanned the shelves for something that looked edible. A couple of apples, half a loaf of bread. I made a peanut butter sandwich but after a few bites, standing near the sink, my stomach turned. The phone rang. I thought it must be Daniel, telling me he was on his way home.

"Gwen, it's Jamie."

"Jamie?" She didn't sound the same. And there was noise in the background. Traffic? "Where are you?"

"I'm at a pay phone, down the street. I told Rose I was walking the dog so I only have a few minutes."

"Where were you tonight? Even Cat didn't know."

"You talked to Cat?"

"After class we went to Fido's," I said.

"The little scheming bitch," Jamie said playfully, but perhaps with a bit of an edge. "I leave you alone for one minute and she pounces."

"She told me you and Rose got married. Did you?"

"Not legally, of course, since we can't be. But we did have a commitment ceremony."

A tinge of relief pinged in me like a fingernail against a wine glass. She came out clearly, no hedging, and said it. She wasn't hiding it. I just hadn't thought to ask.

"What was it like, the ceremony?"

"We wore long white wedding dresses with veils."

"You did not."

She laughed. "We wore burgundy linen pants and shirts. It was at her church, officiated by a minister friend of hers. We and had sparkling cider in the lobby afterward. It's embarrassing to even talk about it, Gwen. It was three years ago, and I didn't want to do it."

"Why did you then?"

"I guess I didn't want to hurt her feelings. We were living together, after all. It was important to her. No, okay, here's the real reason. She pressured me, and I was weak and gave in."

"Seems like you're whipped. You're whipped, aren't you?"

"No!" She laughed. "Besides, only a man can be whipped."

"Is that so?"

"I still can't believe Cat took you out for a drink."

"She didn't take me out. I paid for my own."

"Yeah, well, you don't know Cat. I'm sure she's all worked up about you. She's still pissed at me. She refuses to talk about the studio incident. Ha, 'the studio incident.' I'm sure that one will go down in the Jamie and Cat history. Anyway, she made it clear to me that you're not off-limits to her. She says I have no right even imagining, well, being with you since I'm with Rose."

Being with you. My heart pulsed, sending a current through my whole body.

"You know," she said. "I *am* with Rose. And you *are* with Daniel."

I didn't say anything.

"I'm sorry I haven't called, that we haven't been able to see each other," she said. "It's been horrible for me keeping away from you. I need to see you." She paused. "Gwen, Rose got a job offer, to be minister at a church in Arizona. We've gotten in a terrible fight about it."

"Did you say something to Rose? I mean, about—" I couldn't quite finish that sentence with "us." It sounded too presumptuous.

"She's very guarded, let me put it that way. And—and she should be. Gwen, I need to see you. We need to talk."

"I couldn't wait to see you tonight. I couldn't believe you weren't in class. I have something for you." A flush of shyness. "A poem, an Emily Dickinson poem about madness."

"*Madness is the divinest sense.*"

"You know it! How is it possible you know both that and the *Happy Hollisters*?" Was it true that my whole body was lighting up over talking about poetry on the phone with another woman? Was it possible that I might lose this, that she might move away from

California?

"When can I see you, Gwen?"

"Can you come see me after work on Friday? I should be done around five. Why don't you come there?" I told her where the learning center was.

I heard a dog bark. "Peanut, no," she said.

"Your dog?"

"Someone just walked another dog by."

"Peanut. Is she little?"

"She's a one-hundred pound yellow lab. But she was the runt of the litter. She's so huge, it's hard to believe she was ever that little. I've had her since she was six weeks old." I imagined Jamie, wrapped in her coat, leaning into the phone booth. All the trick-or-treat kids were now home, counting their candy or sleeping with over-full stomachs. There was no moon tonight. She was probably surrounded by darkness. I was glad she had a huge dog with her.

"Friday's good," said Jamie. "I'm sorry, I need to go."

"Whipped."

She laughed. I was only half-kidding. I remembered her needing to go that night in the studio, too. What a contrast to my life, where I could come and go as I pleased, no questions from Daniel. Did this mean that she and Rose were more connected than I'd like to admit? Daniel had never talked marriage with me, much less shared sparkling cider in a lobby.

"It's so good to hear your voice, Gwen. I'd like to stay on the phone with you all night."

"Then let's do," I said impulsively. "Call me back, collect. I'll accept. I'll run up a thousand-dollar bill and we'll talk all night."

"I'd love to. But I can't."

"Why? What would happen?" I felt myself pushing her, playfully, but a little forcefully too. I wanted her to choose me.

"It wouldn't be pretty," she said. "Trust me. Gwen, I'll see you Friday. We'll sort a few things out. I think it'll all be okay."

"Stay on, just a little longer. If we run out of things to say, we can just listen to each other breathe."

"You're bad," she said. I could hear the smile in her voice. "Watch the sky tomorrow night. There's supposed to be a meteor shower."

"Okay, I will."

After we hung up, I went into the bedroom. I sat up in bed and opened my poetry class folder. I looked through the papers and found several of my poems with Jamie's handwriting on them. *This image is astonishing. Nice line.* I followed the loops of her handwriting with my eyes and wondered what it would be like to touch her, to kiss her. Not only her, but a woman. To press my body up against the body of a woman. My body felt like it was being filled with warm water. I reached beneath the sheets and touched myself. In the distance somewhere, a car roared by, faraway music thumping. My heartbeat, my body. Deep down, a whole other self was blooming.

Daniel's keys rattled at the door. I turned over, facing the wall, blood pumping in my ears. I heard the thud of his bag dropping to the floor in the hallway, the movement of his feet across the carpet to the living room, the clink of his keys on top of the T.V., then a click and muffled voices, a sound connecting us, separating us, the subdued cadence of the T.V. on low.

Curled on my side I brought my hand back between my legs to finish what I'd started.

The closest place to have a drink near the learning center was the lounge of a hotel down the street. The lounge had a Vegas feeling with its dark ambiance and deep red upholstered booths and walls covered in burgundy, flocked wallpaper. The servers were all busty women, dressed in short black skirts and white ruffled blouses that framed their cleavages. Our server was a blonde in her early twenties, wearing several gold necklaces that snaked seductively over her skin.

"Hi, I'm Emily. What can I get you ladies?" she asked.

"A pitcher of margaritas, extra salt," said Lucy. "Is that okay?" she asked me as an afterthought, as Emily turned to walk away.

"Sounds good," I said.

"Damn," said Lucy, watching Emily lean over a table of men in suits who clearly were enjoying an eyeful. "Sometimes I feel like I wasted my twenties. I could have been playing the field, sewing my wild oats and all those other clichés, but instead I married Will. Why did I get married at twenty-two? Why did you? What were we thinking? No one forced us. My mother tried to talk me out of it, even. What the fuck was my problem?"

"I guess things aren't going too well with Will?"

"That's an understatement. At therapy yesterday he said he thinks I'm frigid. Can you believe he used that word? That anach, anach-asm—what the hells's the word?"

"Anachronism?"

"Yeah, that. What does he think I am, a 1950's housewife?"

"What did you say when he said you were frigid?"

"That I think he's addicted to sex. That his wanting sex all the time has nothing to do with me. That he could be getting sucked off through a glory hole for all he cared."

I laughed. I'd hear about what goes on in the gay baths but was surprised that Lucy knew.

"You did not say that!" I said.

"Indeed I did." She dramatically shot her eyes around. "Where's our booze? I need booze."

As though on cue, Emily appeared, serving up a glistening pitcher of margaritas along with her cleavage. When she left, Lucy said, "I'd love to have a job where I could dress that way. See, I'm not frigid. It's just Will. I love him, but … Shit, I don't know. I'm not even sure I know what love means. I'm not sure what I want." She licked salt off the rim of her glass then took a long drink.

"Be careful, cold headache," I said.

"I dare you," she said, looking at me straight in the eye, "to drink that whole glass down, right now. I'll race you."

On impulse, I downed my whole drink. She did the same. We looked at each other then grimaced simultaneously, cold headaches gripping us.

"Ow, ow, ow!" she said.

"Look what you made us do! I feel like we're back in the dorms."

"Every once in a while a little rebellion is good," she said. "But damn, that hurt! Here, let's be more civilized." She poured us more margarita then took a refined sip. "So, Gwen, what's up? I've been waiting weeks to hear, so spill it."

An invisible hand squeezed my stomach. I was dying to tell her. But this would be so different from sharing all our other secrets. Those were all about men, stories that giddily connected us. It seemed that telling her about Jamie had the potential to break us apart.

"It must be big," she said. "You're getting skinny. You only get skinny when you're stressed about something."

I felt a tenderness toward her. We were about to leap into unknown territory, and it felt like saying goodbye.

"Well, Lucy," I said, stalling to sip my margarita again, "I think I'm falling for someone else."

"Good for you!" She grinned, her light dusting of freckles spreading across her nose. "You know I like Daniel, but you need to be happy. Tell me about him!"

"That's just it," I said. "Wrong pronoun."

"Pronoun? Don't throw that esoteric grammatical language at me. You're going to make me sit here and admit that when I fill in for an English tutor I have to fake it? You're going to make me remember my high school grammar class? Pronoun. In place of a noun." She looked at me. "Wait. Are you saying *him* is the wrong pronoun?" She froze, her glass halfway to her mouth.

"That's what I'm saying," I said, trying on a confidence I didn't really feel. "Her name's Jamie. I met her in my poetry class. I can't believe it, Lucy, but I think I'm falling in love with a woman." I was dizzy saying this out loud. Or maybe it was the margarita.

"My god, this is great!" she said. "Tell me everything, and I don't want you to leave out one detail. What's the sex like?"

I flushed. "We haven't had sex," I said. "Or kissed. Or even touched."

"What? I'm outta here," she said, feigning reaching for her purse. "Get back to me when you have some juicy details." She laughed. "Don't look so stricken, Gwen. I'm just kidding." Then, tenderly: "Tell me all about what's going on with your heart."

I felt my eyes fill. "Lucy, I don't know what's going on with my heart. I don't know what's going on with *her* heart." I wiped my eyes with a napkin.

"Are you waiting to find out what's going on with her heart before you consult your own?"

I smiled. "What, are you channeling your therapist?"

"Maybe so. I might as well be getting something out of spending a hundred bucks a session. But don't derail yourself here, my dear. Talk to me."

"I don't want to leave Daniel for someone else," I said, surprised at what felt like a new truth coming out of my mouth. "If I leave him, I want it to be because I've decided it won't work between us, that I can't get what I need from our relationship. I don't want to regret leaving him for someone else, if that someone else doesn't work out."

"Have you talked to Jamie about this?"

"No. Not really. Kind of. She's with someone else, too. A woman named Rose."

"Sounds a little messy. A lot messy."

I told her what I knew about Rose the minister, about the fact that they'd had a commitment ceremony. I told her about meeting Jamie in poetry class. I told her about our day at the beach, about last night's phone call, how tomorrow we were meeting to talk. I realized

I was reciting details, like the CliffsNotes of my life. I still hadn't told her what she asked for. I hadn't said much about what was in my heart.

"It's so different," I said, "when I'm with Jamie. Different from Daniel, I mean. I feel like there's something about me that she understands that Daniel never will. Because he's a man. Lucy, I never imagined myself with a woman before. But, now I can. And it's really beautiful ... and exciting." A blush crept up my neck.

"Gwen, I never thought I'd tell you this. But about a month ago, I had a dream. A dream about us, that you and I were, well, making out. Making love, I mean."

I looked at Lucy and remembered one time in college when she'd had the flu. I'd brought her orange juice and 7Up, and I'd held her hair back as she got sick in a pan by the side of her bed. I'd lightly rubbed her back, as my mom used to do for me when I was sick.

"You probably don't remember," she said, "but I was flustered at work all day that day. It was hard for me to look at you, to sit next to you. I was embarrassed, but kind of—well, kind of aflame with the memory of the dream. What I mean is, it was the hottest dream I ever had. It had seemed so real I almost expected you to say something about it that day. But of course you didn't. And now, well, it's bizarre. You're sitting here telling me this."

I was amazed at Lucy's bravado. I squirmed, uncomfortable but a little thrilled.

"Oh, wow, okay. I don't know what to say."

"I know, I know, I'm not your type," she joked. I could see she was diffusing the awkwardness of the moment.

"Have you ever really wanted to be with a woman?" I asked, and the moment it came out of my mouth I saw something sad in her eyes. I wanted to reach out and touch her, to sit gently holding her hand. I wanted to hold her hair back from her face, like I had that night she was sick, long ago. She sat in her sadness for a minute or two, a vulnerability she rarely revealed. But just as quickly I saw that she pushed it aside, like closing a window blind. She sat up a little straighter, tucked her hair behind her ear, and sipped at her drink. The best I could do was to try to help her protect herself, a gift I wanted to give.

I forced a little giggle then said, "What would Will and Daniel think if they were flies on the wall for this conversation?"

She grinned. "They'd probably be rooting us on, asking if they could watch."

That night as I drove home I wondered where Jamie was, if she was looking at the same dark sky, watching for the meteor shower. I looked as I drove, but I saw only motionless stars. Maybe she sat at a window or in her backyard with her big yellow dog. I tried to erase Rose from the picture, but her presence stubbornly shadowed the scene in my mind.

I came to the exit that would take me to Daniel's lab and felt a flicker of an urge to take it, to go to him. Daniel had told me he'd be working late into the night. I imagined him and Ellen listening to music I'd never heard before, chatting in French, her dark hair grazing her cheek as she looked across the room at him. He'd hold a test tube up to the light, Ellen's white lab coat refracting off the glass like sparks of a shooting star.

I didn't take the turn-off, just kept driving toward home, leaving Daniel behind.

CHAPTER NINE

NEANDERTHALS

When Jamie walked in, I saw Lucy look at her and register right away who she was. No one else who looked like Jamie had been in the tutoring center, with her short, spiky hair and leather jacket. Lucy and I were dressed in our usual business attire—slacks, heels, silk blouses and blazers. Most of the parents who came in were dressed the same way, on their way home from work in Silicon Valley. There were no parents there at the moment, though. The last child had just been picked up by her mother. Yolanda, the algebra tutor, had been opening the door to leave when Jamie came in.

"Can I help you?" Yolanda had said, and Jamie, eyeing me at the book rack in the back of the room, had said, "No, thanks." And Yolanda and Lucy watched as Jamie made her way over to me. I stood there, a book in my hand. As Jamie moved between the tables toward me, I was struck by the sudden juxtaposition of her in this part of my world. With her here, the tutoring center stood out in relief. The tutors' chairs were high-backed upholstered desk chairs on wheels, the sleek gray aesthetic of corporate CEO's. The children's chairs were mini-versions of these chairs. Every book on the book rack, every binder on the shelf—each had its exact spot, and each was adorned with the eager blond boy logo, relentlessly smiling. We had a script for answering the phone, a script for selling the program, a script for interacting with each child based on that child's test scores and subject matter. Children and parents weren't *children* and *parents*, but *clients* or *potential clients*. We weren't allowed to listen to music, or to wear jeans or denim shirts or tennis shoes. And suddenly I remembered: we weren't to have non-family members visit us in the center. But there was Jamie, her thick black boots calmly making their way across the severe gray carpet, toward me.

She smiled, said hi. Feeling shy but electrified, I said hi back. I could sense her energy as though her face were right against mine, even though she stood a few feet away.

I realized Lucy was hovering over the corner desk, waiting to be introduced. We were the only three in the room; Yolanda had left, shutting the glass door behind her.

"Lucy, this is Jamie," I said, aware that I omitted a descriptor, like *my friend from poetry class* or *the woman I've been telling you about*. A chill crept into me when I realized Lucy might say something like, *I've heard so much about you*. Instead, though, she said, "Hi, nice to meet you." I flushed with gratitude, realizing that Lucy was being gentle with me.

"Give me a minute, I need to change my clothes," I said, pointing to myself to indicate my green-jacketed, brown nylons-and-pumps attire. I went into the office and closed the door and the blinds to change into jeans and my favorite zip-up extra-soft black sweater, positioning the zipper just so to reveal a little cleavage. Funny how I was ambivalent about men looking at my body, but I clear-headedly hoped that Jamie would look and look and look at me. For some reason, her gaze struck me as different from being ogled by a man. Maybe because I was ogling Jamie back, coveting her long neck, her full hips, the shiny scar on her forehead, the wave tattoo on the back of her hand. I thought about how she looked, not just how I looked to her. To look at a man in the same way he looked at me not only seemed awkward, but not quite possible.

While changing, I could hear Lucy's and Jamie's voices coming from the other room, murmuring, then Lucy's loud, sharp laugh. Quickly, I brushed my hair and went out to join them. Lucy was sitting on the top of the big desk, this particular position exhibiting her striking legs crossed at the knees. She was grinning at Jamie who leaned against a bookcase, her hands in her jacket pockets, that casual sense of being fully in her body filling me with a familiar yet surprising charge, every one of my pores pulsating.

Lucy had obviously said something funny because Jamie was finishing off a laugh, too. With a shiver of jealousy, I was sure I detected something between her and Jamie, a kind of energy. Sheepishly I realized that I'd thought jealousy was something I'd only feel with men—because of the way men looked at other women, because women were socially designed to compete for men. How silly, I realized, to imagine that the supposed equality of desire between two women would erase all of the puerile elements of opposite-sex attraction. Still, I doubted that Jamie would, say, subscribe to *Playboy*. But what if she did? Would I get pissed off? Would I join in? After Daniel's and my blow-out over his *Playboy*, I'd found his hiding place for it, in the bottom drawer of his desk beneath a file holding reams of paper listing all the books he'd ever read and albums he'd ever listened to. I'd flipped through the pages of the magazine and felt a bodily surge. Did it matter that these women were placed on the page for this very purpose? Did it matter that this magazine might make men see women as objects? I wasn't sure anymore. I'd tried to put men out of my mind. I'd tried to pretend the women on the page—with their voluminous breasts, olive nipples, glassy lips—were posing for other women. Posing for me. My fantasy had a hard time staying there, though. It kept slipping into imagining myself as one of the Playmates, which zipped a small thrill up my spine, countered by a kernel of disgust. Frustrated, I'd jammed the magazine back into Daniel's drawer and kicked it shut.

Now all I knew was that I wanted to get out from under the florescent lights of the tutoring center and into the night with Jamie.

"Good to meet you, Lucy," said Jamie, as we walked toward the door.

"You too. Have a good night, girls," Lucy said, and again I was grateful for her. The way she said "girls" suggested she was giving us her blessing. I thought of her going home to tough, handsome Will tonight, to their clean, organized house, and their two special-breed cats with elongated bodies. One of those cats once bit me. A manifestation, in my mind, of the tension in that house. I squelched an urge to invite Lucy to join us.

Mad Mary's was packed. People crowded in at the bar and tables. Dance music in the front room blasted, competing with what sounded like country-and-western music pouring in from the back room. Mad Mary's was a restaurant and bar tucked in an industrial corner of town. I'd driven by it a couple of times and had noticed the sign portraying a comic drawing of a busty waitress with a pencil tucked into her upswept hair. But I had never been in, and I'd had no idea it was a gay establishment.

We were greeted by a young black guy wearing eyeliner, cornrows decorated with multicolored beads, black leather pants and a tee-shirt reading "Faggoty" in sparkling pink script. His name-tag read "Billy."

"It's going to be a few minutes, girls," he said.

He wrote down Jamie's name and told us to relax at the bar. The ceiling of the bar and adjacent dining room was draped with hundreds of hanging green plants, some adorned with yellow or pink flowers.

"Wow, that must be quite a job to water all of those," I said, looking up.

"Or dust them, if they're fake," said Jamie. "One of Cat's and my customers has about fifty plastic plants in her house."

"Do you have to dust them?"

"Occasionally, and it's a bitch. But the woman is eighty-five years old and set in her ways. It makes her happy when her plants are all spiffy."

"What do all those old people make of you and Cat?"

"Well, some of them think I'm the wife and she's the husband. One, who has really bad cataracts, thinks it's the other way around. She always calls Cat 'Cal.'"

I laughed. "Does that bother you?"

"Sometimes, a little," she said, "but not really. They're generally good people. They're from an entirely different generation. Some of them are lonely. They're glad we're there, no matter what."

"Are you really so saintly?" I asked, playfully squeezing her arm. It was surprisingly exhilarating to touch her.

She looked taken aback. "I'm not sure you could call a former cocaine addict saintly. Believe me, I've done plenty of things in my life that would keep me out of a fundamentalist's version of heaven."

"But their version of heaven is your version of hell. What I mean is, it sounds like you're really nice to all the old people you work for. Don't all those old people ever get on your nerves?"

"Sure, sometimes. I guess I'm just used to old people, though, having spent most of my childhood being raised by my grandparents."

"I love my grandmother," I said, "But she's always clicking her dentures and talking about her bowel movements. I wish I were more like you, more patient with her."

We walked toward the back room toward the sounds of country-and-western music. It overtook the front room's dance music as we approached. We squeezed through bodies in a long hallway and entered the room. There, dozens of cowboys danced in couples, decked out in cowboy hats, tight jeans, boots, red bandanas tied around a neck here, a thigh there. They were all skilled, dancing to the twanging music in unison, stomping their boots to the floor at one point to emphasize a beat of the song.

The guy nearest to me, holding his partner's hand aloft, looked a lot like a guy I'd danced with once, years ago. I'd been a camp counselor at a rural Northern California summer camp. It had been my night off, and a co-counselor and I had gone to the small town bar. We were only eighteen, but we weren't carded, so we hung out near the jukebox with our beers, as local guys watched us, occasionally approaching us to dance. They had black grease beneath their fingernails and wore a John Deere or Coors baseball caps. Their politeness made them appear handsome, even if they weren't particularly. The cowboy who'd asked me to dance wore a cowboy hat, a tucked-in plaid shirt, and tight Wrangler jeans. He had a little bump of chaw in his mouth. I was awkward on my feet as he tried to teach me dance steps. I'd gone home with him that night, and he'd shown me pictures of his dogs, horses, and family in photo albums before we'd had sex on his leather couch. He'd seemed almost like another species to me: hyper-male, yet with a surprising undercurrent of vulnerability.

I looked again at the cowboy dancing near me and, for a disorienting moment, was confused about where I was, who I was. Was he about to break away from his male dancing partner to ask me to dance? Where was I, who was I, watching a sea of male cowboys dancing without women?

"Can't you just feel the cowboy love?" Jamie said, cupping her hand around my ear to get her voice to me, above the blaring music. Her breath warmed the side of my face. I turned toward her, her eyes and her gelled hair glistening in the pulsing dance-floor lights.

"Who would have known there were so many cowboys in the

Bay Area?" I said.

"I think by day they wear business suits and work in cubicles at computers."

"Wow, it's a sight. I wish I could film this for prime time T.V. People need to know this exists."

When Jamie's name was announced, we squeezed through the bar crowd to a spacious back dining room and followed Billy to a table, the beads on his corn-rowed braids clicking as he walked. It took my eyes a minute to adjust to the dark room, illuminated by dim overhead lights and a twinkling candle at each table. The huge hanging plants draping from the ceiling created the atmosphere of a forest.

"You've been in here before," Billy said, pointing to Jamie with his pen, once we were seated.

"Yes, with my friend Cat."

"Oh, yes. *Me-ow*! It's such a shame she doesn't have boy equipment. She'd make such a hot boy. I'd be all over that in a minute."

"I'll be sure to let her know," Jamie said, smiling.

"You do that, doll. Who knows, maybe we could start something new, rock the queer world."

"It's been known to happen," Jamie said.

"Now *that's* the truth." He looked around the room. "Miss Bruce has a zillion tables. I'll help her out and get you girls started. What would you like?"

"Are you hungry?" Jamie asked me.

"I can answer that," Billy broke in, "she's *really* hungry!"

"What makes you say that?" I retorted, doing my best to enter the rhythm of his banter.

"I can see it in your eyes, girl. You hunger for her." He pointed his pen at Jamie again. "And now you're blushing. See, Billy's always right when it comes to matters of the heart."

Vaguely pleasurable embarrassment overtook any bravado I'd been working up. I looked over to the menu, propped up on the table in a plastic frame.

"You girls could not be a cuter couple," he said.

"That's what I think, too," said Jamie. I looked over at her and caught her eye. She was smiling, but I could feel something serious in the way she was looking at me.

We ordered beer and food, as though we knew we needed to eat and would give it a good try. But I could already tell my stomach was going to reject anything non-liquid.

"I wonder what his parents are like?" I said as Billy turned and disappeared into the crowd. "I mean, what do they think of having a flamboyant gay son?"

"Did you know that Cat hasn't come out to her parents?"

"What? That seems unbelievable. I mean, look at her."

"Well, of course they know. She's always lived with women. In fact, her parents have always been great to her girlfriends—inviting them for dinner, buying them birthday and Christmas presents."

"So they know but they've never talked about it? Really?"

"They've never used the L word. Or even the G word. Her parents are really … Ozzie and Harriet. Very nice, polite. Very much of a different generation."

"I have a hard time imagining that. I wonder what it's like for them to have a—"

"A dykey daughter?"

"Yeah."

"They seem to love her a lot. They just don't talk about it."

"What about you? How did your grandmother react?"

"She wasn't too happy about it," Jamie said. "But she got used to it. I told her when I was eighteen. That was my birthday present to myself, to get it out in the open, now that I was an adult. I'm sure my grandmother already had a suspicion because I'd never had a real boyfriend. I was tired of pretending, so I told her. At first, she wanted me to go to a therapist, when of course she was the one who should have gone since she was having a hard time dealing with it."

"Did you go?"

"Yes, just to appease her. And the therapist told my grandmother that she should be happy that she had a well-adjusted lesbian granddaughter."

I laughed. "No, really?"

"Really. I realize how lucky I was. It would have been possible, especially back then, to end up with a therapist who felt differently— one who would want to ship me away to a clinic in the Midwest that would beat the dyke out of me."

"Are there really such places?" I felt a chill.

"Yeah. They present the pretense of being medical establishments, and they try to de-program people. Or should I say, program them to be straight. I don't know much about them, really, but I know that even in this day and age there are places like that."

"But your grandmother wouldn't really have sent you to one of those places, would she?"

"Who knows? If some authority figure had insisted that it would be best for me, she might have listened. Anyway, that was fifteen years ago. Before she died, she'd more or less accepted that I'm a lesbian, but she would have liked it, I'm sure, if I became a wife and mother."

So she didn't think of herself as Rose's wife. I found myself hung up on these words, *wife and mother*. If I chose to be with a woman, would I never have to wonder about those roles again? I'd been a wife once, and that role had felt like trying to pull a wet bathing suit onto my body. But still, I grappled with the idea of being a wife to another man, to Daniel. Could I be a mother with him as the father? If I were with a woman, would *wife* and *mother* disappear from my repertoire? I thought of books I read as a child where a character finds a secret passageway in a false wall behind a bookshelf. Perhaps a whole other possible world existed behind the obvious.

"She had a thing for big, hairy dark guys," Jamie was saying, and I realized she was still talking about her grandmother. "She always pointed out a man on TV or even on the street and said, *Isn't he handsome?* And I'd always tease her that he'd be perfect for her, and she'd drop it. She never dated another man after my grandfather died. She was alone for almost ten years. Maybe that's why she found peace with my being a lesbian. She didn't want me to be alone. She was always nice to my friends and girlfriends. Even," she paused, as though debating whether or not to continue, "even Rose. She liked Rose. I was with Rose for just about six months when my grandmother died."

"Here you go, girls," said Billy, putting our beers down in front of us. "Enjoy your social lubrication." He turned and rushed off to another table.

"Do you feel bad when we talk about Rose?" I asked, sipping at my beer.

"A little," she said. "Sometimes more than a little. She, well, depends on me. Not in the way you might think. I mean, in terms of her career. Rose, well, as I said, she got a job offer in Arizona. To seal the deal, she needs to go out there to meet the congregation. And of course, I'm supposed to go with her, as her life-long partner." She looked down at the table then back up to me. "Before I met you, Gwen, I'd been thinking of leaving Rose. You've just added some extra impetus. But there's this job now for Rose, the perfect job, really. And if I left her right now, it might screw things up for her. I don't know exactly what I'm saying. But I do think that next week I'm going to go with her to Arizona to help her out. Then I'll figure out what I'm going to be doing with my life. All I know is that I'm so drawn to you, it's crazy. Disorienting. I feel like I need to clear my head, but I'm not sure how."

Irrationally, I was a little irritated. I wanted her to talk about what a bad person Rose was, and how she was definitely leaving her. I wanted her not to care if she hurt Rose. But I knew that was hypocritical. I had similar wavering feelings about Daniel.

"I've been thinking about this, too," I said. "And what if, what if we agree to not—well, to not act on how we feel about each other until we do what we need to do with Rose and Daniel."

"You mean not see each other?"

"Well, no. We can do—this, dinner. Poetry class. I'm just saying

…" I didn't know how to say it exactly, but I felt like if we touched, I'd fall into the well of her, drop and drop and never be able to climb back out. "Maybe we need to separate what might happen between us from Daniel and Rose. Take care of those relationships first, before you and I do anything to, well, try—"

I was interrupted by two big platters of veggie burgers with fries and fruit descending onto the table.

"Enjoy girls!" enthused Billy.

I looked at Jamie over the voluminous steaming food. Her hands were wrapped around her beer mug, the wave tattoo dark green against the skin of her hand. Her eyes reflected the jumping flame of the candle on our table.

"You mean, no kissing," she said, a small smile forming on her lips.

A warm thrill zipped up my spine. "Right," I whispered. Where had my voice gone?

"And no touching."

I nodded. She reached her arm across the table and, feather-light, ran a finger across the top of my hand. I felt a strange sensation watching her touch me, as though I were underwater, everything muted and slow.

"I think you're right," she said, her finger still circling softly across my skin. I reached up my fingers and interlocked with hers.

"You mean, stopping here," she said, "at holding hands."

I nodded again. Her hand was a little cold from having held her beer mug. How did we get from sitting across each other in poetry class to this moment? I felt a little dizzy.

She moved across the booth over to me. The sharp smell of her leather jacket reached me at the same time our lips met. The kiss was insistent—her face, velvet. Kissing her felt new but familiar. I reached my hand into her jacket and placed it on the back of her tee-shirt and felt something I'd definitely never felt before when kissing someone—the outline of a bra. In the midst of losing myself in our kiss, I retained a fragment of self-awareness that there I was, in a gay restaurant, adjacent to a gay bar where cowboys danced together, and I was kissing a woman by candlelight, beneath an explosion of plants. Even with my eyes shut, I could feel the plants hanging above us, draped over our heads, shadowing us. We could have been a world away, in a forest or a jungle. We could have been Neanderthals, early humans, in the act of discovering the kiss.

That night I lay awake in bed, in the dark, next to Daniel's sleeping body, a pillow over his head. Or, half of me lay in bed. The other half was reliving, over and over, the events of the night. Jamie and me, kissing. Jamie taking my hand and leading me through the crowd and out the door of the restaurant, across the parking lot, and into her car. We'd taken off our jackets and felt each other's bodies through our thin shirts, kissing like two deep-sea divers without tanks, surfacing from the water, gulping oxygen into our air-deprived bodies. We'd kissed for only seconds, or forever. Then—as though my words about not touching until we'd decided exactly what to do with our lives had suddenly reached her—Jamie pulled away. It was late. She needed to go home.

That weekend, Jamie left to go to Arizona with Rose. She called me from the pay phone down the street from her house before she left and told me she'd be thinking about me the whole time she was gone. She said she couldn't stop thinking about me, that she felt crazed, that being away was going to be really hard, but she felt she was doing the right thing. Although maybe she wasn't. She just couldn't know.

I had the sensation that I was in the same world, but everything was just a little askew. Just like I'd when I'd returned from Japan, I felt as though a little something had been tweaked, and it changed everything. And, like the Ray Bradbury story, only the people who had time-traveled could see the change. Being around Daniel made me feel like a wobbly time-traveler, as though I had no firm ground to walk on. But I wasn't around him much, anyway. He was in a big push at the lab and came home very late each night. And of course, as always, we didn't see each other in the mornings. Or if we did, we didn't talk.

The weekend Jamie was gone, Daniel spent at least twelve hours each day in the lab. I was relieved. Besides, I had precinct work to do. I walked neighborhoods, hanging fliers on the doorknobs of houses and apartments, fliers that reminded people to vote on Tuesday. Even though I had my hopes up, I had a hard time believing that this charismatic governor from Arkansas could actually usurp the current administration's twelve-year hold on the presidency.

While I was posting fliers in an apartment building, an elderly woman with coiffed white hair, wearing a spiffy blue suit, gave me the thumbs up when she passed me on the stairwell. I waved to her, trying to return her optimism. Soon we might have a new, young president who had a powerful wife who'd been given a lot of grief over a crack she made about not being the cookie-baking type. I wasn't sure if who the president was would really change my life much. But it was sure to affect others' lives, wasn't it? All I knew was it felt like the country was on the edge of something. That sense of being right at the edge reverberated in my bones as I stepped over the cracks in the sidewalk on my way down the street, past one apartment building to the next.

Chapter Ten

Hunger

I never knew what to buy my father for his birthday. His hobbies didn't involve things like fishing reels and golf balls, as Hallmark seemed to think they should. He liked to read the newspaper and watch history and nature shows on T.V. He was president of his town's Democrats club, and he was on the local school board. He was hard to buy for. I wanted to get him something different this year, something other than the usual shirt, tie or book. Besides, I was filled with fidgety energy with Jamie in Arizona and the election a day away. I had distributed all my Clinton fliers. I knew I could be on the phones in the headquarters, but the image of sitting in a chair on the phone made me feel in advance like I was climbing the walls. I had a poem to write, but I couldn't focus. So I went to the nearby mall, a California conglomeration of high-priced boutiques and cafes, book-ended by two massive department stores that assaulted the nose with overblown perfume scents the minute you entered.

Passing by the gleaming cosmetic center, I felt a zing of

inadequacy. A woman behind a glass counter offered me a free makeover. Her white coat lent her a vague sense of medical validity, a sharp contrast to the rest of her: young and beautiful, her makeup, jewelry and clothing flawless. I walked by her, waving away her offer. It took an effort because against my will I was drawn to her, silently agreeing that every part of me could be fixed. She was flawless. And yet, deep down, "flawless" wasn't truly appealing to me. I was a little fond of my unruly eyebrows, and of Lucy's freckled skin, and Jamie's scar and tattoo. These things added traction to a person's personality. The woman behind the counter looked as smooth as ice you might skate over.

I walked past the men's clothes, fingering a few shirts my dad might like but resisting the obvious. Behind the men's section were tools and small appliances. Every option looked like something he already had or something he'd have no use for. An electric razor? Talk about an obvious man-gift. Next to the razors was an assortment of foot and back massagers. I remembered Lucy telling me a few years back that she had bought one such massager and used it as a vibrator. "That's what they're really for," she'd said. "Look at the bliss of those faces on the boxes. You can't tell me they're feeling so good because they're vibrating their backs."

Sure enough, the woman on one elongated box looked like she was posing for the cover of a porn video, with her ecstatic lips parted and her eyes shut in bliss. Lucy had sworn that a vibrator was a must-have for any woman. At the time I had resisted, saying I enjoyed sex more with a person than by myself. She'd insisted that I didn't know what I was missing.

I picked up the box. Fifteen dollars.

Carrying the box, I went back to the men's clothing section and picked out a shirt for my dad, paying for them together. The guy behind the counter looked like a version of Cary Grant in his prime, and I suppressed an urge to escape. But he didn't seem to care that I was buying a vibrator. Or maybe he was clueless, like I'd been before Lucy clued me in.

Fueling my impulse buy was the fact that it had been weeks since Daniel and I'd had sex. And ever since Jamie and I had kissed and touched in the car—no before that, ever since I met Jamie, really—I'd been in a constant state of arousal. My body wanted something badly, just not food.

I pulled out of the parking lot and into the flow of traffic. At a stoplight I reached over to the bag on the seat and opened the box to the vibrator, an absurdly phallic looking thing with a thick long handle and a head as big as a sunflower's. I clicked the button to "on," expecting it to need to be charged with the attached plug-in, but it shivered awake in my hand. As the light changed and the car moved forward, I lifted the vibrator and placed it between my legs, resting the head on top of the fabric of my pants. An astonishing blossoming of energy burst in me, like I had never quite felt before. My vision dangerously faded for a brief moment, perhaps because blood rushed to or from my head. This was nothing to play around with while driving. I threw the vibrator on the seat next to me and burst out laughing. What the hell was this thing?

When I got home, I rushed to the bedroom and plugged it in. I took off my clothes and lay down on the bed with the culprit. I felt something build and build, something unlike I'd ever felt before, like climbing a ladder. And then it was as though I was at the top looking at a vast turquoise swimming pool, and I jumped, falling and falling and falling, to plunge into the muted underwater, weightless.

I lay on the bed, depleted, the vibrator now silenced. My damp skin picked up a chill from the air.

So that, I thought, *is an orgasm.*

Natasha, our server at Palazzo, set a glass of wine in front of me and a beer in front of Daniel, who had started the crossword puzzle without me. I was watching the bar T.V. showing projections from the election, even though the polls hadn't yet closed in California. Eager reporters looked alive with the news that we might very well end up with a new, young president: the first baby-boomer president, with his baby-boomer vice-president, and their wives, powerful women with unlined faces and good hair who would never, ever wear the anachronistic pearl necklace and vacant, adoring stare of the current First Lady—even in light of accusations about the candidate's unfaithfulness to his wife. Bill Clinton and Hillary Rodham Clinton had handled the unfaithfulness issue so well in interviews that people no longer seemed to care one way or the other.

I leaned over toward Daniel and said, "It looks like 16 Down, *Pearl scribe*, is Steinbeck."

He moved his finger along the squares to check before writing in the word, which fit. I usually got the twentieth-century literary clues, especially if the writer was from the American west. Any early European literary clue he usually knew because at both his elite high school and private liberal arts college, he was immersed in the European canon. I read some of that literature in college as an English major, but I mostly focused on twentieth-century American literature. And in my high school, we read short stories out of textbooks and read books from the F.R.U.I.T. Cart (Free Reading Uninterrupted Is Terrific). When I thought of Daniel's upbringing, I thought of dark, oak-paneled hallways and gray coats and Renaissance paintings. My upbringing evoked redwood decks and bathing suits and *Archie* comic books.

What was Jamie's, I wondered? No matter what I was thinking about, it seemed, my mind would snake over to Jamie. I thought about the stories Jamie told me about her childhood, and what I'd read about in her poems. If my upbringing was redwood decks and bathing suits and *Archie*, hers was shelves filled with her grandmother's homemade jam and bare feet on a hot sidewalk and her brother playing the guitar. Although my middle-class girlhood contrasted with her poor one, we both held the hot, dry central California summers in our bones. We both had experienced anonymous west coast public schools that were imbued in the loose curriculum of the 1970's. Sometimes the three thousand miles between New York and California felt like the biggest chasm between Daniel and me.

I looked over at the crossword puzzle again and saw that Daniel had almost finished it. On the T.V., an authoritative male voice projected three Midwest states as choosing Clinton, and a number of people sitting in the bar hooted and clapped, a few remaining silent. I wondered if the silent ones were in shock that their dynasty might collapse, or if they didn't care about politics. I wondered where Jamie was tonight, two hours ahead of me. Was she watching the returns too? Or was she involved in another sort of politics, schmoozing at a dinner with religious leaders checking out the new potential minister? Was she thinking about me, about the mist that formed on the windows of her car as we created a world of our bodies, of us? With a twinge I wondered if her trip to Arizona with Rose was her attempt to give their relationship one more try. But who was I to talk, as I sat next to Daniel at *our* restaurant in *our* corner of town? He carefully sipped at his beer, as though measuring his sips in equal portions. I had a sudden urge to jump up and run out into the street, into the night—and a curious realization that I often felt that way when we were here at Palazzo's. The dark coziness of the place sometimes morphed into claustrophobia.

A roar went up among the customers and I saw that the news was now projecting Clinton the winner. People jumped up off their barstools and out of their chairs and were hugging and high-fiving each other. On the T.V., a rush of balloons fell from the ceiling at a celebration party. I couldn't believe it. The newly elected President— President Clinton!—would be coming to a nationally televised stage soon to speak. The exhilaration of the moment coursed through my body and I reached over and hugged Daniel. He pulled me in tight and said, "What a great moment for you. I know you really cared about this."

His words both buoyed and deflated me. He was happy for *me* that *my candidate* had won. But his words felt mechanically designed to shield himself from my politics. Even though he'd also voted for Clinton, he'd done so languidly, claiming he was choosing between two evils. I had gone crazy at that, saying how could he even believe such a thing, when Clinton planned to reverse the damaging Reagan-Bush fiscal policies, when Clinton would likely be able to appoint a Supreme Court justice or two who might decide the fate of *Roe v. Wade*, when Clinton wasn't afraid to say the word AIDS out loud? Daniel has said in reply, *You're such an idealist*—words almost identical to Andy's when he'd said I was reading too much and getting too idealistic. I'd said to Daniel, *How is it that what I'm saying is idealistic?* And he'd said, *You act as if politics can really make a difference in the world.*

And now tonight, his saying he was happy for me, brought this all back. His words told me that tonight had nothing to do to with him, that it was all about me. His words conveyed his refusal even at this peak of a moment that meant so much to me, to implicate himself. He refused to share it with me.

That night as Daniel and I lay in bed, I thought he was asleep, but he reached over and pulled me to him and kissed my neck and ran his hand up and down my arm. I lay there, unyielding, then grabbed his hand and laced my fingers through his, both effectively holding his hand and halting his touch. I thought about Thanksgiving, about how he was leaving me to be with his family, a family I had never met and was not invited into.

"When do you leave for New York?" I asked.

He let go of my hand and rolled onto his back. "Two weeks from today."

"Did you make your flight reservation yet?"

"Yes."

I could tell he wasn't about to offer any more information. I wouldn't even be driving him to the airport. I knew, as usual, he'd take a cab. I pushed the covers aside and got out of bed, pulling on my kimono.

"What are you doing?" he asked.

"Nothing." I put on my slippers and went out into the living room. I sat on the couch, its sagging familiarity engulfing me. A sliver of moon shone through the sliding glass door. My bike leaned on the balcony like a shadowy, overgrown spider.

I thought about the T.V. at Palazzo's showing our newly elected President, his face broad and optimistic, holding up the hands of both his wife and our new Vice President, streamers and confetti and balloons pouring down, the propitious strains of their theme song blasting out, *Don't stop thinking about tomorrow* .... And Daniel was watching the T.V. as though it were a *Star Trek* episode, chewing on his pasta, pausing to sip carefully from his beer, and for a moment my irritation had been swept aside as I'd been flooded with fondness for him, for his careful, objective ways, though the feeling was fleeting, like a gust of warm air that can sneak through on a cool bike ride. As that brief moment of affection faded, I'd jumped up from the table and high-fived some of the celebrants at the bar and then Natasha approached me, wiping her hands on her green apron, with her wild black hair and her striking eyes that I always thought lingered on Daniel, but she was smiling toward me, moving toward me, with her hands reaching out, and we wrapped each other in our arms, sympathetically, warmly holding each other in that festive moment of hope, of change.

I'd fallen asleep on the couch in my kimono and woke groggily to Daniel's kisses. It was dark, and it took my eyes a moment to adjust to the dim living room, meagerly lit by a streetlight. I had no idea what time it was. Daniel's body was stretched out next to mine, a blanket over us. I closed my eyes. His lips became Jamie's for a moment, then his again. I pulled back, eyes still closed, and made a sleepy sigh, a half yawn, turning over, my back to him. He spooned against me and I drifted back to sleep, feeling him holding on.

When I came home from work the next day, the message machine light was blinking. Jamie's voice poured out when I hit the play button, a voice that sounded like the colors brown and green, an earthy, steady tone. And necessarily she held back, not saying what she really wanted to say, aware that Daniel might be listening in. I wondered what that was like for her, to hear Daniel's flat voice follow four rings, abruptly, deeply saying only: *Leave a message.* She did seem a little rattled. But that could be because she was in Arizona with Rose, because she was anticipating returning—and then what? All she said was, *Hey Gwen. Just wanted to say hi, and to tell you I'll be back tomorrow. See you in class. I've got a poem. Can't wait to read yours.*

I pressed play again, just to hear her voice again, and to hear her say again she'd be back tomorrow. I played it again and again. When her voice ceased the fifth time I thought, *a poem, I don't have a poem.* I looked around the room, my eyes taking in everything, as though I had never before seen the room, and I was struck by the functional nature of it all, that nothing was beautiful: the slouchy brown couch, the dusty coffee table piled high with books, topped by the remote control, the TV on a wheeled cart, bookshelves crammed with books—mostly Daniel's, but one shelf was mine. I pulled down my anthology fat with poems then grabbed my purse and keys and left, walking down the stairs in the cool night, the moon pricking the dark swimming pool with light. I wasn't sure where I was going, but it had to be away from here. It had to be some place I could write a poem.

As I walked into Lamplight Books, I passed stacks of books laid out and propped up on tables, books thick with invitation, books that tempted me to open them with their bright new covers and pages fragrant with new glue. Books in sections labeled with rich potential: Art, Travel, Memoir, New Fiction, Poetry. I recalled Jamie's and my fantasy of owning a bookstore and café. She hadn't said I was too idealistic. She had egged me on, encouraged me to think about my dreams, to linger on what I loved. I loved bookstores. But a bookstore wasn't exactly the best place to write a poem. Even though I could sit in one of their comfortable chairs with my notebook on my lap, there were too many distractions. Lamplight Books, though, had an adjacent café where I could sit with a cup of tea and write. I'd been headed toward the café—through the bookstore, of course, so I could feel myself buoyed by the stream of millions of words—when I saw that a reading was just about to begin.

The turnout for the reading was high. All the seats were taken so I stood with others at the back of the room. Next to the empty podium was a table stacked with books written by someone named Lisa Lindstrom. The name was vaguely familiar, but I wasn't sure why. The crowd quieted as a man approached the podium and blew into the microphone.

"Good evening," he said. "Welcome to Lamplight Books. We're pleased you're here for this exciting event. Lisa Lindstrom's new memoir has garnered a great deal of attention, especially after her appearance on the Oprah Winfrey Show. As you all know, Lisa's on the forefront of the transsexual movement, an outspoken advocate in this arena. Her book about her transformation from male to female has raised a great deal of controversy. But something lost in all the controversy is the quality of the book. Lisa is a terrific writer. She's here tonight to read and to share her journey. Then she will take questions and sign books. Please welcome Lisa Lindstrom."

To the sound of applause, a woman stood up from the front row and approached the podium. Her shoulder-length hair curled around her face, which was brightened with the force of cosmetics: blue eye shadow and salmon-colored rouge complementing her salmon-colored blouse. Tall and thin, she stood with a little bit of a slouch on her low-heeled shoes.

"Thanks, everyone," she said into the microphone, her deep voice resonating throughout the room. Then she began to read from her book, a section about her childhood, her feeling that she was a girl from the time she was a little boy, how her father spanked her for dressing in girls' clothes, how her mother secretly gave her lacy underwear to wear beneath her boy pants and let her dress in dresses when her father was at work.

She didn't strike me as a man dressed in women's clothes. Nor did she strike me as a woman like Cat, a woman with masculine qualities. What she had in common with Cat, and with Jamie to some extent, was a pushing of the envelope, a challenge to the world that gender might not be quite what we expect. I became conscious of my body, my earlobes lightly weighted by earrings, my breasts held in the cups of my bra, the pooch of my stomach, my narrow hips, the folds of my vulva pressed against the seam of my jeans, my toes touching the tips of my brown boots.

When Lisa finished reading, she answered people's questions: Yes, she'd had breast implants and no, she hadn't had any other surgery; perhaps one day she would but for now she felt like a full woman; no, having a penis didn't necessarily disqualify her from womanhood—other transsexuals had different feelings about that so she didn't want to speak for them all, she just had to do what she felt was right for herself; yes, she experienced discrimination, and the book was replete with examples, including several acts of violence against her; and, yes, she was a little afraid sometimes, but she had to do what she had to do; and no, she wasn't a lesbian, she was a straight woman; no she wasn't a gay man because she was a woman; well, maybe she just didn't fit into society's rubrics and we'd have to come up with others, or abandon categories altogether, a comment that led to rousing applause. People liked these things in theory, I thought, but I wondered how they'd feel about having her as a colleague—or a lover. I could feel myself filling up with all kinds of new possibilities, things I hadn't quite thought about before. The richness of it all was a little beyond words, a little overwhelming, like sitting on a raft in the middle of a huge, dark lake.

I waited in line to buy her book, to meet her and have her sign it. When I got closer to her, I saw a small protrusion of her Adam's apple, which made me want to feel for mine, or to look in a mirror at my profile to see if it was there.

"What's your name hon?" she asked, smiling at me, her full lips and very white teeth the most feminine thing about her, I thought, at the same time asking myself why I thought of those things as feminine. As a man, she'd had those same lips, those same teeth.

"Gwen," I said. "But would you please sign this to me and to Jamie?" I spelled Jamie's name for her.

"Is Jamie a man or a woman?" she asked. The tone of her voice reminded me of Billy's, our server at Mad Mary's.

"A woman," I responded, and for an odd moment I thought to myself, *Jamie's a woman, but I was kissing her—and I only kiss men, don't I? So does that make her or me the man?* And I knew that's what people would think, that if I were with Jamie, because of how we look, the most basic changeable thing about us—me with my long hair, her with her short hair— and they'd think Jamie was the man. They wouldn't see my slim, boyish hips and unruly eyebrows. They wouldn't register Jamie's rounded hips, her long eyelashes. No, Jamie didn't feel like a man at all. And if it was possible, I felt more like a woman when we'd kissed—a Venus stepping out of the half-shell, my body uncovered and full.

Lisa signed the book with a flourish, For Gwen and Jamie— *You go girls! Live the dream!* Here was Lisa, a white, heterosexual transsexual woman, in many ways the complete opposite of Billy, a black gay man. But at that moment they came together in my mind, like two fairy godmothers, rooting Jamie and me on.

At the café, I sat down with my tea and my notebook, my swirling thoughts filling up page after page in my journal. What seemed like unrelated images poured out onto the page: my mother's pink lipstick on my forehead when she kissed me before going out for the night with my father, her short lavender dress interlaced with silver threads; my father smelling tartly of aftershave, his swirling paisley tie; me as a child in the swimming pool, floating; the sense of floating on my bed the other day, me alone with my vibrator, my body so filled-up and electrical with that memory and with the memory of Jamie and me in the dark car, my hand sliding under her bra and holding her breast, her face like velvet against mine ... Words filled the pages, flowed over from one line to the next, as though my hand had a mind of its own.

When the rush of words stopped, I looked up. For a moment the room looked like an odd version of an incorrectly processed photograph. People at the tables around me appeared illuminated from within. It seemed I could suddenly perceive the invisible warm light of the body, which obliterated the particulars. I couldn't distinguish the specifics of each person, just bright silhouettes, as though the person looking down at a book was his or her own sun, as though the couple chatting in the corner were their own individual stars.

God, I'm seeing auras, I thought, although I didn't know exactly what auras were, and even if I'd read about them, I wasn't sure I'd think they were real. But there was something real about this—this, whatever it was. I was literally seeing differently, a transfigured vision.

With my next blink, the room returned to normal. The shimmering was gone as though it had never been there. But a residue remained in my memory, a little echo of a voice lodged in my mind, telling me there is much more to life than we see.

* * *

Sitting in class across from Jamie was surreal. There was extra texture between us that no one else could see, could touch. If they thought about us at all, they probably just thought of us as poetry classmates. Who would think that we'd kissed in a gay bar, that we'd touched each others' bodies in a car?

Cat sat next to Jamie and Vanessa—Vanessa with her long silver hair, Vanessa talking in her gravelly voice about how she wanted to pay attention to line-breaks this class session. "The line is a very important unit of a poem. Where you decide to break the line stresses the last word of the line, as well as the first word of the next line. And you can create surprise and multiple meanings by breaking lines at certain places. Don't always stop the line where you might normally pause. Create some tension."

To my astonishment, she did something she'd never done before: she stood, pushing herself up from her desk, and walked to the board. She began writing slowly with a squeaky piece of chalk. We were more than halfway through the course, and I'd never before seen her write on the board. She looked smaller up there, dwarfed by the traditions of board-writing. Her silver bracelets clattered as she wrote:

Somewhere thy sweet Face has spilled beyond my boundary.

"This is a line, actually two lines, from Emily Dickinson. Where do you think they should break?"

"After 'Face,'" said Leonora, a woman who was probably in her fifties whose poems were always about how much she despised her ex-husband.

"Why?" asked Vanessa

"Because it sounds right. And it emphasizes *Face*."

"I can see why you say that. *Face* is where you take a breath in the line. It's basically the caesura, the place where you might naturally pause. Any other thoughts?"

"I think it should break at *spilled*," I said. "Because then the words on the page are spilling over, and then the line is kind of doing what it says."

"Beautiful," said Vanessa, and I felt the rush of the teacher's praise that I always craved, even as an adult woman. Was I perpetually to be a child? "Now of course there's not one right answer here, and Dickinson in the previous line uses the word *held*, which is a slant-rhyme with *spilled*,—but still, when you can get such double action out of a word or phrase by your line breaks, as Gwen has described, do it. Be attentive to it."

Maybe I wasn't necessarily a child craving the teacher's approval. I realized that my sense of pleasure wasn't only about getting a pat on the head. My pleasure was imbued in this very aspect of talking about language. That the placement of words mattered. That we could evoke so much about life in a poem. And there was Jamie, across the room, looking at me kind of sideways, out of the corner of her eye, telling me many things with that look. There were so many layers in the room, layers between me and Jamie, layers within poetry and language. I never felt quite like this in other parts of my life: the richness, the sense of possibility. And it all came to me, like the opening to a movie that flowers in Technicolor before you, at the moment that you'd been sitting in the cool, dark theater wondering if the movie would ever begin. *I wanted this.* I wanted the world of language and poetry and art. I wanted Jamie. It wasn't about auras, or poetic influence, or the allure of dancing cowboys. It was about the woman sitting across from me. And that meant another choice, I knew, something I could clearly see. It meant not choosing Daniel. Not choosing his dark eyes, his words: *love of my life, you're beautiful.* Something clenched inside me. It was as though he had tendrils in me, roots that coiled through my veins and pointed toward my heart.

An absurd thought swept through me: Did I really have to choose? Could I have them both?

Jamie's poem was being passed around. I took the sheet and followed along as she read it aloud:

hunger

she has a place at this table
a place where cooked beefsteak
wallows thick and red,
where soft potatoes and carrots
tread butter on heavy white plates

but she is hungry.
she wants to feel the sticky wet
drip down her chin
as she bites the fuzzy flesh
of sweet ripe peaches,

to pull back the leathery skin
of a round red pomegranate,
to nibble and suck the juice
from each small white stone.

she wants fresh, raw,
slick in its own juice,
eat it with your hands food,
not comfort food that mashes in her mouth
slides down easy and never
fills the hollow beneath her heart.

Hunger. I thought about my body's resistance to food lately. About Billy at the restaurant, saying I was *hungry*. About the way Jamie and I nearly devoured each other in her car. While the class was talking about the poem, I tried to catch Jamie's eye, but she was looking down at the page, her face a little pink. This poem was way beyond line breaks. It moved right into my body and lit it up. I was sure everyone in the class could see my aura.

After class, Jamie and I walked together to the parking garage. Winter coolness was seeping into the air, the dark blue sky on the edge of black now that the sun was setting earlier and earlier, cutting the days short.

I wanted to touch Jamie's arm or face or hand as we walked, but I kept my feet moving forward. Two women from class walked by and turned to say "good night." I wondered what they would have thought if Jamie and I had been touching.

"It's so good to see you," said Jamie.

"It's so good to see you too," I said. She rattled her keys in her hand then leaned over to me. We moved into each other, our mouths, our bodies. I could feel her soft warmth beneath her clothes as we pressed together. I pulled back, looked into her eyes.

"I loved your poem," I said.

"I'm glad," she said. "Can you believe I wrote it in the bathtub of the hotel in Arizona?"

"I would think you'd have to be naked while writing such a poem."

We both smiled. She moved her lips toward mine.

"What if someone from class sees us?" I asked.

"Then they'll really understand the poem," she said. She kissed me again then pulled back and said, "I have something for you." She reached into her backpack and handed to me a flat package wrapped in dark tissue paper. I peeled the paper away to reveal a small painting, not much larger than a postcard. In the dim overhead car garage light I could make out a deep red pomegranate with black and purple undertones, casting a purple shadow. I thought of the sexual nature of the pomegranate in her poem.

"I painted it for you in Arizona. It made me feel like we were together."

"It's beautiful," I said. "Thank you." I leaned into her and whispered in her ear, "Let's get out of here. Get in my car. I want to take you somewhere."

"Oh, god, I don't know," she said, her voice soft and deep, her hand gripping my arm. "It's so late, I need to go."

"There's a pay phone on the way."

I opened the door and, without saying anything, she got in the car. At the gas station at the corner, she got out and made a phone call. Illuminated by a streetlight, she stood in the phone booth, her mouth moving.

"What did you tell her?" I asked when she got back in the car.

"That Cat and I were going out after class. But even that lie got me in some shit because she hates Cat. God, there's no love lost between the two of them. Sometimes I feel like I'm the mother of two bickering children. I want to put them in a time-out."

"What about a spanking?"

"If that's what you're into."

"You're very funny," I said, smiling and starting the car.

"Aren't you going to make a call?" she asked.

"No need. He doesn't care where I am."

"That's hard to believe," she said. "If you were mine, I'd care." She reached over to me, kissing my neck, tucking her hand between my legs, as I drove us through the night, over the hill, to Santa Cruz.

Chapter Eleven

Pre-Color Time

The hotel room overlooked the silent Boardwalk roller coasters, an edifice of shadows. A streak of silver moonlight draped across the black ocean, waves pulsing darkly with a distant swish, a sound not unlike the whisper of the freeway that I always heard from the balcony of Daniel's and my apartment. But I wasn't thinking about our apartment at that moment. I was thinking about being alone with Jamie, which wiped everything else from my mind—the illusion of a clean slate.

Jamie pulled the curtains closed while I turned off the too-bright overhead light and switched on a bedside lamp. Jamie came to me and we kissed, finally completely alone in a space bigger than a car—no gear shifts in the way, no worries that someone might tap at the window. We fell into each other, helping each other pull off our clothes. Jamie placed her tee-shirt on top of the lamp to create a subtle glow in the room—always the artist, creating ambiance and innovating with whatever was available.

We moved to the bed. Finally, finally a bed, not an awkward bucket seat, not the booth of a restaurant or the dance floor of a bar. Being fully with her in this way I was struck by how the bony angles and gristly muscle and rough five o'clock shadow of a man were replaced by the pliant flesh of a woman, by rounded thighs and breasts, by softness against softness. I felt like I was underwater. It was as though I'd never had a swimming lesson but was thrown into the pool and knew what to do intuitively, primordially.

We made love like the people we were: two women electrified by each other but who had been held apart for months, who had craved complete connection within the tight confines of limited space and time. But now space was open and time was free. I held her hand in both my hands, moving it to my mouth to kiss her wave tattoo. As our bodies pressed together, my face lay against hers, my unblemished forehead pressing into the scar on her forehead. Moving my hand down the side of her body, my fingers found their way into her, and she moved her body against mine. A brief self-awareness flickered in me, that there I was, a woman inside another woman. How could this be? But the thought disappeared like blowing out a candle, and I became no thoughts, only body, all body. In the muted light of the room, we intermingled like the salt water and ocean kelp that churned on the other side of the window.

A sound entered my consciousness, something far-off and deep, like a horn honking. I pulled up out of sleep, and in the dark I realized the sound was a sea lion calling from below the wharf where groups of sea lions congregated. I was on my side, curled up. As my eyes adjusted to the dim light I realized Jamie, too, was on her side, facing me, our knees touching like twin fetuses in a womb. I rolled over to my back and Jamie stirred, inching up toward me and placing her head on my shoulder. I reached around and held her. I'd never before held someone in bed. Was it true I was always the held one, never the holder? I pulled her closer and felt my strength. I could see why men liked this.

"How are you?" Jamie whispered, her breath warm on my neck. It was early morning and I was with Jamie, and she was talking to me, touching me.

"I'm really, really, really…" I searched for an ideal word but then felt satisfied with a basic one: "excellent."

"Me too."

For a moment we were quiet. A sea lion barked. Jamie's shirt still hung over the lamp, which was now switched off. The diffuse light filtering into the room, I now realized, was due to the dawn. It was morning. I felt a tug of real life—of Rose, of Daniel, of my job. All that waited impatiently outside this room.

Jamie ran her hand lightly up and down my arm. It had been years since I'd been touched and talked to in the morning

"I wonder what time it is," I said.

"It's pre-color time."

"What's that?"

"It's a word I made up as a kid. You know, it's the time of the morning when it's so early, when there's not enough light to see color yet."

"I can't believe I never thought about that before," I said, "that you can't see color sometimes."

"See, the blue comforter is actually gray right now. Dawn makes neutrals. Light, the sun, brings color."

"How can it be that I never really noticed it—that you can only see color with light? Tell me something else I don't know, something about art."

"Well. You're really going to make my brain work right now?"

"Yes, please." I squeezed her tighter.

"Well, okay. Hm. Do you know about negative space?"

"Vanessa talked about it in class once, I think. She said it's the absence of something."

"Yeah. Look at my hand." She placed her hand on top of the comforter. "You see my fingers because they're distinguished from what's behind them, the blanket, the negative space. Seeing means not just seeing the object, but what surrounds it, what defines its shape."

"Thank you professor," I whispered.

"You're welcome," she whispered back, reaching under me and slipping her arms around me. As she kissed me, I tasted the sea on her lips.

As Jamie and I walked down the silent sidewalk toward the boardwalk, the air smelled of gray ocean, salty seaweed and damp gray sand. Seagulls pecked at a dark mass at the edge of the white water. My eyes searched for color. The weak sun was lighting up the pinkish quality of an adobe building, a small store, not yet open for that day, that sold postcards, key chains and tee-shirts to tourists. A streetlight lit up a green bench where a man sat, his back a hump, a shopping cart next to him filled with bulging black plastic garbage bags. He lifted his head and watched us pass. I leaned toward Jamie as we walked so our arms grazed. I felt the pressure of her leaning into me, too.

The yellow and red neon sign of a twenty-four hour chain restaurant shone across the street. The smell of grease and coffee greeted us as we made our way from the cool, shadowy outside into the warm, bright inside. A waitress who looked like a caricature of a waitress, with her poofy Aqua Net hair and red lipstick, showed us to a table by the window. The only other customers were two men at the counter who looked like they'd been nursing cups of coffee all night. The clock over the counter read 5:45 a.m.

When the waitress brought us coffee, Jamie chatted with her about what a nice morning it was, all the while holding my hand beneath the table. The waitress smiled as she took our orders, revealing teeth speckled with red lipstick. As the waitress walked away, Jamie said, "She reminds me of a waitress my grandfather used to flirt with when he'd take me to a diner to get pie. We'd go in the middle of the day. I think he sometimes wanted to escape my grandmother who was always asking him to go get this or that at the store, or to pick some peaches and plums from the tree and bring them in."

"What did your grandfather do for a living?"

"He was a gardener. Sometimes I'd go with him to work, help him rake, or pull weeds, or water. I used to love helping him out, but my grandmother didn't let me go that often. She wanted me with her to help her clean or can fruit. I loved my grandfather's big old station wagon that smelled like cigarettes and cut grass."

"My dad once taught me how to use a chainsaw," I said. "A tree fell on our property and he wanted to cut it up for firewood. I almost never went outside to help him with things like that, but for some reason I did that day. I must have been about twelve or thirteen. It was fantastic—I felt so powerful holding that chainsaw and cutting through a tree trunk."

The waitress set on our table plates heaped with fragrant, steaming pancakes and eggs. "Here you go, girls."

As we ate, pouring thick syrup onto our plates and sopping up egg yolk with buttered toast, I said, "My god, I'm starving."

"Me too."

And we grinned at each other in recognition that for the first time, we were able to eat food together. The clenched feeling in my stomach that had kept me from being able to eat much had dissipated. Had my full sexual connection with Jamie untwisted my twisted stomach?

"I can't believe," I said, "that it's morning, it's early, and you're talking to me, touching me, eating with me." I stopped myself from finishing my thought—Jamie already knew it anyway, knew how much I was bothered by Daniel's need for separation and silence in the morning. And Jamie was telling me about her family life; I knew almost nothing about Daniel's family except what his parents did for a living. Maybe it was inevitable that I'd compare my life with Daniel to this new part of my life. Maybe Jamie was doing the same thing, silently comparing me to Rose.

"For a lot of my childhood," she said, "I had a paper route. All those years of getting up early turned me into someone who loves the mornings."

"You liked doing a paper route?"

"For the most part, when my bicycle was working. When it was broken and I had to walk, I didn't like that."

"I think as a kid I would have resented having to do a paper route. Didn't you ever just say you wouldn't do it?"

She looked at me. "We needed the money."

"God, I'm such an idiot," I said.

"No, just middle class. Or upper-middle? Or rich?"

"Not rich. But, well, I had everything I could have wanted, I suppose."

"You were lucky you never had to think about money as a kid."

"Yes I did! I spent a lot of time trying to persuade my parents to give me more allowance."

"What a princess."

"That's Princess Gwen, to you. You may kiss my hand."

She pulled my hand up to her lips, which were sticky with syrup. "We are now betrothed," she said.

"Our very own fairy tale," I said.

"A happy ending. I always love it when the girl gets the girl."

Carefully, I unlocked the door then peeked into the bedroom. There lay Daniel, a pillow over his head. I could see only his elbow, pointing right at my heart. The familiar musty smell of him reached my nose, and a whiff of sadness injected me with even more anxiety than was already coursing through my veins. Quietly I backed out of the room and walked to the kitchen. Something smelled bad. I opened the refrigerator door and saw a bowl of something black and hairy, half covered in fuzzy saran wrap. I closed the door, picked up the phone and dialed.

"Wellstone Learning, where your child comes first. This is Lucy, how may I help you?"

"Lucy, it's me. I'm really sick this morning. I have a terrible sore throat and a fever of 101."

"You do not. Good use of authentic details, though."

"No, really." I coughed. "I feel awful."

"Okay, I'll be right over with chicken soup and aspirin."

"Very funny," I said, tucking the phone to my shoulder. I opened the refrigerator again to the mold-ridden bowl of rancid food, pulled it out and dumped the entire thing, including the bowl, in the garbage.

"As long as you promise you're not abandoning me forever," said Lucy, "I grant you the day off."

"Bless you. But I need more than a day off. I need two weeks, until after Thanksgiving. But it won't really be a full two weeks, since we have four days off for the holiday."

"That's a damn bad cold you have."

"Lucy, I need to go home, to see my parents. I'm losing it. I feel fuzzy, like I don't even know who I am anymore."

"Oh my god, you finally had sex with Jamie."

"You scare me."

"Well I'm right, right?"

"You're amazing. Your psychic abilities are right up there with Dionne Warwick's. You should start your own 1-800 line—you'd make the big bucks."

"I'm going to need them since Will and I are getting divorced."

"No. Oh, Lucy, really?"

"Yes. I found an apartment. I'm moving out right after Thanksgiving."

"Oh, Lucy. God, I'm sorry. But I'm also happy for you. You get to start all over. Everything will be really good. I'll come over and help you move when I get back from my parents'."

"Okay, then we'll celebrate all these life changes. Champagne's on me."

"Are you really okay, Lucy?"

"I'm relieved. The decision has been made, and there's no turning back. I just want to get on with my life. Shit, look at the time, I have to run—especially since it's just me, all alone, to take care of *everything* here at the center."

"I'm sorry, really I am. But I—"

"Knock it off. Have a safe trip, you slacker."

"Thanks so much, Lucy, for everything. And you have the number at my parents'—call me if you need to talk."

"Yeah, yeah, just hang up now."

I kissed at the receiver and hung up. Then I searched the kitchen for a pen and some paper, opening a drawer stuffed with a tangle of utensils, and another with a riot of mismatched Tupperware. Finally I rooted through my purse and pulled out a pencil and a deposit slip.

Daniel, I wrote on the deposit slip. *I went to my parents' house.*

It seemed like there was something I should tell him. But I didn't know what. So I left it at that, tucking the edge of the deposit slip beneath the phone. The whole time I snuck a few clothes from my closet to throw in a plastic bag—my impromptu luggage—I held my breath, sure I'd have to face Daniel the second he woke up. But he slept hard, pillow over his head, and I left the apartment with time spread out before me to think.

Driving north on I-280, I passed the massive statue of Father Junipero Serra, a big white sandstone figure kneeling and pointing over the freeway like the West's version of the eyes of Dr. T.J. Eckleberg. Funny that I'd be pointed at accusingly by the pioneer of the California missions on this morning, the morning after Jamie and I—two women who were raised Catholic—had made love for the first time. All those years of Father Serra converting the California natives to Catholicism—and just a little over one hundred years later, the freeway was in existence. As were anti-Father Serra protestors who objected to the deification of a murderer of Native Americans. As was the woman driving her little red car who lived with a male scientist and had sex with a woman artist.

I wondered what Jamie was doing right now, and in spite of my messy array of guilt and anxiety—and my worries about what the hell I would tell her and Daniel about my two-week escape—an image of Jamie and me in bed together sent a shiver of bodily memory through me. On Jamie's and my drive back from foggy Santa Cruz into the brown-tinged skies of the Santa Clara valley, I could tell we were both worried about what we were about to face at home with Rose and Daniel. But we hadn't talked about it. We talked instead about poetry class, about how Cat had written on my poem, "We are intrigued by you." I wanted to know whose idea that was. Of course it was Cat's—"that's definitely a Cat move," Jamie said. "And quite effective," I countered. And Jamie reached over and kissed me, and I'd almost veered right into a semi, which would have been a tragedy of the proportions of Juliet and Juliet, Jamie said. And she said she wanted me not to leave her, and she didn't want to leave me. I told her to call in sick—and I'd do the same—and we could spend the day together. But she said she couldn't, the old people were counting on her—she had to grocery shop and wash windows for an old woman in what I imagined was a silver bullet of a mobile home, followed by a house-cleaning gig for an elderly man who chain-smoked and was hooked up to oxygen. Even though that seemed not only un-cheery but dangerous to me, Jamie hadn't seemed too concerned. I'd driven her back to the campus parking garage, whose blank-faced enormity shone brightly in the harsh wintry sun.

And that's when she broke the news: She and Rose were leaving tonight to go to Florida for two weeks, an extended Thanksgiving. She'd already told Vanessa she'd be missing class next week; the week after that there was no class due to the holiday. So two weeks with no poetry, two weeks without me, but she was compelled to go. Even though they'd just gotten back from a trip to Arizona.

"It's horrible, I don't want to go. But it's been so long since I've seen my brother and his family—I need to see them. They're my only family, and they've been expecting me. I don't know what's wrong with me. I should have said something to you sooner, but we were swept away into Santa Cruz, and leaving was the last thing I was thinking about, only staying, being with you. I didn't want to cast a pall over the whole thing. Oh, Gwen, I have to go. But I'll try to call you when I'm there. And when I come back, after Thanksgiving, can we see each other? Please? We can be together, we can figure this whole thing out."

And even though there was part of me that was relieved—like I had pulled my hand away from a hot burner just in time—another part was disappointed and anxious. After our time together Jamie would be spending days on end with Rose? And I'd be back in the apartment, surrounded by Daniel's books and dark eyes? Would I really be able to sink into that futon again? Would I really be able to leave it forever? What in the hell would I do with myself with Jamie gone? I'd imagined myself at work, jumping to the phone every time it rang—or worse yet, at home, pacing the cluttered apartment. And the whole movie in my head of me attached to the phone by my pulsing body was enough to get me in my car, away from phones.

I needed to act. I needed to do something. The best answer to it all was getting in my little red car and driving. Yes, I thought, as I gunned it up the hill, above Crystal Springs Reservoir, upon which a fluffy white cloud skimmed making me feel I was in an airplane. Yes. Yes. Whenever I had the question clearly formed in my head, the answer would be yes.

Chapter Twelve
Little Pea Toes

Funny how people like to honor their famous men with huge statues that overlook the freeway. As though to mirror Father Serra, another eminent man greeted me when I hit Suffolk. Claude Dupree, founder of gold in this Gold Rush town, loomed over the passing cars, an enormous kneeling effigy holding in his hands a gold pan big enough for people to sit in. Indeed, as I drove through Old Town, a group of people were seated in Claude Dupree's gold pan for tourist photos— likely to be followed by a walk along the wooden planked sidewalks to gaze at souvenir gold nugget jewelry.

I made my way up past the high school, where a million ghosts flew at me. Through the large cafeteria windows I could see lunch was in session. Memories crowded my mind until a few sifted out, echoing their emotions in me as though they had happened yesterday. I remembered my friend Kaye sitting stiffly next to me, miserably trying not to stare as the newly-elected cheerleaders made their way to the front of the cafeteria and sat at the head table, like royals. Kaye had spent all summer working on her cheers and had performed flawlessly in front of the whole student body at our first whole-school rally. But that wasn't enough. Cheerleaders at our school were voted in by the students—and not enough ballots had been cast for Kaye. Her popularity quotient wasn't as high as the five who were chosen: Tammy, Linda, Nancy, Karen and Joan. All were nominally our friends, positioning us on the edge of popularity. I'd sat next to Kaye, flushing with embarrassment for her, and grateful that I had been too chicken-shit to test my own popularity in the way she had. In reaction, Kaye had become a hippie that year, growing out her Farrah Fawcett feathered hair and trading in her high-waisted flared jeans and platform shoes for long quilted skirts and Birkenstocks.

In my mind, that moment in the cafeteria morphed into the cafeteria cleared of tables and chairs, the lights dimmed and a DJ booth positioned—condensation curtaining the windows, and teachers positioned at the doors, checking student IDs. All our school dances had been held there, and I'd gone to one after another, year after year, after each football game, each basketball game, embracing one perspiring boy after another, his sweaty neck pressed against my nose, his hands pressed into my lower back, his hardening penis pushing against my pelvis. I'd had a series of boyfriends in high school—I'd been chosen to dance with, or go out with, the almost-popular (and very occasionally the supremely popular) guys—guys I'd drunk beer with and smoked pot with at concerts and parents-on-vacation-parties; guys I'd made out with, had sex with, in vans in dark parking lots, on blankets in vacant lots, on living room floors when parents were gone for the weekend or were asleep upstairs, and in anonymous bedrooms at keg parties, the room illuminated by a bonfire flickering in the front yard.

Just past the high school, at the edge of downtown, I passed the charming white-steepled Calvary church where Andy and I had been married. Neither of us was religious—and I wondered why it hadn't crossed our minds to marry somewhere other than a church. We'd just launched into the usual: flowers at the altar, minister in robes, me in white dress and veil and Andy in a black tux, organ music, champagne reception—a small-town stereotype, a pigeonhole of a wedding. Perhaps the weight of traditions that preceded us was so unwieldy that we were unable to discern what we really wanted and who we really were.

Passing the church and all the memories that resided in my body like DNA, I approached Whispering Winds where my parents now lived. When I was in Japan, they abandoned the house I grew up in—the house with its redwood decks and swimming pool and sliding glass doors—to move into a townhouse. Whispering Winds had been a field when I was growing up. A field of rolling hills crowded with blue oaks, manzanita and poison oak. Now mammoth placards announced new condos and family homes for sale in the developments: Oak Point and Whispering Winds and Gold Nugget Estates. Planted near the banners, little colorful flags on sticks, like at car dealerships, snapped in the breeze. Even the sidewalks were new—not grey and buckled as in other parts of town, but pristine white and smooth.

I parked my car, spattered with freeway bugs, near the curb next to a recently planted spindly tree tied to a stick. The past—high school cliques and sex, me driving my grandfather's old car, my friends and I smoking pot in a field, our split-level house inhabited by my parents and sister, my church marriage to Andy—lived only in my mind like ghosts. Materially, it was all gone. Dissolved. It didn't take long for the future to arrive.

It was odd to have to knock on the door of my parents' house. That's how I thought of the condo: their house, not our family house, not home. I was just about to tap on the door a second time when my mom flung it open, her lips pink with lipstick, her purse over her shoulder. She was wearing her gold Real Estate sales jacket.

"Oh, Gwen! You scared me! How long have you been standing there?"

"I just got here. Hi, Mom." I bent over to give her a hug and she stiffly embraced me, patting my back with manicured fingers. Hugging was something new in our family. Now that my sister and I were adults, perhaps hugging was an expected transition: hugging to pretend our seditious adolescence hadn't really happened, that my mother had never angrily swatted me with a broom after I'd called her a *bitch*, that my sister had never slammed her bedroom door so hard it flew off the hinges, that my mom had never screamed red-faced at me, "You should be ashamed!" after a hickey the shape—and in her eyes, the size—of Texas had appeared on my neck.

"I don't remember you saying you were coming today," Mom said as she walked with me into the kitchen, a perfectly clean kitchen installed with futuristic appliances. Shiny new pans hung above the stove.

"I got a chance to take an early vacation, so I did."

"Well, that's good, dear. I'm so glad to have you here, but I have a house to show in—" she looked at her thin gold watch "twenty minutes."

"That's fine, Mom, don't worry about me."

"There's stuff for lunch in the fridge. Your father's at a school board meeting. Then he has choir practice." *Choir practice* was what he and his friends called their poker games. "If he'd known you were coming he probably would have cancelled."

"Really, Mom, that's okay, I have almost two weeks with you. I can keep myself entertained."

"I really didn't know you were coming today."

"I know, Mom, it was a sudden change of plans."

Mom rooted around in her purse for her keys—she appeared organized to other people, but I knew she was always misplacing things. When she finally found the keys, she triumphantly held them up. "Wish me luck!" she said.

"Break a leg."

"I wish you had called. I'm only baking a chicken for dinner. I would have planned something more spectacular."

"It's okay," I said, "See you." I felt irritated at her constant references to food preparation. Once she'd said to me that she thought I might be able make Andy happier if I cooked more.

She threw a little wave in my direction and was gone, leaving behind a zesty whiff of perfume. In light of her sudden absence, it felt like I was in a foreign house, not the house of my parents. I remembered how I used to feel when I was home alone as a kid. I nestled into my world, free to watch T.V., to eat scoops of peanut butter from the jar, to read alone in my room without worry that someone would call out to me from the bottom of the stairs to tell me to wash the dishes or water the plants. We'd had plastic runners in the hallway that, alone, I'd turn over to walk on the plastic spikes for a pleasing pinch of the feet. But now that my parents no longer had kids or dogs or all the accoutrements of the middle-aged married, there were no plastic runners—besides, it wasn't the 70's anymore, and plastic runners seemed to have gone the way of bean bags and love beads.

I walked into the living room and sat on the new stiff sofa. For a moment I imagined Jamie here, sitting next to me, but the thought was ungraspable. How would she fit here in this living room with its gleaming piano topped with photos of my sister's wedding and her kids? In one photo, I stood in a stiff aqua-colored bridesmaid's dress, my head piled with hair-sprayed hair. My parents used to display Andy's and my wedding photo on the piano, too, but after we divorced it disappeared, probably stuffed in a dark closet or box. Could they have thrown it away? The only photo of me was me in my college graduation cap and gown, my body obscured by all that fabric, my hair pushed into my eyes by an awkward mortarboard.

Rising from the couch, I walked through the rooms, restless. This townhouse was small compared to the four-bedroom house I'd grown up in. Pacing around in it made me feel like a lion in a cage. I should go somewhere, I thought, but the idea of driving around Suffolk, with all the ghosts of my past chasing me, made me feel unsafe. I picked up the phone and called the lab.

"Hey Sullivan," Daniel said in his happy, pretend-coach voice that he knew made me smile, coming from a nerdy scientist. My throat tightened. It felt like he was trying to reach out to me over the lines. "Why did you suddenly rush off to your parents' house? How long will you be gone?"

"I don't know," I said, "it was just an impulse. Things have been slow at work so I decided to come spend some extra time here. I was thinking I'll stay through Thanksgiving."

"That's two weeks." He said this like he was reading a newspaper headline that he didn't have much interest in.

"Yeah," I said.

"Did you come home last night?"

I was stunned that he came out and asked me that way. I really hadn't thought he'd notice. "Yes. I slept on the couch. I didn't want to wake you." The lie came easily, too easily. He seemed not to notice.

"You got a phone call from some person named Cat. Is that a man or a woman?"

"A woman, silly. Have you ever heard of a guy named Cat?"

"She has one deep voice. Anyway, she said she wants you to call her. I think I put the note somewhere in my pocket. Hold on."

In the background, I could hear punk rock music playing—and I thought about how all the scientists in the room were dressed in tennis shoes and wrinkled lab coats, lost in the microscopic world of the usually-unseen; how they could wear whatever they wanted, could listen to music; how their foil-wrapped sandwiches were tucked in the refrigerator along with bottles of noxious lab liquids. Maybe each one of them was slowly getting poisoned, ruining their chances at healthy children. One of Daniel's jobs was to check for, and clean up, small radioactive spills. I'd asked him if that ever worried him; he'd said, no, there's more radioactivity in stones and the sun than most of what he uncovered in the lab each week.

"Found it," he said into the phone, and I wrote down Cat's phone number as he recited it to me on a piece of cream-colored notepaper with "Mr. and Mrs. Ralph Sullivan" embossed across the top.

"Thanks," I said, noticing my hand was shaking a little. From every angle I was feeling assaulted, overwhelmed: Jamie and I had slept together, and now she was gone; Daniel doing his usual thing, working in the lab and talking to me, his voice on the phone so familiar yet distanced, foreign; Cat, unlike a woman I'd ever known in my life, was calling me: Why? Could I bring myself to call her back? I sat down on a firm kitchen chair, my thighs squeaking against the newfangled fabric that covered the cushions.

"Sure," he said. "Okay, I have to run—a lot to do today. A lot to over the next week or so before I go home."

The word burned my ears. "Do you realize you call your parents' house *home?*"

"I do?"

"Yes, you just did it. You said you have a lot to do before you go home."

"I see."

"You see what?"

"I see what you mean."

"Okay, well, I'll see you later. In a couple of weeks. At our apartment. Which apparently isn't home."

"Gwen, you're relentless." He paused, cleared his throat, then said, "Oh, and Gwen? I'm going back to the city again in December, around Hanukah. My sister will be in town then, too. And I was hoping you might want to come with me."

"You were?"

"Yes. Do you think you'd be up for meeting the parents?"

I thought about all the times his mother called and he took the phone out onto our messy patio to talk to her. I'd watch his mouth moving silently through the sliding glass door, and when he came back into the apartment, his mouth would be tight and his eyes dark. Just like making noise in the mornings, talking about his family was taboo. He'd said only a few things about them in our years together—that he didn't like the "family thing," that his grandparents wanted him to marry a Jewish woman, that his parents had worked a lot when he was a kid and he hadn't seen them much, which he claimed to be fine by him. And now, of all times, he was inviting me to meet his family? To go to his *home* in New York?

"You mean go to New York? This seems strange, Daniel. You don't invite me for Thanksgiving but you do for Hanukah?"

"When I realized my sister would be there in December, I thought it might be a good time for you, for us, to go there together." He was tripping over his words, as though his ideas, for once, were unscripted. "What do you think? You think you'd want to come? I could tell my parents when I go there for Thanksgiving. I'm sure they'd be glad to have you."

So they did know about me. And they'd be *glad*? I wasn't sure I'd ever heard Daniel use that word before, much less in relationship to his parents.

"Well, maybe," I said, with an odd feeling in my gut that I was betraying Jamie and Daniel simultaneously.

"Okay, good," he said, seeming to take my *maybe* to mean *yes*. "I have to run. Call me again soon. Or I'll call you."

"Okay," I said, hanging up the phone, slumping to the table. The straw place mats pinched my forearms as I hid my face in the dark cave of my arms.

* * *

My friend Kaye tried to hug me when she answered the door, but with her eighth-month-pregnant belly jutting out in front of her, the hug was awkward. Her long blonde hair was braided thickly down her back and secured at the base with a leather tie, a visual testament to her ongoing embrace of her high school hippie identity.

"It's amazing to see you," she said, as she handed me a cup of steaming herb tea. "You look amazing. Life must be good, huh?" I shifted on the couch to take the tea without spilling it and felt the extra weight as Kaye and her about-to-be-born baby pulled down the other side of the couch. "I'm so glad you finally came to see me! Can you believe this?" she said, pointing at her hump of a belly. "Last time I saw you I thought I was pregnant, but I didn't want to jinx anything. And—well, we just haven't talked. Why haven't you called me?"

"I believe that's a phone hanging on your kitchen wall."

"I know, I know, I'm sorry. It's, well, with Lennon's school being a co-op, and with preparing for the new baby—you know, getting the doula all set up and all."

"The what?"

"The doula. She'll work with me and with the midwife. She does all kinds of amazing things—massage, aromatherapy, advice—anything that will help make the birth a better experience." She pulled her braid over her shoulder and fingered the leather tie.

"Are you sure," I teased, "that you don't just want to go to the hospital, get knocked out by anesthetic and wake up with a baby in your arms?"

"Epidural, anyone? Forceps? Drugs? Caesarean? Dear god, whatever happened to being there when one of the most amazing experiences in life is happening? I so regret that I didn't have a home birth with Lennon. But David insisted we do the hospital." David was her first husband, father of Lennon. "That episiotomy was the worst thing ever. I'm never going through that again. Thank heaven for Brad." Brad was her new husband, father of this in-utero child.

"Where is Lennon?" I asked.

"At preschool. In fact—" she glanced at her turquoise-embedded watch "—I have to go pick him up in about an hour. It's a co-op, so I put in a number of hours each week. It's a fantastic set-up, with wonderful teachers. There's no pressure, honestly, but Lennon's already reading, can you believe it? At three years old?"

"Amazing," I said, aware that I rarely used that word but that she did all the time. Unconsciously I had mimicked her terminology, become a Suffolk girl again just minutes after entering her house. "So you two—you and Brad—are doing well?" I asked, honestly curious but also my heart racing, hoping she'd asked me about Daniel. A sense of dread and excitement swept over me; I needed to talk.

"We're so good," she said. "We're excellent. Brad is so unbelievably excited about the baby. This," she pointed to her belly, "is a girl. Her name's Luna."

I bent over toward Kaye's belly and said, "Hi Luna."

"Brad couldn't be more excited that we're having a girl. His work is going really well—construction around here is booming. Life is just, well, just amazing. And we have another project—well, come here, I want to show you something."

As she struggled to stand, I jumped to my feet and helped pull her up. She led me through the house, with its glossy hardwood floors and high-beamed ceilings. In the kitchen, two fragrant loaves of newly baked bread sat cooling on the butcher block island. We passed Lennon's room, a riot of books and wooden puzzles and cloth stuffed animals. Kaye and Brad believed that plastic toys were toxic. If I ever got cancer, I wondered if I could blame all my years of playing with Barbie, Midge, Ken and green-haired trolls.

Kaye led me through the laundry room into the backyard. It was a cool, sunless day, the sky gray-white. Beyond the herb and vegetable garden loomed a newly-built fence penning in a number of large, grazing animals.

"You have llamas?"

"No, alpacas. They're very sweet," she said, as we approached the fence. One with a brown body and long white neck waddled over to us. Kaye reached out her hand and stroked its brown head. I followed suit.

"Wow, so soft," I said. It stared at me with guileless black eyes.

"We're raising them for this very reason, their fleece," she said.

"Can you believe we can write off everything related to them—supplies, vet bills, even the computer we bought to keep track of our investment? And we can depreciate on our investment for the first five years."

"I had no idea you were a capitalist at heart," I said, continuing to stroke the silky fur.

"Brad's quite entrepreneurial," she said. As she spoke about his *amazing* ability to invest, to predict the market, to make plans for the future—all for her and the children—I found myself drifting away a little, hearing just the sing-song quality of her voice and feeling the soft fur beneath my hand. I thought about all the guys we dated in high school, and how Kaye had been dying to go out with Chip Knightly, who was extremely popular in spite of his raging acne. As a testament to the mysteries of popularity, his tallness and cute smile and letterman jacket had apparently usurped his bad complexion. Kaye had been sure that if she became a cheerleader she would win him—ergo, her devastation at not being voted in. I barely remembered classes in high school, but indelibly marked in my mind were experiences with boys, boys, boys: a senior, Robert Major, asking little sophomore me to dance at one of the ubiquitous cafeteria dances; and later, Robert sliding his hands down my pants in the back of his van and the utter shocking thrill when he touched me; the humiliation of getting violently sick from drinking Mad Dog at a concert and then having my boyfriend Wally break up with me soon after; all my days of waiting by the phone, hoping Wally would change his mind ... The memories went on and on, and I could lose myself in them. Yes, that's what it felt like—that in high school I had lost myself in boys. I shuddered, trying to shake off all the memories, trying to bring myself back to Kaye, pregnant beside me, stroking the absurd head of one of her and Brad's "investments," trying to pull myself back to the realization that I had a whole life elsewhere, in the Bay Area—or did I? Did a poetry class really exist somewhere? Did Jamie?

"—and isn't it strange, they have no top teeth in the front?" Kaye was saying, and I realized she was talking about the alpacas. "And their feet are so soft and padded that they're gentle on the pasture. Ooh, I'm cold, let's go back in." A little wind had picked up, reminding us it was mid-November.

Stationed back in Kaye's beautiful house, looking around at all the child accoutrements—finger paintings pinned to the wall, a wooden rocking horse near the front window, a pink and white bassinet at the ready in the corner—I wondered if Kaye was doing life the right way. And if so, was I doing everything wrong? My parents had been married for thirty-five years. My sister for fifteen. Kaye had been married for ten years now—granted, eight of those years were to one man and two to another—but look at her, she had a house, she had investments, she had children, she had a future.

"God, I've just been babbling, babbling, babbling about myself," said Kaye, blowing on her cup of herbal tea. "What's new with you? How's your job? And Daniel? Am I ever going to get to meet the elusive Daniel?" She lay her hands on her belly, settling back for a story from me. I was sure she wasn't expecting the one I was about to tell her. As nervous as I was, I marveled at my compulsion to tell her about Jamie and me. Yet she'd asked what was new—and that's what my friends and I did: talked about our lives.

I began slowly unraveling the story—beginning by repeating some things that were already familiar to her: my hopes that things would be different after Japan, my frustrations with Daniel's and my relationship, Daniel's sudden desire to take me to New York in a couple of weeks to meet his parents.

"That's a positive step!" she enthused, beaming her bright pregnant mother-smile. I wondered if she really was as happy as she seemed—and if she ever still thought about how she'd never become a cheerleader. Had she ever told Brad? He hadn't grown up in our town, so Kaye was able to start with a clean slate.

"It's ironic," I said, "that Daniel would finally offer up something I think I wanted—a chance to meet his parents."

"What do you mean you *think* you wanted?"

"I'm not so sure anymore. Something has happened."

Kaye leaned forward and fixed her blue eyes on me. "Oh! Do you mean some*one* has happened?"

My heart knocked furiously at the door of my chest. "Yes, someone." I could see in Kaye's gaze that she was suddenly living vicariously through me—me, the single woman who was still making choices in life about which direction to go. Or was she relieved that she was past all that and settled in her child-husband-homemade-bread-alpaca life? "I met her in a poetry class."

Did Kaye lean back to get into a comfortable position, or was she moving away from me? "Did you say *her*?"

"Yes. Her. Her name is Jamie. I know, it's a shocker, isn't it? I mean, even to me."

"Are you feeling you're a lesbian?"

"I don't know. I don't know. I don't know." The record needle of my voice skipped over the scratched surface of my heart. "I mean, I can't believe how I feel with her. I care so much about Daniel but I feel so restricted around him. With Jamie I can be who I really am—I mean, I can say what I believe, about politics, about women's lives, about art and poetry—and she doesn't resist me, doesn't judge me, doesn't shut down. She just takes it all in and gives me something back. In the morning she likes to talk, to observe the world—"

"You slept with her?"

"Yes, once."

"Gwen, don't make a decision based on that. I had sex with a woman once—and look at me now. I'm really glad I made the decision I did, to be with men, not women. There's a lot less to have to deal with in life this way."

"Wait a minute. You had sex with a woman? And you never told me?"

"I almost told you a few times. I came really close once when we were at the Low-Down, having a drink, remember? I was engaged to David? We got a little sloshed on rum and cokes, if I recall. I wasn't sure how you'd take it, the fact that I'd had a little thing with Debra Robinson—"

"With Debra Robinson?" I saw Debra Robinson's freckly face in a broad smile, legs kicking a perfect can-can in a pep rally—Debra the cheerleader. "You're shitting me," I said.

"No! Debra's a big dyke. Sorry, I mean a lesbian. I didn't find that out until one night we were both drunk on senior cut day, down at the lake. We'd been laughing and talking, and I followed her into the bushes, and well—"

"You mean that when I was sucking face with Danny Esposito in an inner tube, you were having sex with Debra Robinson in the bushes?"

She laughed. "Yes! And it's such a relief to finally tell you! I thought you'd judge me. I mean, a few times I've tested the waters with you, brought up the subject of lesbians, of women together, of bisexuality—"

"You have?"

"Yes! Earth to Gwen! Yes I have! And each time you glossed over the idea, or changed the subject so I thought you were uncomfortable with it."

Could this be true? That I had absolutely no recollection of Kaye raising this issue and that she had tried to talk to me about it several times? Were there really parts of my life that were stuffed in the back of a dark closet like old shoes?

"I—I don't know what to say," I said.

"Is this Jamie woman really the first woman you've ever felt attracted to? Haven't you ever had crushes on women before?"

"Yes! No! I mean—yes, Jamie's the first woman I ever felt like this about. I was sitting in poetry class and suddenly I realized I thought she was beautiful. And not in the usual way. It was, well, sexual. And I'd never felt that before."

"Are you sure? I've felt that a million times."

"A million?"

"Yes! I had a huge crush on my obstetrician for a while."

"Wait a minute. Are you saying you still feel these things for women?"

"Well sure. It's normal. My theory is that society usually beats the bisexuality out of us. Where on T.V., or in commercials, or in books, do you see same-sex love? Nowhere! Well, unless you count the way it's presented as freakishness on talk shows. But where is it presented as normal? Does anyone ever ask a little girl if she has a crush on a little girl? No—but they say, *is he your little boyfriend?* About another kid! It seems awfully early in life we instill heterosexuality into people, don't you think? I think almost all people could go either way, could have crushes on men or women."

"Kaye, you are blowing my mind."

"Alright, but now that I've said all this, my advice to you is this: You're at a crossroads where you can choose either Daniel or Jamie. I say, choose Daniel. Your life will be easier. You won't have to deal with society's wrath, its prejudices."

As Kaye continued to talk about society's prejudices, I closed my eyes for a moment. The room spun. When I opened them again, there was Kaye, her hands on her voluminous stomach, talking away. She looked a little different to me somehow, a little like a stranger, her mouth moving. How could it be that I talked to only two of my friends about this—Kaye and Lucy—and both of them had had lesbian desires? Was this a skewed sample, or did all women secretly desire other women? Was Kaye right about bisexuality? Here I thought I'd been holding a secret, a uniqueness inside, but I wasn't so special, not really. I wanted to say something—something about the hope I felt now that we had a new President. Maybe the world would be different. But this wasn't really about the world, was it? It was about me. And Daniel. And Jamie. And Rose.

"It's not a decision to take lightly," Kaye was saying. "Of course I don't even know Jamie. But this goes beyond her. It goes to you, and what you choose to do with your life. So those are my two cents."

"I don't know what to say," I said.

"You don't have to say anything. Just promise me you'll think about what I've said." Her face skewed, as though she'd just seen something horrible, like a car accident or a murder—and then she grinned. "Oh, oh! Luna's moving—feel."

She reached over, grabbed my hand and placed it on her belly. Beneath her skin, an unmistakable foot with little pea toes slid beneath my hand.

CHAPTER THIRTEEN

THE MERGE

It was the day before Thanksgiving. By the time my sister Barbara and her family had arrived, I'd already helped my mom prepare the turkey stuffing, the fruit salad, the green Jell-O salad, the yam casserole and the green bean and mushroom casserole. The rest of the day stretched before us, quiet and still, as though time were on pause. There wasn't the usual uproar when Barbara, her husband and kids came through the door because four-year-old Thomas had fallen asleep in the car. Barbara's husband, Bill, took Thomas into my parents' room to rest on their California King bed—and Bill had promptly fallen asleep beside him. When we saw our parents nodding off on the couch in front of the football game, Barbara and I decided to go for a walk to shake off the contagion of drowsiness. We were instantly refreshed by the cold air, but baby Toby wasn't—he promptly fell sound asleep in the stroller.

Wrapped in blue blankets, Toby slept as Barbara and I walked through the streets of my parents' neighborhood. Our breath puffed white before us, and I was glad—I liked the wintry cold. The sharp chill of this day pinched our cheeks, leading us on with a promise of snow it had little chance of delivering.

This neighborhood—with its rows of town homes fronted by well-manicured lawns and bordered by brand-new mini-mansions with three-car garages—had not existed when Barbara and I were kids. When we were growing up in a neighborhood just a mile away, this had been the undeveloped outskirts of town.

"There," I said, pointing to a gray house, "is where I parked under a bunch of oak trees with Danny Esposito and tried pot for the first time." In the front yard towered one of the twisted oaks that had been saved. It was draped in white Christmas lights. A Christmas tree glittered in the house's front window.

"I hate it when people shove aside Thanksgiving in their rush to get to Christmas," Barbara said. "They have their priorities all wrong. They're rushing through life to get to one holiday instead of cherishing the one they're in."

"I wonder who lives there?" I asked. As we passed the Christmas twinkle, there was no evidence of people around.

"Used to be we knew everyone in Suffolk," she said. "Now I can go to the store here and not even see someone who looks familiar." She stopped for a moment and tucked the blanket more securely around her sleeping son before we continued down the street. "But what was that you were saying, about your first time smoking pot?"

"Oh, nothing," I said. "Nothing really. I was just remembering."

"This place does that, doesn't it? Bill tells me to shut up sometimes when I've mentioned for the tenth time that we're driving by the building that used to be the restaurant where I had a summer job. Or whatever. I guess when you live away, all that stuff comes back to you with a lot of force when you're visiting." My sister had just articulated something I'd often felt. While reveling in our sisterly connection, I was also struck by a sense of doubleness—that part of me was here with her, while another part of me was watching us. The watching part was the part that had slept with Jamie, the part that felt like I was falling in love with a woman. The silent watching self was the part of me that had thought and thought about what Kaye had said last week, her advice to choose Daniel instead of Jamie. I had turned this over and over in my mind these quiet days in Suffolk while I read in the bedroom, played cards with my parents, ate dinners with them, grocery shopped with my mom, and watched movies with my parents in the evenings while we ate ice cream or popcorn. I had dreams of Jamie and Daniel. I didn't remember the details, but I was haunted by feelings. I'd wake up remembering that the dream had been imbued with a sense of danger and betrayal.

Daniel had called me a few more times before he left for New York. Each time I thought about trying to call Cat afterward, to see if she had a number for Jamie. But it was too risky to call Jamie. She was with her brother, and Rose.

I wasn't sure Kaye was right. She'd said life with Daniel would be easier. But was easier necessarily better? And would it really be easier, anyway? *Ease* was actually the last word I'd use to describe my relationship with Daniel. *Ease* fit my relationship with Jamie much better. Although it was true, *ease* most fit when Jamie and I were alone. I remembered being in the restaurant in Santa Cruz, after we'd left the hotel. Jamie had held my hand beneath the table, and it had crossed my mind that we might, somehow, be in the waitress' way—that we might somehow *disturb* her—if we held hands on top of the table for all the world to see. This, I knew, was the essence of the *ease* Kaye had meant.

"How's Daniel these days?" asked Barbara, as we walked past a newly sprung-up small corner park. The grass and the see-saw sparkled with frost.

"He's alright," I said, my heart picking up its pace in my chest. I was sure this discussion was going to lead me to open the door on my life. Once again I marveled at my desire to tell. This desire felt a little like the times I'd been to confession. Pulling the heavy red curtain aside, I'd sat in the dark little booth, my heart pumping with anxiety and excitement before the priest—smelling like dried flowers—spoke. And now, on the edge of saying something to my sister about Jamie, my palms grew hot. "Daniel invited me to go to New York for Hanukah."

"It's about time!" said Barbara. "Does that mean he might deign to show himself here sometime, too?"

"I don't know."

"He's really an odd one, isn't he? Oh, I'm sorry, I shouldn't have said that. But it's true, isn't it? Tell me what you love about him. Help me understand what you find so compelling about a man who won't come visit your family."

"I don't know," I said, a wave of inexplicable sadness sweeping over me. It was like my emotions lately were not anchored to concrete reality—sadness, joy, desire would grab me like an attacker in a dark alley. "I'm not sure I do love him anymore."

Barbara looked at me, her chubby pink face framed by her orange knit cap. I knew this admission would get a reaction. It had from Lucy, it had from Kaye. Besides, my sister was a believer in marriage, monogamy, family. In my gut, I knew this was the moment of shifting gears.

"Really? Why?"

"Well—there's something in him that's untouchable."

"There's something in everyone that's untouchable. You always want to merge with the men you're with, Gwen. That's not necessarily how relationships work."

I resented the preachy tone in her voice, the posturing as older-and-wiser-sister. Just because she was married and a mother didn't mean she knew everything. There was something I knew that she didn't, and I was now especially compelled to tell her.

"Maybe not," I said, as we crossed the street, past the billboards for Whispering Winds and the other new developments, the little car dealership-like flags bright yellow and red in the white day. "Or maybe it's just relationships between men and women that have that untouchable thing. Maybe it's not that way between two women."

She stopped. Right in the middle of the crosswalk. "Two women? What do you mean, two women?"

I kept walking to the other side of the street and turned. She still stood in the middle of the crosswalk. I heard no cars coming, but you never knew when one might come barreling over the hill. Toby's stroller jutted out in front of her.

"Barbara, come on."

"I'm not moving from here until you tell me what the hell you mean."

"What's your problem?" I said, my burning throat growing tight. The last time I'd seen her like this was years ago, when she discovered I'd snuck her green sweater out of her room and put it back after wearing it, hoping she wouldn't notice the greasy stain created by a dropped French fry dripping in ketchup. That memory calmed me a little, because she had quickly forgiven me for the stolen, ruined sweater.

"Listen," she said, her voice edging to a screech, "are you dropping some kind of bomb on me here? Because I can't handle it. I'll just have you know right now, I can't handle it."

"Barbara, a car is coming." A large white van was rolling toward her, slowing down to let her cross. She turned the stroller around and, her back to me, walked the other direction. I held up my hand at the van and raced across the street to catch up to her. I had to continue to either lightly jog or walk fast to keep up with her.

"Barbara, why are you freaking out?"

"Freaking out? Don't tell me I'm freaking out. You're the one who's the freak. You're the one who's—" She swallowed whatever she had intended to say and kept walking at a frantic pace.

"But I haven't even said anything!"

"You've said enough. Why are you so goddamned selfish? We're here for a nice Thanksgiving, a nice family gathering, and you—you. You always have to be *different*, Gwen. And you just steam roll over people around you. Did you even think about Mom and Dad? Did you even think about my sons? You just do whatever you want—get divorced from Andy, just pull him out of the family like yanking a tooth. And you go flying off to Japan when Dad has to have surgery—"

"Surgery? You mean getting his appendix out?"

"And then you're dating this—this weirdo, who won't even be part of this family. And now you're talking about women with women? What are you saying, Gwen, are you saying you've decided to become a lesbian so you can be even more different, so you can push us all even father away?"

"Oh my god." My face was numb but I thought there might be tears rolling down it. "I had no idea you felt this way about me."

"Well, think, Gwen. Just think. You don't fucking think."

Toby began to cry. We were almost back to my parents' house. I stood, frozen in front of the too-soon-Christmas house, the colorful tree lights blinking, while Barbara fumbled with Toby's blankets as she lifted him out of the stroller. I reached over and handed her a corner of a blue blanket that had almost slipped to the ground. I could see she was crying, too. All three of us, crying in front of a cheery holiday display, the cold air biting us.

"So is that what you're saying?" she asked, her voice now the sotto hush of a new mother. She looked at me. For a moment we were young—her nine, me six. She'd washed her suntan Barbie's hair and had placed her on the fireplace mantle to dry Barbie's long blonde hair. When she pulled the doll away, a hunk of Barbie's hair stayed behind, melted to the fireplace screen. While crying, she'd thrown the now defective Barbie at me, hitting me on the head. The utter unfairness of that action had bloomed hate in me, until I'd seen Barbara's face, contorted with frustration and sorrow. A sudden pang of empathy had run through me, partially shadowing my intense sense of injustice.

"Is what, what I'm saying?" In spite of feeling some sympathy for her pain, I wasn't going to make this easy for her. I knew hardening myself would only make things worse, but my heart and body tensed beyond my control. "Barbara, is *what*, what I'm saying?"

"That you're a lesbian?"

"Did I say that?"

"Goddamn it, Gwen, this isn't something to play around with."

"I'm not playing around with anything. It's just a fact that I may be falling in love with a woman." I half-expected her to follow suit with Lucy and Kaye, to admit to me a same-sex attraction she'd once had, perhaps for her best friend Wendy. They used to wash each other's hair and braid it to create the effect of long, wavy hair that looked more frizzy than wavy. I could feel the energy leaking out of me. Barbara's intense reaction made me feel like I was a snowman whose head she'd knocked off onto the cold, hard ground.

"God," she whispered. "Just don't tell anyone, okay? In fact, I'd rather we pretend this discussion didn't happen."

For the rest of the day, Barbara kept herself busy playing blocks and puzzles with Thomas, or nursing Toby, or putting dishes in the dishwasher, or watching football with Dad and Bill. I played Scrabble with Mom, but it was hard to focus. The tiles were hard to grab onto. My hands didn't feel connected to my body. And it was as though I had temporary dyslexia—U's looked like V's, E's looked like F's. After my mom won two games, I excused myself and went to my room to read *Leaves of Grass*, which I'd tucked into my bag of clothes. Walt

Whitman always helped to center me with his long, rhythmic lines and his celebration of abundance, his embrace of all, of everything. A professor had once told me that the word most used in *Leaves of Grass* was "and." I could use some "and" thinking right now, some rejecting of "either/or." Although when it came to Jamie and Daniel, I knew "and" wouldn't cut it.

My dad peeked his head into the room and asked if I'd like to go with him to pick up Grandma. I begged off, saying I wanted to read. When he left the room, I glanced down at the page and read, *Who need be afraid of the Merge?*

Merge. The word that Barbara had accused me with. The very word. A numbing chill spread down my arms. *You always want to merge with the men you're with, Gwen. That's not necessarily how relationships work.*

And here was Walt Whitman, telling me to merge. And to not be afraid.

The next day, I rose early to help my mom put the foil-covered turkey in the oven. Then Mom and I sat at the table with cups of coffee. She asked me about my job, about Daniel, about the poetry class I was taking. Trying to force the monotone from my voice, I did my best to answer her cheerfully. She told me about the two houses she sold last month, and about a big celebration the town's Democratic party threw on election night.

"It was the first time in years I drank too much champagne," she said.

"Did you get drunk?" I asked, trying to go along with a

playfulness in the conversation, trying to negate the sting I still felt from Barbara's shaming harangue of the previous day. I was glad to have something light to talk about—champagne. I'd seen my mom tipsy at my cousin's wedding a few years back, but other than that, my whole life she'd been a pillar of self-control when it came to alcohol.

"Actually, I did." She smiled, lines spreading out from her eyes and down her cheeks. "I sure paid for it the next day. But it didn't matter, because I took some aspirin and floated around the house filled with the realization that we defeated Reagan-Bush."

"I know, Mom, I felt the same way—still feel it. I can't wait for the inauguration."

"Now, honey, I know we're all excited about this, but I have to ask you, please let's not talk about politics later, around everyone, I mean."

"Around Bill, you mean." Whenever we had family gatherings, he was the only Republican in the room. My chest constricted at the realization that I was now being directed by both my mom and my sister to shut up about something they didn't want me to discuss.

"Yes, that's what I mean. Let's not ruin Thanksgiving."

An impulse to tell her about Jamie scooted up my spine, but then a wave of exhaustion hit me. I had to force myself to keep my eyes open as we continued to chat.

Barbara entered the kitchen and poured herself some coffee. She joined us at the table, ignoring the thick air between us by regaling my mom with stories of the children. I was frozen to my chair, numbly and intensely sleepy. I wanted to get up and go back to the guest room but my body felt immovable. Soon everyone was up and about, my grandmother in her purple robe, my father in his jogging suit, Bill feeding Cheerios to the kids who wore footie pajamas. All the activity thawed me a bit, and I excused myself to take a nap.

Lying in bed in the guest bedroom, I heard the electric knife buzzing. I glanced at the clock. I'd been asleep for four hours. I was surprised, and grateful, that no one had awakened me. Escaping into sleep was not the accepted behavior in my Horatio Algier-inspired family. Then again, there was often a relaxing of standards on the holidays in my parents' house, a sense that chaos and sloth were okay for a day or two.

I could picture Dad carving the golden-skinned turkey on the counter next to the sink, wineglasses dangling over his head from the rack on the ceiling. But no, that was in the house where I grew up. Here at my parents' townhouse he was probably carving away on the butcher block island, lifting slabs of white meat onto a platter. Also filtering into the bedroom were voices: My mom sing-songing to baby Toby; Barbara's sharp bark of a laugh; Thomas making *vroom-vroom* car noises; Grandma saying something about a turkey wing. The roar of a crowd and raucous sports talk rose and fell—football, being watched by Bill and Dad.

Part of me was awake, the other part still wrapped in the fugue of sleep. I stretched and forced myself to sit up, leaning against the headboard. I had the sensation of being in a hotel room with the bleach-scented sheets, the nondescript bedside stand that looked like it belonged in a model home and the generic framed print of pink and green flowers. The only thing I recognized from my parents' past life in the house I grew up in was the pink princess phone that had been in Barbara's room. Everything else that had been in Barbara's or my rooms we'd either carted away when we'd moved, or my parents had sold in a vast yard sale. I'd been in Japan when they'd had the yard sale, when they'd rid themselves of the accumulation of years.

In spite of my long nap, I felt tired, deep-down tired in my bones. Barbara's red, crying face loomed in my mind, followed by a flash of Jamie's face, her eyes, her wave tattoo, followed by a warm-water bodily sensation at the memory of Jamie's hands on my body. Where was Jamie right now? I had no idea what I would do with my life. All I knew was that I craved being next to her.

The piece of gold notepaper on which I'd written Cat's number lay crumpled next to the pink princess phone. It had been more than a week since Daniel told me she'd called. I'd avoided calling her back because the whole idea of talking to her over the phone from my parents' house seemed odd, absurd, awkward. But now I picked up the receiver and dialed, my heart thrumming in my throat. The phone rang and rang, and then Cat's machine answered: *Hi, I'm not here. Please leave me a message.* A startlingly common message.

"Hi Cat, it's Gwen, returning your—"

"Hey, Gwen." Cat picked up. While answering machine feedback screeched in my ear, she said, "Hold on." I heard a few clicks and then, "Hi, how're you doing?"

"I'm okay. Is something wrong? Daniel told me you wanted me to call you."

"No, nothing's wrong. Are you okay? You missed class."

"Oh, I'm fine," I said, wondering if Cat intuited that Jamie and

I had slept together. Or had Jamie told her? "I'm at my parents' house for the holiday."

"Up in Suffolk, right?"

Had I told her that? "That's right." Embarrassment infused me for some inexplicable reason. I wanted to deter the discussion away from myself. At the same time, it felt comforting to have Cat on the line. It made me feel closer to Jamie. "So how was class? I'm sorry to have missed it."

"It was pretty good," she said. "We read yet another poem about that woman's asshole husband." She laughed. "And one of Vanessa's poems, too."

"Vanessa shared one of hers? Damn, I wish I hadn't missed that."

"Yeah, it's pretty remarkable. I'll give you a copy next class. At first I thought it'd be weird to be taking a class from Vanessa, but it's turned out to be good."

"What do you mean, weird? Why weird?"

"Well, you know, since she's Jamie's ex." She paused, clearly judging my reception of this information.

"Do you mean ex-girlfriend?"

"Yeah. Oh, Jamie didn't tell you?"

"Vanessa? Is Jamie's ex?" My throat felt suddenly dry. "How old is she?"

"Hm, good question. I'm not sure at this point. I think she must be close to sixty. I think she's probably twenty-five years or so older than Jamie. Yeah, I think twenty-five years. They lived together for a couple of years, after she and I broke up. Then she was with, hm, what was her name, Lila, Lilly, something like that. Yeah, a girl she met at the hotel where she worked. And then there was that girl Cecelia who is the granddaughter of one of our clients, Mrs. Wallerston. That girl must have been only about nineteen or something. Jamie went out with a couple others, too, I think before getting together with bitchy Rose. I really don't get what she sees in Rose."

The phone was slick in my hand—my palms were sweating. I tried to swallow but my throat burned tightly.

"Cat, it's time for dinner, I have to go."

"Oh, yeah, okay. Happy Thanksgiving. Have a good one. See you soon."

As I hung up, nausea burned my chest. I thought about Jamie sitting in class next to Vanessa, Vanessa's hand touching Jamie's poems, Vanessa's long white hair and silver jewelry. Jamie leaning over to say something to Vanessa during class. Jamie and Rose walking down the aisle—the slant of light in the chapel like the slant of light in the classroom, illuminating the dust motes and then fading. Merging in my mind, Vanessa and Rose—and there were others, too? Was I merely one of the many others? Who was I to Jamie? She was in Florida, with her brother and his family, Rose there as her partner, her love. Again, I was on the outside of someone's family, kept separate. A secret. I knew nothing about Jamie. Her body and mine had merged for a few moments, but she didn't love me. I was just another in a line of women.

I would go to New York with Daniel for Hanukah. I would meet his family, see the house he grew up in, look through his old yearbooks at the girls he had crushes on, get every single detail I could about all the women he ever loved—and I'd make him, force him to hear the sordid details of my past, of every man I'd ever placed my body against.

Thanksgiving was the usual: Grandma piled her plate high and hardly took a bite of the fragrant abundance; Dad, not I, brought up politics and Mom stood up to clear the plates when Bill's and Dad's voices lowered to growls full of pinch and tension; Thomas spilled his milk and after it was cleaned up and a new cup placed in front of him, he sniffed and whined until Barbara frowned and lifted baby Toby out of his high chair and took him into the living room to nurse.

And me? I sat numbly, not getting sucked into the political discussion, not standing to help Mom clear the plates, droning out answers to Grandma's questions about Japan. She wanted to know if the Japanese were racist against the Koreans, like she'd heard. It was as though I were watching the whole thing through binoculars: Look! It's *Mammalia Sullivan,* a species of turkey-eating, politics-discussing humans. See how they bare their teeth at one another. See how they walk away from one another. See how they dip their hands in soapy water to wash away the detritus of too much togetherness.

Chapter Fourteen

Self-Help

Lucy had more china than Gump's, more books than Border's, more clothes than Macy's. Helping her pack was no small feat. We were buried in boxes and newspapers in the living room, my fingers blackened from newsprint. I wrapped quickly to hide my dark fingerprints that marked her crystal. She was very protective of her crystal. But she probably wouldn't have noticed that I was dirtying it, anyway, because she was weeping. Or more like seeping. Tears leaked out of her eyes as we worked, but she kept talking as though she wasn't going to allow the crying get in her way. Besides, she was drinking beer after beer after beer, so perhaps she didn't even notice that she was crying. And I wasn't about to bring it to her attention.

"So what the hell is going on with you and Jamie? And Daniel?" she asked, wiping her nose and eyes with her sleeve then taking a swig from her beer bottle. She reached into the china cabinet and pulled out a butter dish that I knew was part of her wedding china set. I'd always thought Lucy would be the type to throw her wedding china against the wall or off a bridge as a comment on divorce. But instead she lovingly wrapped each piece and placed them in boxes with copious packing peanuts. All this wrapping added an ironic holiday flair to the event, especially since it was raining outside and a fire crackled in the fireplace, throwing dancing shards of light on the wall.

"I've only seen Daniel for what seems like a few minutes since he returned from New York. He's neck-deep in work. Jamie's back from Florida, but I haven't seen her."

"And she hasn't called you?"

"Actually, she's called me a few times and left messages—but I haven't called her back."

"What's wrong with you, girl?"

It was hard to look at her—my best friend, her eyes and face glittering wet with divorce-tears. With all she was going through, I was being self-pitying. But she'd asked. So I told her what Cat had told me, that Jamie had been in a relationship with our poetry professor and had never bothered to tell me. And that Jamie had had a bunch of other girlfriends she hadn't told me about either.

Lucy cradled a cut-crystal vase in her hands. "Have you told her about all the men you've fucked?"

My face got hot. "No. But she knows about the important ones, about Daniel and Andy."

"Well maybe this professor lady wasn't important to her."

"But we've been sitting in this poetry class all this time. And it just seems so weird that she never said anything. I really like Vanessa. But. She's, well, she's old."

"How old?"

"I don't know, fifties, sixties."

"Since when are you ageist?"

"I'm not ageist! It's just that—it makes me feel funny, that's all. I can't explain it." Something in me slammed shut. I really didn't know why I was so upset, and I didn't want anyone else telling me not to be.

"Damn, you're one jealous mama, I can see it in your eyes. You must really have a big thing for her if you're so jealous."

I didn't answer, just grabbed a handful of self-help books off her bookshelf. I began reading aloud the titles as I placed them in a box. "*Women Who Love Too Much, Women Who Run with the Wolves, Women Who Want More, The Co-Dependent Woman.* Holy crap, Lucy. I had no idea you were into these."

"My therapist recommended them. I keep meaning to get around to reading them."

"You mean you haven't read any of these?"

She absently wiped her wet eyes with her sleeve. "Nope. They're probably filled with a bunch of bullshit, but buying them felt like I was doing something."

I opened one up at random and read: "*Women need to get in touch with their inner wild woman, the part of them that can love freely, without expectations, the part of them that can give without feeling depleted.*"

"Give me that!" Lucy grabbed the book from my hand. "What is this shit? Why does it say *women this*, and *women that*? What about men? Where the hell are all the self-help books for men?"

"Well, there's that *Iron John* thing."

"That's not self-help. That's men jumping around, celebrating their penises. Nothing new about that. What else is there?"

I thought for a minute. "Hm. Good question."

"Damn right it's a good question!" She took a vigorous swig of her beer, then walked over to the fireplace and threw the book into the fire. Instead of inflaming the fire, the book nearly snuffed it out. Lucy took off into another room of the house. I heard her opening and closing cabinets, the clinking and clanging of bottles and cans.

"What are you doing?" I yelled out. No answer—but seconds later she appeared, a silver can of something in one hand and a wild look in her eye. She took the whole box of books and dumped them into the fireplace, then doused it with what I could now see was barbecue starter. The fumes invaded my nose.

"Lucy, be careful."

"Fuck careful!" she shouted, grabbing a box of matches and unsuccessfully trying to strike a light.

"How many beers have you had? Were you drinking before I got here? Let me have that." I tried to grab the matches but she turned her back to me.

"Ah ha!" she yelled, striking a flame and throwing it into the fireplace. The thing flashed up like a bonfire, the heat flushing my body. I stumbled backward, bumping into a stack of boxes and almost losing my balance. Lucy's arms were spread out, her wet face glistening in the reflection of the flames.

An orange ember popped out of the fireplace and landed on newspaper crumpled on the carpet. Lucy didn't move, as though entranced by this turn of events. I grabbed the closest thing at hand—a heavy coffee table book—and swatted at the flames. I knew I'd be able to keep it under control; I was more concerned about the look in Lucy's eyes. They reminded me of the eerie eyes of a statue in a wax museum.

I was successfully smothering the errant fire on the carpet when something exploded in the fireplace and more embers flew out onto the carpet and the curtains. Smoke burned my eyes. I thought about running into the kitchen to get a pan of water to pour onto the flames, but I was afraid they'd get worse if I left.

"Lucy, help me!"

She snapped out of her daze and began swatting at the flames.

Suddenly, everything turned.

One minute it had been like we were blowing out candles on a birthday cake, and the next minute we faced an inferno. I grabbed Lucy's hand and pulled her through the burning smoke, past the curtains that were now a conflagration. A window cracked like a bad tooth, then exploded in a shower of glass as we reached the front door.

The firefighters worked hard, but in the end, in spite of the trickling rain and their efforts, the house transformed to a dark skeleton. A paramedic treated Lucy's hands on site—she had swatted at the flames with her bare hands and had a few small burns, now wrapped in gauze. The paramedic's name was Jack—a full-faced, dewy-eyed guy who had asked Lucy for her phone number. She pulled a sheet of paper out of her pocket that had her new phone number and address printed on it and recited the number to him.

"Good thing I had that piece of paper," she said, "otherwise, I wouldn't have been exactly sure where my new apartment was. You know me and directions."

We were now sitting on the carpet of her new apartment. A few boxes leaned in the corner—things she had brought over days before. But everything else she owned had burned up in the fire. Fortunately she'd taken her crazy-looking elongated cats to her mother's house the previous week since the new apartment complex didn't allow animals.

"Are you okay?" I said. As much as I had the urge to go home and snuggle up in my bed, I had a hard time imagining leaving her in this virtually empty apartment. "Why don't you come home with me? You can sleep with me on the futon, and Daniel can sleep on the couch."

"I'm not sleeping with no lezzy."

"Don't flatter yourself. Remember, you're not my type."

"I'm going to drive down to my mom's to spend the night."

"Tonight? It's late and it's raining. You can't drive all the way down to Monterey tonight. Come over, get a good night's sleep. Besides, that's a long way to drive back in the morning for work."

"I need to see her, to tell her what I need, give her a list. She'll shop for me, buy some new things while I'm at work. She has impeccable taste, and a nose for great sales."

"Just spend one night at my place. Come on."

"It's no big deal," she said, scratching her ear with a bandaged hand.

I wondered how Will was going to feel when he came back to

see his charred house. He'd planned to stay with a friend for a few days while Lucy cleared out. A police officer had let Lucy use his car phone to call Will. Will had said he was coming right over, and we had quickly escaped to her new apartment. Lucy hadn't wanted to see him.

"It's very strange, Gwen," she said, "but I feel so good. Why do I feel so damn good? I have a hangover, my eyes are burning from tears and smoke, and almost everything I own has been burned to a crisp. But I feel happy."

"You do? Really?"

"Yes, I feel really, really happy."

I thought about when I had a yard sale to sell most of my belongings before I left for Japan—how free I'd felt, and a little scared and vulnerable, with just two suitcases to my name.

"I'm glad you're happy, but you really can't drive all the way down to Monterey tonight."

"I'm fine!" she said, holding up her car keys in her bandaged hand. "Quit babying me! I'm fine!"

"I'm not leaving here until you agree to come with me."

I saw a look float over her face, perhaps a sudden recognition that she was exhausted, that she'd been through so much—and she relented.

When Lucy and I walked through the door, Daniel was in front of the T.V. with the headphones on and the *New York Times* spread out before him on the couch. He looked up, removed the headphones and offered a bright smile for Lucy's benefit.

"Hey you two, what's up?"

While Lucy joined Daniel in the living room and regaled him with a riotous version of what had happened that evening, her bandaged hands slicing the air for humorous effect, I put on the teapot. When the teapot began to sing, Lucy stopped her story mid-sentence and said, "Tea? How about a beer?"

I was about to ask her if she really needed more, but then I figured she might. In the fridge, behind two withered apples, I found two beers. "Want one too?" I asked Daniel.

"Sure," he said, his voice upbeat. When I handed him the beer, he smiled. Even though the smile was directed at me, I only saw that particular, broad smile when there were other women around. He smiled that way when Ellen was in the lab, or Natasha was serving us at Palazzo's.

"Thanks," he said, taking the beer. "Hey Gwen. There are a couple of messages on the answering machine for you. Your sister. And that Jamie woman from your poetry class."

Lucy didn't miss a beat. She launched back into her *I-burned-my-house-down-isn't-it-hilarious* story. I excused myself and went into the bedroom with my tea. It was only 9:00—not too late to make a call.

Jamie answered. My mouth was suddenly dry, and I had to take a sip of tea before I could talk.

"Hi Jamie, it's Gwen."

"It's so good to hear from you, finally. I've been going crazy. I need to see you."

My body felt pulled to her voice, in spite of myself.

"I can't believe you didn't tell me that you and Vanessa used to be lovers."

She was silent for a moment. "Cat. That's the only explanation. Cat must have told you."

"Yeah, well, was it a secret or something?"

"Gwen, please, can we talk about this in person? Rose is going to come through the door any minute. Tell me where I can see you tomorrow."

"I can't tomorrow."

"Please, even if for just a few minutes. Meet me at five, okay? Please? At Mad Mary's?

"I don't know if I can."

"Please, Gwen. I'll be there. Please show up. Shit, I hear Rose's car. Please meet me there. I have to hang up."

A click, then the sound of dead air.

I stood and pulled off my clothes. My whole body ached and my ears droned with something like the after-sound of a thunderous concert. I took my kimono from the closet. Even the dragon looked tired.

In the living room, I found Daniel placing a blanket over Lucy, who was sprawled out on the couch, her face contorted in sleep. Daniel's tender action of placing the blanket over Lucy dizzied me, sweeping me into something that felt like a memory but clearly wasn't—of Daniel placing a blanket over our own sleeping child.

I took Lucy's half-drunk beer from the coffee table and put it, with Daniel's empty bottle, in the kitchen. Something smelled bad in there, but I didn't have the energy to do anything about it.

In the bedroom, Daniel sat at his computer. Dropping my kimono to the floor, I crawled between the futon's sheets.

"You two have had quite an adventure," said Daniel.

"Uh huh," I said, closing my eyes. Bright splotches whirled in the darkness behind my eyelids.

"I wanted to tell you. I had good news today. My paper has been accepted in *Cell*."

"That's great," I mumbled, turning over, feeling myself beginning to drift off.

"It's a turning point, Gwen. Things are going to be different now. This is really big. Everything's changing."

In the middle of the night, I woke for no reason. I hadn't been having a bad dream. The traffic wasn't louder than usual. Daniel was sleeping soundly, a pillow over his head. The darkness before my eyes swirled with little objects, like pond water under a microscope. Sometimes I'd get insomnia during my period. My period. When was the last time I'd had my period? I ran through an imaginary calendar in my mind. My period was late. Very late. I never missed a period in my life. My heart beat in my throat. Daniel and I'd had sex with no condom. When was that? And I wasn't taking the pill anymore. What the hell had I been thinking? I touched my breasts. They didn't feel tender. I'd had no morning sickness. In fact, since I'd stopped taking the pill, I'd noticed I was no longer nauseous in the mornings. I couldn't really be pregnant, could I? I forced the thought from my mind. I was exhausted and needed sleep. I imagined waves at the beach breaking on the shore, one after the other after the other, to lull myself back to sleep.

The next morning I expected Lucy to be hung-over and depressed, her manic high from the fire depleted. But her eyes were as bright as her hushed wit (*hushed* since Daniel was still sleeping), and after a cup of coffee and a change into some of my too-small clothes (that were too big for her), she hugged me and said, "See you at work."

I stood still in the dusty apartment. None of the furniture was mine. I hadn't been the one to suffer a fire, yet a year after returning from Japan, I still had no furniture to my name. I pulled down *Leaves of Grass* from the bookshelf, followed by my anthology of American poetry. Quietly, in the bedroom I filled a bag with some of my favorite clothes, leaving the rest hanging there like ignored sale items. In the bathroom I filled another bag with my makeup and toothbrush. In the kitchen I found two coffee mugs that were mine, and my blue sweater hanging over a kitchen chair. I stuffed them, too, into the bag. Glancing at my bicycle leaning in the drizzle on the balcony, under the gray sky, I turned and walked out of the apartment. Cradling nearly all of my earthly possessions in my arms, I closed the door quietly behind me.

Chapter Fifteen
Man Action

Mad Mary's was almost empty. The lights hadn't yet been dimmed for evening dining; they brightly illuminated the eruption of plants hanging from the ceiling. Two men sat in a corner booth and one woman at the bar. No Jamie, yet. The clock over the bar read 5:05.

"Hey, long time no see, sweetheart!" It was Billy, who'd been our server last time. His beaded cornrows were now gone—as was most of his hair, shaven closely to his scalp. His lack of hair accentuated his eyes, which were lined with glittery blue eyeliner.

"Hi," I said, feeling a little shy. "I'm surprised you remember me. I was only in here once."

"I never forget a beautiful face. Is your sweetheart joining you today?"

It took me a second to realize what he meant. "Oh, Jamie? She should be here any minute."

"Don't look so glum, dear. Why so serious? You women are always so serious!" He sat me at a table and thrust a menu at me.

"That reminds me of a joke! How many feminist lesbians does it take to screw in a light bulb?"

I took the menu and said, "I don't know, how many?"

Crossing his arms against his chest, he fixed his face with a faux-humorless stare. "One. And joking about it is *not* funny." He burst into a laugh.

I smiled and said, "Okay, I have one for you."

"Tell it!"

"If there was an earthquake in San Francisco in the morning, who would get out first?"

"Who?" he said.

"The gay men because they had their shit packed the night before."

Billy screamed with laughter. "That's more like it, sister!" I smiled back but cringed inside, feeling strange about having shared with him a joke that had been told to me long ago at the expense of gay men. But there was something funny about it, wasn't there? It was a witty play on words. And Billy had thought it hilarious. Maybe when telling jokes, context was all.

"What are you two laughing about?" Jamie slid into the booth across from me, smiling her movie-star smile. My stomach skidded when I saw her. She looked great, her spiky hair gelled, her skin ruddy, the scar on her forehead shining. She shrugged off her leather jacket while Billy replayed both jokes for her, laughing at his own telling of them.

"Okay, I have one," said Jamie. "A straight guy is making love to his wife. In the middle of it, he stops and says, *I'm sorry, did I hurt you?*

And his wife says, *No, why?* And he says, *Well, because you moved.*"

Billy screeched out another laugh. "Now *this* is a good day!" he said. "A day of dykes telling jokes. I love it!" His eyes followed a group of six people walking through the door. "Oh, excuse me," he said. "I'll be right back for your orders."

Jamie reached across the table, squeezed my hand, and let it go. "It's so good to see you," she said. "It's wonderful to see you."

I pushed back tears that I could feel building in me. Everything was hard right now. I didn't know where to turn. I could feel an intense connection to her, but there was part of me that held back because clearly I didn't know her. She was a stranger. A stranger who hid things from me.

"I know you want to talk about Vanessa. I have nothing to hide. I wasn't hiding it, Gwen. Ask me anything. I'll tell you."

"Why didn't you tell me before?"

"Gwen, I told you things about my mother, about my grandparents—things I've never told anyone, not even Rose."

"But it seems weird to me. We've been all these months in this class with Vanessa—and you never said anything."

She shifted in her seat, bumping my shin with her boot. "Sorry," she said, and I wasn't sure if she was apologizing for accidentally hitting me or for withholding information about Vanessa. Billy reappeared with ice water for us, took our orders then left.

"How long were you together?" I asked.

"Two years," she said. "We met at a Planned Parenthood rally, a protest against all those fucking psychos that stake out in front of Planned Parenthood with their Bibles and those shocking images on signs—you know, of dead babies?"

I nodded. I'd seen them and had averted my eyes. But the images of bloodied, tangled limbs had burned in my brain. They were effective. They made me wonder if abortion were truly evil.

She continued, "Well, for a while a group of us were staging counter-demonstrations. We were also helping to safely escort women into the clinic. That's where I met her." As politically involved as I'd been in my life, it had never crossed my mind that pro-choice groups might respond to the anti-choice groups in that way. It sounded vaguely dangerous—especially in light of abortion clinic bombings and murders of doctors who provided abortions. "Vanessa and I connected through our activism. And our loathing of the way religion is forced on us in this society. We are also both artists."

My face was suddenly hot. "It sounds like a good match."

"It was, for a while. But then, well, Vanessa's former partner, Theresa, reappeared. They'd broken up only because Theresa had gotten a position in another state—I forget where, in the South somewhere. Theresa's a math professor. Vanessa hadn't wanted to move there so they broke up. After a few years, though, Theresa got another position, at Berkeley. When she came back to the Bay Area, they got back together." Jamie fiddled with the straw in her ice water.

I suddenly understood. Vanessa had broken her heart. No wonder she hadn't wanted to talk about it.

"After that, you two became friends?"

"Yeah. It took a while. But when Theresa was diagnosed with cancer—breast cancer—well, it was a hard, hard time. It brought us back together. I felt terrible for both of them."

"What happened?"

"Theresa died. Three years ago." Visibly weighed down with these gloomy memories, Jamie talked about how all of their friends had rallied around Theresa and Vanessa, had brought them food and books, had accompanied Theresa to chemotherapy appointments and had spent weeks on end at their home once Theresa was on hospice. As she spoke, I realized how foolish I'd been when Cat had told me about Vanessa and Jamie, when all of this was behind the story.

"I'm sorry," I said, "sorry for all you and Vanessa have been through, and sorry for what I said on the phone to you. It was petty of me. You're talking about death here, about losing someone."

"Yeah, the whole experience with Theresa was really hard. But it's part of life," said Jamie, as though she simultaneously accepted mortality and wished it weren't so.

Billy placed our food in front of us: veggie burgers and milkshakes. "I leave for just a few minutes and you girls are so somber again! You're so pretty when you smile, the both of you! Are you sure you don't want some drinks—some liquid happiness?"

We both shook our heads no. A milkshake had sounded good to me—something that might soothe my whirling stomach. Jamie had liked the idea and had ordered one, too. Billy threw his hands up, a gesture that said, *I give up*, and turned away.

"I have something to tell you," I said, tracing a cold line down my milkshake glass with my finger. "I—I moved out this morning."

Jamie kept her eyes on me. "You did?"

"I think so."

"You *think* so?"

I smiled, my throat clenching. Everything felt bittersweet these days. "Before work, I left Palo Alto and came to a hotel here in San Jose. I don't know what I'm going to do. Daniel doesn't even know yet. I suppose I need to talk to him. Or write him a letter. Or something. I have a little bit of savings, but no furniture or anything. I think I'm going to go apartment hunting."

"I can help you try to find a good place," said Jamie. My heart plunged with the realization that she wasn't saying anything about moving out, herself. In fact, she hadn't said anything about Rose since we'd been here. I imagined myself alone in an apartment—where? Santa Cruz. The salt air, the redwood trees, the honking sea lions. A whiff of desolate loneliness accompanied the romantic image of me alone in my own little apartment, a narrowly winding mountain road separating me from smoggy San Jose—separating my old life from my new one. Part of me liked living alone. When I lived in Japan, my tiny studio apartment with a futon mattress on the floor had been my haven. The whole time, however, I'd had Daniel in my life, even though he was on the other side of the world. Could I really live fully alone—alone in my apartment, and alone in my love life?

Jamie stood and slid into the booth next to me. She smelled like lemons, with a whiff of fireplace smoke. We put our arms around each other and kissed, my body once again blooming into hers under the explosion of Mad Mary's plants.

When I opened my eyes in the dark, I detected a faint dark blue shadow. As my eyes adjusted I could see it was Jamie, her head propped on her elbow in the bed next to me. It took me a moment to place myself. The hotel, my temporary home. We'd come here from Mad Mary's.

"What are you doing?" I whispered.

"Watching you sleep," she said. She reached over and kissed me. I reveled in the intermingling of our smells. Never before had I paid much attention to how my lover smelled, except for the overpoweringly unpleasant smell of Daniel's and Andy's sweat after they'd physically labored. There was nothing about Jamie's tart and mild scents that bothered me—in fact, her smells were alluring.

We lay back on the pillows, her arm around me. I could see by the hotel's glow-in-the-dark clock numbers it was 2:30 a.m. I was surprised Jamie was still here with me. Didn't she need to go home to Rose? But I didn't want to ask her about it.

"My sister and I had a terrible fight over Thanksgiving," I said.

"What happened?"

"I told her that—well, I don't remember exactly what I said, but she got the idea I might be interested in being with women."

Jamie rolled toward me, pulling her arm out from under me to face me eye-to-eye. "You told your sister? About us?"

"Well, not quite about us—but about my, well, interest in women."

"Women plural? Who else is there?"

"Jealous, are you?"

"Damn right I am." She kissed me again. Then she said, "So what happened with your sister?"

"She told me I was dropping a bomb. She called me a freak—and told me not to tell anyone else." My body tightened with the memory. "That was the day before Thanksgiving. On Thanksgiving she basically gave me the cold shoulder."

"You mean she didn't announce it in front of your whole family? She didn't hit you? She didn't go running back home to get away from you? It could have been worse." I registered both the joke and the seriousness in Jamie's tone.

"Have any of those things happened to you?"

"That's the reason I hadn't seen my brother in all those years—my brother Bob, who I just saw in Florida, and his wife and my two nephews. They're four and six, and it was the first time I met them. Bob and his wife didn't want me around their children. At first Bob was okay with my being a lesbian, when we were in our early twenties and I came out to him. But after he got married, he got distant. And once he told me that he thought I'd be a bad influence on his kids—and this was even before he'd had them." I had a heavy sensation in my body as she talked, like when the dentist drapes a lead blanket over you before taking x-rays.

"So what happened? I mean, why did you suddenly spend Thanksgiving with him?"

"I just never gave up. Over the years I sent birthday presents to the boys. Eventually I would call and Bob would talk to me, fill me in about what they all were doing. Then he'd let me talk on the phone to the boys sometimes. Eventually they began asking about when Aunt Jamie was going to visit. Finally, this year, I got an invitation. So I went."

"How was it?" I noticed she didn't mention that Rose was there too, but I let it slide.

She was quiet for a moment, and then when she spoke, I could hear her voice was full of something—happiness, maybe? "It was great. The boys are great. We played a lot of games together, and I taught them both how to make pinch pots with clay. And of course, it being Florida—Miami—we went to the beach and had a great day throwing the Frisbee and playing in the water. A few nights in a row, after everyone else had gone to bed, Bob and I sat up drinking Scotch and talking about the past. I can't tell you, Gwen, how good it felt to talk to someone else who remembers my grandparents. It was as though my memories exploded into living color. Someone had shared my past—it wasn't just me, alone."

We lay there quietly for a few moments, our bodies touching, the word *alone* resonating in the air. Then Jamie said, "I guess these things take time, sometimes."

"I suppose," I said. But I didn't know how she could stand it, to be so judged by her brother for all these years—and to keep reaching out. I had no desire to talk to Barbara, to reach out or to try to explain myself. She had called my apartment and left two messages, and I wasn't about to call her back. At least not for a while.

"Jamie?"

"Yes?"

"Tell me about some of your other girlfriends, other than Vanessa and Cat."

"Okay, but for every one I tell you, you have to tell me about one boyfriend."

"What makes you think I had that many boyfriends?"

"Just a guess."

I smiled and pinched her shoulder. "Ouch!" she said.

"Sorry. Okay. You go first," I said.

"Alright." She shifted a little and pulled the sheet up to her neck. "The first woman I ever had sex with, when I was nineteen, was named Beata. She was twenty-nine, had a German accent—she'd moved to the U.S. a few years before. We were together for about six months, and the whole time she was also having sex with other people—women and men. At the time I'd just thought that's the way some people were. I didn't realize I could have said something to her about what I wanted."

"Wow, I don't know if I can match that—a German bisexual lover. Although I did have a boyfriend for a while in college, a guy named Nico, who I intuited had attractions to guys. After we broke up, I heard rumors he had a boyfriend, but he'd moved away so I wasn't sure. Your turn."

"There was Cecelia, the granddaughter of one of our clients."

"Yeah, Cat mentioned that."

"She did? The little bitch! She's trying everything she can to get to you."

"She is?" I smiled to myself.

"Of course, haven't you noticed? You're not really that naïve, are you, Gwen?" She kissed my forehead.

"Are you still fighting?"

"Not really. We're ignoring the elephant in the room. We have to work together, and we know that, so we're both just trying to not churn up the waters too much. Okay, where we were?"

"The granddaughter."

"Right, Cecelia. We went out for a few months. We met through her grandmother, who wanted to introduce us."

"That's one liberated grandmother."

"Mrs. Wallerston was a great lady. Is, I should say. But she no longer lives in her mobile home that Cat and I used to clean. She's now in a nursing home."

"What happened with Cecelia?"

"She went away to college."

"Ooh, cradle-robber." I pinched her arm again, but lightly.

"Your turn," Jamie said. "What about when you were in Japan?"

"Well, you know, Daniel and I were still together then, kind of. And I never had sex with anyone there, but there was a guy I met, an Australian named—what was his name? Nick. That's right, Nick. He was in Japan to study, and he was fully bilingual. He'd become a bit of a local celebrity on a morning T.V. show, offering the *gaigin*'s point of view about Tokyo."

"What's *gaigin*?"

"It means *foreigner*. We were both pretty drunk, and we took the train to his place. He showed me some tapes of his T.V. show. It was funny seeing him there, all blond and blue-eyed, speaking Japanese with two Japanese television anchors. I told him about Daniel, that I didn't want to cheat on him—and he said all he wanted was to hold me."

"Did he really say that?"

"Yeah."

"Did he mean it?"

"I guess so because that's all we did. We slept with our clothes on in his futon. Okay, there may have been a little kissing. To be honest, I was pretty drunk and out of it. All I know is I woke up with my clothes on."

"So was that your extent of man action in Japan?"

I laughed. "*Man action*? Where'd you get that? Anyway, it's your turn, not mine."

"Oh, right. Okay. Let's see. There was a guy whose name I never knew."

"A guy? You've had *man action* yourself?"

Jamie laughed. "Not quite. It sounds a lot like your adventure in Japan with the Australian. We met in a bar, and we were both drunk. Except that it was a gay bar, and we were both gay. So, needless to say, not a lot happened when I went home with him. Just some kissing and sleeping."

I tried to picture Jamie kissing a man—and then I saw an alternative version of her in my mind. Jamie with the same haircut but with mascara and eye shadow, and wearing a silk blouse with tight jeans. No tattoo—or maybe one of a butterfly on her ankle. With the right costume, she could pass as a straight woman. I could see her driving a mini-van, taking her kids to soccer practice, kissing her husband when he came home from work.

"I think I'm done talking about our pasts," Jamie said. "All I want to think about right now is you and me." She pulled me to her, pressing our bodies together.

A few days later, I was pushing open the door into Bookshop Santa Cruz. I closed my umbrella and set it with the others on the floor. The wet rain smells mingled with the scents of gluey book bindings and wet hair and clothes. The place was packed, humming with conversations. Removing my wet raincoat, I held it over my arm so that my professional outfit of a black blazer and black skirt would be on display.

I passed the literary magazine section, the children's section, the New Fiction section. I passed the newspapers, all displaying the ebullient face of our new President, juxtaposed with a small tight-lipped photo of the now Lame Duck President. At the Information Desk, I waited in line behind two customers. The guy behind the desk wore black, blocky glasses that somehow looked chic, torn-up jeans, and a shirt that said "Keep Santa Cruz Weird." I squirmed in my business attire, certain I had overdressed. When I finally was able to approach the desk, I asked the guy—whose name-tag read "Teal"— for a job application.

"Do you have any experience as a bookseller?" he asked.

Oh, so that's what I'd be. A bookseller, not a clerk at a bookstore.

"No. But I have a bachelor's degree in English, and I love books." Was it my imagination, or did he cock an eyebrow? I wanted to tell him that looks were deceiving—that I was weird enough for Santa Cruz, that I had a lesbian lover. "I'm moving to Santa Cruz," I added. "Currently I work for a tutoring center, which involves a lot of contact with the public, and a lot of work with books." I was rattling on. This guy probably wasn't one bit involved in hiring decisions.

"Here you go," he said, producing a pad of applications. He tore one off and handed it to me. "How can I help you?" he said, and I realized he was talking to a customer behind me.

I took the application to one of the wing-backed chairs set up throughout the store for customers to sit and read books. From the adjacent café, an espresso machine roared. Carefully I filled out the application. Which phone number to leave, I wondered? I put down the one for the hotel, and Daniel's number. After just a few days of being away from him, I was thinking of our former apartment as just his again. A pang of guilt shot through me. I hadn't talked to him. I'd merely left a message on the answering machine when I knew he'd be at work, telling him I needed some time alone and that I was fine. I had told Lucy to tell him I wasn't there when he called me at work each day. He had no idea where I was, no way to contact me.

When I finished the application, I stood and realized I was in the poetry section. I pulled down a few books and leafed through them, breathing in their new-book smell. Marilyn Hacker. I recognized that name; perhaps Vanessa had mentioned her. Titled *Love, Death, and the Changing of the Seasons*, the book's cover immediately made me remember the postcard-sized painting Jamie had made for me, as well as her poem "Hunger": pomegranates split open revealing ample black rubies inside. I opened the book. Sonnets. I read one, then another, then another. I had never before read sonnets like this. Sonnets that were about love between two women, sonnets that explicitly described passionate woman-to-woman sex.

I gripped the now-closed book in my hand and went to the information desk. Teal looked at me through his thick glasses, which suddenly didn't look quite as chic as before. "Thanks," I said, handing him the completed application and paying for the book. I turned away, grabbed my umbrella and walked to my car. There I sat and read the book front to back, the rain splashing at my windshield.

I wasn't ready to go back to San Jose, back to my dreary hotel. I drove through downtown Santa Cruz, my windshield wipers a rainy metronome. White holiday lights sparkled from the trees, brightening the gray day. I passed through a neighborhood of low-slung beach houses, punctuated by a wide-porched Craftsman here, a Victorian of points and spirals there. A few blocks later, the ocean lay out before me, gray waves churning. I turned onto West Cliff Drive, coming upon the hotel where Jamie and I had first made love, had first spent the night together. It seemed like yesterday, and also a lifetime ago. Nothing felt anchored right now. Was I really thinking I could leave my life and come here to live in Santa Cruz? Why not? I had left this country and lived in another for a year, a place where I didn't even speak the language. But the stakes felt higher now. What I would be giving up I could never claim again. What was that? What exactly might I be giving up? *A normal life.* That's what rang through my mind, *a normal life.*

I made my way over to the East side of town and parked near a huge cement whale perched on a span of lawn overlooking the ocean. Getting out of my car, I saw that the whale was the mascot of the Santa Cruz Natural History Museum. The pungent air smelled like life and death mixed. A place between. I could have stood there a long time, breathing in the thick air, touching the broad, thick side of the whale but I was getting wet in the rain.

The museum had no other visitors. Rain tapped at the windows. A volunteer—a woman with white hair—greeted me at the front desk, took my two dollars, then went back to reading a book.

Freeze-dried hawks hung by invisible wires from the ceiling, and a pair of golden-haired coyotes hunched in the corner. I passed shells, fossils and animal specimens, and an odd cantaloupe-sized object that, I read, was a hairball that came from the stomach of a cow. A massive white skull, I read, was from a giant mastodon that had roamed the area 100,000 years ago.

On the wall was displayed an old photograph of a woman in a long skirt and bustle, wearing a hat with a bow. An expanse of ocean before her, she leaned over a tide pool. I read that her name was Laura Hecox. Her mother and father had traveled across the plains in a covered wagon and arrived in Santa Cruz in 1856. When her father died in 1869, she became the Santa Cruz Lighthouse keeper, where she lived alone for many years. A self-taught naturalist, she'd wandered the shore, collecting shells and marine specimens. She opened her own museum in one of the rooms of the lighthouse, displaying her curios and others given to her by various people over the years. In 1905, eleven years before she died, she donated her treasures to the city, the origins of this very museum in which I was standing.

I studied the picture. Something about her looked sustained as she stood alone before the vast ocean. Was she about my age in the photo? It was hard to tell. Women from those times, with a mound of hair and all those clothes—they could have been any age. Still, I fancied her exactly my age, thirty-one. In her day she would have been called a spinster. It was here in Santa Cruz that she'd created her life, had collected and displayed what was important to her. Here, living alone, she'd created her meaning.

I took a few steps and came across an unassuming wooden chest. The plaque said it has once belonged to her, the woman lighthouse keeper. I opened its doors and pulled out the shallow drawers. Under glass were displayed shells. Gleaming abalone. Tiny sea snail. Miniature fossils. One perfect sand dollar.

Evidence of a life. A unique life. A woman alone, making her way.

Chapter Sixteen

Keep Santa Cruz Weird

When I told Lucy that over the course of a week I'd gotten a job and an apartment in Santa Cruz, she didn't respond at all as I had expected. I'd been keeping the whole thing secret from both her and Jamie. I didn't want either one of them to try to talk me out of it. I wanted to make my own decisions, unencumbered.

"What a fucking relief!" she said, turning from where she'd been aligning binders with the smiling boy logos on the shelf.

"Thanks a lot," I said. "Here I'd been agonizing over telling you because you were begging me not to abandon you. And now you're glad to be rid of me?"

"I'm quitting too!" she said, flopping down on a chair next to me, tucking her thin legs beneath her. "I was afraid to tell you because I thought you'd think I was abandoning you."

"You're quitting? What? Why? What are you doing?"

"Will and I are going to move in with my mom, in Monterey." The house-burning fiasco had brought Will and Lucy back together.

"And we're going to work on having a baby. My mom wants us to live with her—and she's dying for grandchildren. She has a huge place—and if we're living with her, I won't have to work. I can help her with the catering business she wants to start up. And Will is going to be doing consulting work, so he'll only have to drive over to San Jose once a week or so. So, new changes in life! It's all good!"

Thou doth protest too much, I thought, but I reached over and hugged her. "I'm happy for you, Lucy, I really am."

"And we'll almost be neighbors," she said. "We can go for walks on the beach, and have margaritas afterward. Well, until I get pregnant. Then it'll only be wine. I've heard a glass of wine now and then is good for a fetus."

"I don't think so," I said, pushing away the dizzying thought that I, myself, might be pregnant. My period still hadn't come.

"Okay, okay, but the minute that sucker pops out, we'll pop open a bottle of champagne."

I was packing my few belongings into a garbage bag when Jamie knocked at the hotel door. I let her in. She held me and we kissed.

"What's wrong?" she said, pulling back and seeing the odd look on my face. I saw her eyes fix on the bag I was filling with my things. "You're leaving? Are you going back to Daniel?"

"No," I said, sitting on the bed. "I found an apartment and I'm moving to Santa Cruz. I got a new job. At Bookshop Santa Cruz. I'm actually going to be working in a bookstore." Jamie sat next to me on the bed but didn't reach for my hand. "Do you remember," I said, "the first time we were alone? We walked across campus."

"We talked about your dream of owning a bookstore."

"I don't know if I'll ever really own my own bookstore," I said. "But, at least for now, I'll be working in one. And I'm going to go back to school. I'm applying for master's programs in English Literature."

"Gwen, that's great, that's really great."

It was great? It was great that I was leaving? A surge of fire ran up my back and I jerked around to face her head on.

"I'm sitting here telling you I'm leaving San Jose! I'm telling you what I'm doing. I'm changing my life, I'm making a move. And you say nothing! You say not one goddamn thing about what you're doing! You just keep coming here to have sex with me in this hotel and then going back home to Rose." I stood and paced the floor. The hotel room felt like a cage. "We sit like strangers across from each other in class," I continued, my ranting now like a runaway train. "Neither one of us has hardly been able to eke out a poem. There's so much weirdness! And you haven't said one word to me. I've waited and waited for you to say something. But all you've done is ask me about me, and talk about the past. What about the present? What about the future?"

Jamie lay back on the bed, her eyes fixed on the ceiling. "You never asked," she said.

"Don't throw this on me! What do you mean I never asked?"

"You never did." She sat up and rubbed her hands against the thighs of her jeans. "I take that back. You just did. So I'll tell you. Here, sit." She patted the bed next to her. It was hard to sit, to stay seated. Fiery nerves jumped under my skin.

Jamie said, "Rose and I broke up."

278

"What? You broke up, and you didn't tell me? When did you break up?"

"Three days ago."

"Why didn't you tell me?"

She turned her head to me, her forehead scar flashing under the hotel's overhead light. "Because, Gwen, I want you to do what you have to do." I could see that her eyes glimmered with tears. "My life right now is a complete mess. Don't base any of your decisions on me."

"What do you mean, your life is a complete mess?"

Tears dripped down her face, but she made no move to wipe them away. "It was really, really hard to end my relationship with Rose. I knew I had to do it, but it was terrible. As hard as she was to love, I did love her. There was a time when we were very, very close. At one time, I'd thought we'd be together forever. It wasn't easy to let that go. She's taking the job in Arizona." Her silent tears reminded me of Lucy's, the night we'd been packing away all the flotsam and jetsam of her marriage, just moments before the fire. Maybe like Lucy's returning to her husband, Jamie would go back to Rose. Or maybe like Vanessa's lover Theresa, Rose come back one day and claim Jamie.

"Do you want to move in with me?" The question appeared so spontaneously on my tongue it was almost as though someone else had said it. "I don't have any furniture yet, but we could buy a bed and some chairs on my credit card. We could live together in Santa Cruz. I'm sure there are plenty of old people over there who need their windows washed and rugs vacuumed."

Jamie looked down at her hands. She was so still I couldn't see her breathing.

"Jamie?"

My calling her name seemed to spark her into movement. She curled up on the bed on her side and began to sob. Her body shook, earthquake tremors of grief.

I reached around her and held her, burying my face in her damp neck. She cried and cried and cried for a long time. Then, like a princess who'd swallowed a potion, she fell hard asleep, with me holding on to her.

Jamie was in such a deep sleep that she didn't move when I got up. I stretched out my body, which ached from holding her for so long. How long? I looked at my watch. At least two hours. I felt exhausted to my core, as though I'd been the one who'd had the hard cry.

In my purse, I found the crumpled up piece of gold paper. Unfolding it, I picked up the phone. Jamie didn't move when I dialed, or when I talked softly into the receiver. It was as though she were underwater, or nestled in the amniotic fluid of the womb.

While waiting, I packed all my things from the bathroom. I checked under the bed and found a stray shoe. I checked the drawers to make sure all I was leaving behind was the complimentary bible.

When I heard a tap at the door, I opened it. There stood Cat in her black leather jacket, silvery from the rain.

"Thanks for calling," she said. "Where's Sleeping Beauty?"

I stepped aside so she could see Jamie curled up on the bed.

"I didn't want to wake her," I said. "Not that much could wake her at this point. She seems to be in the sleep of the dead. She had a very intense cry and then dropped off into this deep sleep. I'm really glad you came. I didn't want her to wake alone in hotel room. I told my landlord I'd be there by now, in Santa Cruz, so I really have to run." I scribbled out my new address and phone number on a piece of hotel stationary and handed it to Cat. "Would you give this to her?"

"Sure," she said. A passing thought that she might not give it to Jamie swept over me. But she placed it next to the phone, next to Jaime's wallet and keys, in full view. Besides, it seemed Cat emitted a vague air of disinterest in me now. Perhaps she was concerned about her friend. Perhaps she knew something I didn't. I wasn't going to try to figure it out, though. Jamie's pain was bigger than I could have ever guessed it would be. That had meant her love for Rose was huge.

I wasn't sure she had space left for me.

"Thanks," I said to Cat and turned to leave. I needed to go, to get started on my new life.

* * *

The apartment I found in Santa Cruz was a converted basement. The house had been built on a hill. The front windows of my basement apartment were small and up high, at ground level, letting in little light. People's feet walked by on the street at my eye level. But the downhill wall, the back wall of the apartment, was dominated by a sliding glass door that looked out from the living room onto my very own deck, an expanse of lawn behind it. Light and sea air flooded in through the screens. The people who lived upstairs—two men and a woman—all worked in computers. At night the dialogue of the T.V. shows they watched drifted down, as did the sweet and sour smoke of pot.

It had been almost two weeks since I'd last seen Jamie, rock-asleep on the bed of the hotel room. It was obvious she didn't want to see me since she hadn't called. I thought about her words, *my life is a mess*, and about the way she sobbed over her loss of Rose. She'd been devastated. Maybe she regretted being with me. Maybe Rose was the love of her life. Maybe they'd gotten back together. Maybe I was just another one in a line of women for her. I wanted to see her, I ached to see her—but I also felt like I had to avoid her, as though I was in her way, as though I had caused her devastation. I'd called Vanessa at the university to ask if I could take an Incomplete in her class. She said yes, I could clear it up for a grade in a month or two by sending her four new poems.

I had also called my sister when I figured she wouldn't be home. To my relief, I was right, and I left a message on her answering machine. I told her I'd moved and that I'd gotten her messages. I said I'd call her in a few weeks, perhaps. I needed some time.

My period still hadn't come. I'd resisted getting a pregnancy test. My body didn't feel any different—no tender breasts, no morning sickness. I couldn't be pregnant after only one time of unprotected sex, could I? I knew that was the wishful-thinking question of a teenager, but it was the only one I had to hold on to. As much as the thought of being pregnant terrified me, I entertained a fantasy of Jamie and me raising the baby together. I'd even imagined telling her I might be pregnant, just to see if she might come to me. A few times

I picked up the phone, tempted to dial her number. Once I went so far as to dial the numbers, but I hung up after one ring. What would I say to her, anyway? I didn't want to sound like I was begging. I was trying hard, very hard, to turn over a new leaf. Never again would I step on eggshells in my own house until noon. Never again would I try to force someone to love me.

I was finally ready, though, to call Daniel. Ellen answered the phone at the lab.

"Oh, hi Gwen. How have you been?" I could tell by her tone of voice she knew what was going on with Daniel and me.

"I've been okay." It was true. I was okay. Not great, not perfect. Not horrible. But okay.

"Daniel's grabbing at the phone." She laughed. "I have to turn it over!"

"Gwen?" he said.

"Hi Daniel."

"I've been so worried about you. Where are you?"

"I'm at my new apartment in Santa Cruz."

He was silent for a moment. I could hear The Ramones playing on the boom box in the background.

"You really have a place, your own place?" he said.

"And a new job," I said, "at Bookshop Santa Cruz. You should come by sometime. I look very official in my *Keep Santa Cruz Weird* tee-shirt." I felt a flash of shame for being so flip in the middle of our first conversation in weeks. I didn't want to hurt him.

"Gwen, what's happened?" His voice was so quiet I had to press the phone against my ear to hear.

"Daniel, I had to leave. I had to live my own life. You must have known I wasn't happy."

"But you just disappeared. Why did you just disappear?"

"I don't know."

"Can I see you? Can we talk?"

Had something new opened up in him? This was the first time I'd ever heard those words from him, *Can we talk?* I was the one who always asked him that question. Sometimes he'd said no. Sometimes he'd said yes.

"Okay, when?"

"Can you come over tomorrow? Around 6:00?"

"Alright."

When I hung up, my heart thumped in the cave of my chest. The idea of being alone with him in his place—in our old place— made me dizzy. A collision of lives. I stood and put the receiver in the cradle on the built-in bookshelf which held Walt Whitman, Marilyn Hacker and Jamie's pomegranate painting, its black undertones, its purple shadow.

The next morning, I woke with an ache in my lower back. I rose from the mattress on the floor that I was using as a bed until I would be able to buy some furniture. On the sheet, a stain of dark red blood. The usual cramps, the usual headache.

My period.

I limped to the bathroom and sat on the toilet, gripped by sadness, flooded with relief.

Chapter Seventeen
I Do

I used my key to open Daniel's door. The apartment was dim and smelled of something cooking.

"Hello?" I called out.

Daniel appeared from around the corner, manifesting as though from another dimension. I felt a little woozy, as though I were stepping back in time. I did have an apartment and a job in Santa Cruz, didn't I?

"Hi Gwen." He approached and gave me a hug. Something bittersweet swept over me. This was Daniel, the man I'd thought I might marry one day. My face felt like it belonged against his chest. Part of me wanted to stop time, to stay there forever, my ear to his breastbone. I stepped back and looked up at him. His hair looked odd. When we stepped into the kitchen, I realized he had a yarmulke pinned to the back of his head.

"Are you cooking?" I asked, feeling like I was in some strange parallel universe.

"Latkes," he said. "It's the first day of Hanukkah."

I sat at the table, moving into the familiar rickety chair. An unlit menorah, fitted with nine white candles, was perched on the table. Grease sizzled as Daniel flipped latkes on the stove.

"I thought you were going home for Hanukkah this year."

"I couldn't go anywhere," he said, "without knowing where you were." He turned from the stove and sat across from me at the table. "Gwen, what happened?"

I suppressed an urge to reach across the table and hold his hand. Who knew where holding his hand might take me? Images whirlwinded through me: Daniel and me in his car after sex; Daniel in a Kyushu hotel, a deep, quiet darkness in his eyes; Daniel with the headphones on, his face in the newspaper as I passed by him, hoping to make a breeze stir the pages so he'd look my way …

"Daniel, were you happy with me?"

"Happy? Gwen, I'm not sure I believe in happiness."

Hadn't Lucy once said something like that? Maybe I could have a friend who didn't believe in happiness—but a lover? "See, that's how we're so different. I do. I believe in it. I've felt it. I know it exists. Are you saying you were never happy with me?"

"Gwen, I love you. You know I do."

Somehow the words didn't quite reach me like they used to, as though the camera lens of my heart were glazed with Vaseline. *I love you. You're beautiful. Love of my life.*

"Gwen," he said again, "You know I do, right?"

"Sometimes I know it. Knew it. Daniel, we fought so much. We had days on end when we wouldn't talk. That's not normal. At least I don't want it to be my normal."

"I wanted you to come with me to New York. I wanted you to meet my parents."

"Maybe it all just took too long," I said, a pinch in my throat. "It was too late."

He patted his yarmulke on the back of his head as though to assure himself it was still there. "Is there someone else?"

I looked down at the table, at the dent in the wood that always caused me to punch a hole through a piece of paper with my pen as I wrote. The pinch in my throat grew tighter as though my body were rejecting speech. "No. Well, yes. Well kind of. I don't know what's happening with us. Daniel, I didn't leave you for someone else."

He didn't say anything, just stood and slid potato pancakes, sparkling with grease, from the pan onto a platter. After placing them on the table, he set plates and silverware at our places, the places we always sat when we ate together. Finally he looked at me, and I could see he was gearing up to speak.

"What do you mean?" His voice was tight and whispery. "What do you mean No and Yes?"

My throat was so tightly clenched I wasn't sure I'd be able to get the words out. "I've been with a woman," I said. "Her name's Jamie. I met her in my poetry class."

"A woman," he said.

"Yes."

"A woman. Gwen, you're a lesbian?"

Something oddly funny and sad twisted inside me. The question felt absurd, coming from him, the man I'd had sex with so many times—and usually pretty good sex, too.

"I don't know. I guess so."

"You don't know. You guess so."

"That's what I said."

"You're not sure."

"I don't know what word to use for myself."

He sat silent for a moment, and then another. Again he touched his yarmulke.

"Excuse me," he said. He stood and opened and closed drawers in the kitchen.

"Can I help you find something?" I asked. He didn't answer, just went into the living room and rooted around, then into the bathroom. I recognized the sound of every drawer, the squeak of every part of the floor. The sad familiarity of it all: the sounds of the apartment, the sound of his silence. When he returned, he held up a book of matches and set them on the table.

"Hanukah," he said, "means *dedication*. It commemorates the victory of the Maccabees over the Syrians. The victory was considered a miracle. Afterward there was only one jar of sacramental oil to rededicate the temple, only enough for one day. Miraculously, the oil burned for eight days. Thus, the eight days of Hanukkah."

He picked up the matches and began to chant in Hebrew as he lit the middle candle. These were the first Hebrew words I'd ever heard. They sounded ancient, like they were echoing from a deep well. Continuing to chant, he lifted the burning candle from its holder and used it to light one more candle. The candlelight spread shadows over his face and stirred in his dark eyes. His eyelashes cast shadows on his cheeks. The Hebrew words—part song, part chant—poured out his mouth, sounding like eons of human lives. His breath made the candle flames dance.

The whole drive home, I blasted the heater, but it couldn't quell the icy air coming in through the back of my car. Daniel and I had been unable to close the hatchback because my bike stuck out, a piece of twine holding the whole contraption in place. And now, because the night was so dark and cold, it was extra difficult to extract my bike from the back of my car with my icy hands. For some reason, the city had not installed streetlights on a number of streets in Santa Cruz, including mine.

How oddly beautiful it was that Daniel and I'd had Hanukah together for our first time. Perhaps our last. But maybe not. He'd told me he knew I had to make my own life. But he'd also said that if I decided that I wanted him in my life, to let him know. *As lovers or friends?* I'd said, my insides lurching at the hope we might be friends. Could I really stand to see him with another woman? Could I really go and have a cup of coffee with him and his wife? Maybe someday I could. *As lovers or friends?* I'd said. And he'd answered, as though reading my mind, *Right now it's hard to say for sure, but I think I might be able to do friends.*

And now, as I struggled with the bike on my dark Santa Cruz street, I thought about how he would be the one to remove the bike if we were still together. He wasn't physically stronger than I was, but he would do it anyway. I was so cold, my fingers so stiff, that I was temped to leave the bike in the car overnight and to risk it getting stolen. But the thought of that—of losing my bike, now that I finally had taken it off Daniel's balcony and into my own world—provided me with enough extra strength to wriggle it free from the buckle, or whatever was obstructing it, and to yank it out of the car.

"Good job! You're one strong woman!"

I turned. Jamie, bundled in a thick down jacket and a hat, was seated on the lawn chair at my front door, illuminated by my porch light. My heart, already racing from my wrestling match with my bike, pounded a few extra beats.

Was she really here for me? I barely dared to wish for it.

"Well, thanks a lot for helping out," I said.

"You looked like you were handling it just fine."

She was right. I was.

And then my eyes, adjusting more to the night, took in that she wasn't sitting on one of my lawn chairs. She was seated on some boxes next to the lawn chair. Other boxes were piled around her. A big yellow dog that I knew must be Peanut lay on the ground, her chin in her paws.

Then I registered that there, next to one of my neighbor's cars, was Jamie's truck, filled to the brim with a snarl of roped-in furniture.

"I heard you might need some furniture in your new place," she said.

"Does that furniture come with a girlfriend?" I asked.

"It does if you want it to."

As I walked toward her, I said, "I do. I do."

Acknowledgements

The idea for this novel was sparked in Janelle Melvin's Cambridge home. Together we brainstormed for for a few hours. The character sketches and chapter mock-ups I jotted down during that time are the skeleton beneath the flesh of this book.

Thank you to Paul Robert Mullen for your encouragement and inspiration (in China, of all the unlikely places), which led me to re-release this novel.

Jan McCutcheon: You are a book goddess. A million thanks.

Thanks to Susanne Tobin for reading and editing the galley proofs and for granting permission to reprint her poems "Grandma's Spoons" and "hunger."

Love to my sisters Crystal and Ann and to the memory of my parents. It was under my mother's wing that I fell in love with books.

Without Bev Hamel, Collin Kelley, Nancy Larrew, Merry Gangemi, Cynn Chadwick, Jayne Pupek, Susan Gabriel, Gary Shapiro, Merry Gangemi, Julie Enxzer, Jan Steckel, and Nicki Hastie, my novels would not be as enthusiastically blurbby and publically embraced. Kisses to my former manuscript group: Martha Engber, Kathryn Madison, and Jana McBurney-Lin.

I'm grateful to all my former students and colleagues who still inspire me every day. Ben Malto, I appreciate you heaps.

A penultimate, special shout-out to JP.

And all my love to Dave, who read this book when we first met. He has never wavered in his support for all I do.

ABOUT THE AUTHOR

Kate Evans is the author of *Call It Wonder: An Odyssey of Love, Sex, Spirit, and Travel*, awarded Best Memoir at the Bi Book Awards, where she was also named Writer of the Year. Her other books include two novels, a collection of poems, and a nonfiction book about teaching. Her essays, stories, and poems have appeared in more than fifty publications. She holds a PhD in Education and an MFA in Creative Writing. A former writing and literature teacher at U.C. Santa Cruz, San Jose State University and SCIC/Guangxi University in China, she now serves as a writing coach and book editor. Half the year she lives in Mexico, and half the year she travels. She blogs at *Living the Journey*. Visit her website at kateevanswriter.com.